The Dead's Unfinished Business

Gloria Oliver

COPYRIGHT PAGE

LAST STOP

The Dead's Unfinished Business

Book 01

ISBN: 978-1-957230-26-9 (Kindle), 978-1-957230-27-6 (Trade Paperback), 978-1-957230-28-3 (Hardback)

Cover design by Deranged Doctor Design

Story editing by Serenity Editing Services

Contents

Chapter 01

¡Idiota, idiota, IDIOTA! Why did I *ever* listen to Jay? My breath came in ragged, hot, painful gasps, the rain beating on me like wet admonitions as I ran for all I was worth.

Hot tears burned my cheeks, branding me with each step. Never trust a single source. Check and double-check all facts. But I hadn't! So running half-blind in this crazy storm on blasted high heels was my reward. I grimaced as a painful stitch complained in my side.

Everyone in the group was well aware that doing jobs not approved by the boss might come with blowback. But Jay had sworn his source was legit and that Pierson would never find out.

He couldn't have been more wrong! The moment I'd spotted Pierson amongst the partygoers, we were screwed. We might still have gotten out of there, no harm, no foul, if not for that smug-faced *pendejo*, Bobby.

I rounded a corner, the water collecting on the sidewalk from the deluge splashing my legs with every hurried step. The stitch stabbing my side grew more painful, but I didn't dare slow down.

There were bigger things to worry about than that traitor. I flinched as thunder battled against the dampening sound of the rain, my fear spiking. Every shadow or noise might be a harbinger of doom. I had no way to know if those searching for me were ahead of me or behind me. But I was one hundred percent sure that being caught would mean "The End."

I shivered, soaked through, the oppressive rain having already chilled my skin numb. Whether I was being hidden or hampered by the weather, I couldn't tell. Not that it mattered.

Pierson's information network spread like a web to catch unwary morsels of intel and spin them together for later consumption. His greedy fingers plucked at all levels of Miami and beyond. If he didn't have information on something, he knew how to find people who did—like the VIP whose party we'd crashed.

My life was over—there was nowhere I could run, nowhere I could hide that he wouldn't find me. The certainty of that fact hung like chains off my body, trying to freeze me in place. But

I kept running, even as my heart tripped and lurched inside my chest. I couldn't bear letting it end like this. All we'd ever wanted was a chance to be free!

Daniela la tonta. A fool was exactly what I was.

One of my useless high heels caught in a crack. I gasped, struggling to retain my balance as it almost sent me flying face-first onto the wet concrete.

Breathless, the stitch in my side now a burning brand of agony, I leaned against a rough brick building for a second. At least the bullet graze on my arm was now clean and only lightly throbbing thanks to the cold rain. That minor wound was but a taste of what would happen if I got captured. Pierson wasn't typically the violent sort—not unless you crossed him. And not only had we inadvertently hampered our boss in his dealings, but we had *embarrassed* him. Something he would never forgive.

Throat burning, hopelessness nipping at my heels, I pushed away from the rough wall to get moving again.

The distinctive flickering light and buzzing sound of a neon sign made me glance across the street through the falling curtain of water. Was someone still open at this time of night? The lights beckoned to me, and it surprised me how easily I could make out the words in the middle of this torrent. The warm, glowing letters spelled "Last Stop." I would have laughed at the irony, but I didn't have the breath or energy.

Last Stop—yes, if I stopped moving, it would be the final thing I ever did. Yet the sign promised somewhere dry and warm out of the downpour. But as I took a wobbling half-step in that direction, I hesitated. If the business was open, rather than it being a case of some underpaid kid who forgot to turn off the sign, I might put those inside in danger just by being there. I got myself into this mess, so why dig my hole any deeper by bringing strangers into it?

A lightning bolt struck a transformer with a resounding boom. Sparks went flying everywhere.

¡Ay bendito! I swallowed a startled scream, throwing my arms up in a useless attempt to protect my head. The pungent stench of ozone crowded all around. Florida was the state with the most lightning deaths a year, and I positively did not want to become part of *that* statistic. My odds of survival were already zero. So why make them even lower? *Come on, Dani, get a move on!*

Still shaky from the transformer explosion and with my ears still ringing, I steered well clear of the still falling sparks as I crossed the now darker street. Though everything else around the area looked to have lost power, blanketing the zone in darkness, the place across the way was still miraculously lit. The beckoning letters seemed to glow brighter, again promising safety, warmth, and, best of all, escape.

I had a vague idea of where I was despite my mad dash through the streets constantly looking over my shoulder to check for headlights or figures running in the dark. Yet I was sure I had never heard of this "Last Stop," which was odd. Pierson always kept us informed of all the venues opening in the area, as they might lead to new spots for the *wire mob*, our group of pickpockets, to ply our trade. Tourist traps were our bread and butter.

When I reached the safety of the shop's awning, I stared at the storefront, positive I had never seen it before. The entire façade was made of dark wood, with the entry door set to slide sideways rather than open in or out. The slats at the top third were interspersed with vertical strips of frosted glass. Well taken care of, but weathered and faded.

A two-foot statue of some kind of furred animal, sporting a white potbelly and wearing a straw hat, sat on the right side of the sliding door. The statue wore a gentle smile and had wide, dark eyes that gave the impression they saw everything—both the good and the bad—and that he'd gleefully tattle on you at the first opportunity.

By the door's opposite side sat a dark red lacquered umbrella stand. A couple of normal umbrellas were nestled in it, but there was also one made of bamboo and what had to be some kind of treated paper. Surprisingly, a typical red and white Help Wanted sign had been taped to the wall above the umbrella stand.

Not being pelted by the rain anymore felt great, but a sideways wind suddenly drove a blast of water beneath the awning. The cold, wet fingers of the rain reached for me, making me shiver. Turning, I realized that both ends of the storefront had lights tucked under the awning, though I hadn't noticed them before. Anyone glancing in this direction would easily spot me standing there. *¡Coño!* I needed to decide *this second* whether to go in or not, assuming it wasn't too late already.

"Welcome. Welcome."

My gaze snapped up as my heart jumped in my chest at the unexpected voice. I spotted a *crow*, of all things, staring at me from one of the awning's struts where it sheltered from the rain. I knew that they could mimic human speech, but hearing it firsthand was eerie.

Snippets of music whispered out from inside the place, though I had heard nothing coming through until that moment—"Stay" by Rihanna. Goosebumps peppered my arms. The weird statue's happy stare now seemed more pointed, which was *loco*. Hoping I wasn't making a big mistake, I slid the door open just enough to slip inside.

Blessed warmth hugged me like a long-lost *abuela*. My eyes closed of their own volition as I wallowed in it. The song I'd made out only seconds ago was gone now. Had I imagined it?

"Goodness," said an unexpected and scratchy female voice on my right. "You look like an escapee from a disaster movie."

My eyes snapped open as fear ate me from the inside, robbing me of breath. I spotted an elderly woman coming my way. Tuning out like that would get me killed.

Then I gasped in surprise, catching the reflection of my face in a round-framed mirror hanging from a wooden column near the end of a U-shaped counter. My bouncy, wavy brown hair lay flat, plastered to my head like limp spaghetti. The eye and face makeup I had so carefully applied for the evening's event was smudged or washed away, while the cheap mascara had left black trails down my face. My eyes widened, and my lips twisted as I realized I resembled something out of a nightmare.

The short, curve-hugging wine-red tube dress that had looked so good on me when I left my apartment was soaked through and darkened into a ruddy brown by the rain. The hem was askew and had ridden halfway up my thigh. A drowned rat would have looked better.

As it was, I was dripping water all over the polished wooden floor.

'Ida, be a dear and go fetch some towels for the poor thing.' The new voice was crisp and clear, but rang out all around me rather than coming from a specific direction.

"Okey dokey!" The elderly, slightly stooped woman shuffled away down the narrow hall on the right.

Forcing my gaze away from the nightmarish reflection in the mirror, I examined the odd place. The walls were a dark mustard stucco with reddish-brown wood used for the moldings, panels, sliding doors, and the U-shaped counter. Another umbrella stand was on the inside of the door, as well as a large coat rack with a built-in seat. Wooden, barrel-back stools ringed the counter, and I glimpsed low shelves on the inside of it, full of plates, glasses, and dispensers.

Narrow hallways ran on either side of the counter, but something that might be a kitchen lay recessed behind the U itself.

A dark blue partition curtain, hanging from the ceiling between columns and reaching only halfway to the floor, separated it off from the front. Five vertical slits that went from the bottom of the partition to almost the top split the stylized white-capped waves depicted on the dark cloth.

Everything was neat and clean, but it suffered from wear. The corners were smoother than the rest of the trim, and the colors were faded. An established, long-standing business, then. Which made no sense at all. My fingers twitched.

Though I had heard two distinct voices before the woman left, no one else was in the room—except for the largest cat I had ever seen. She lounged on a cushioned, wrap-around shelf set three feet from the ceiling. The feline had deep green, emerald eyes and a gorgeous white and silver coat. The fur around her collar was so long and thick it looked like a stole. Stretched out, she had to be at least three to four feet long.

She was a *reina*—a pampered queen overlooking her kingdom. But how was she so big?

An answer came to my unvoiced question. '*A Maine Coon. Surely* *you've heard of the breed before?*'

I blinked, my gaze darting around, but no one was there. I still couldn't tell what direction the voice came from, which made no sense. Wiping roughly at the water still dripping over my face, I blinked a few more times. Had I hit my head while running away? Or had I been hit by lightning after all? Was I currently dying in a ditch and just didn't realize it? Because this *chica* would be totally *loca* if I even thought of considering that the explanation had come from *the cat*.

"Here we are!" The old woman shuffled back into the room with several fluffy, folded towels cradled in her arms. She wore a muted pink housedress, a full white apron, bobby socks, and, of all things, bunny slippers. Her white and gray-streaked hair was pulled back into a bun, and a foot-long unlit Churchwarden pipe hung from the side of her mouth. Her thin face and prominent Romanesque nose hinted at beauty lost to time—much like the entire place. Yellowed teeth from too much tobacco showed in a pleasant enough smile, though her light brown eyes seemed unfocused as she stared at me.

"*Gracias*." I took the offered towels, but kept my distance. Though I couldn't say why, there was something not quite right about the woman. Keeping half an eye on her, I used one of the towels to briskly dry my hair.

"I'm off to get a mop!" she said in a sing-song tone and did a quick little jig like a child. "Be right back. Don't go anywhere!" And off she went. *La vieja* might be a few cards short of a deck.

I checked that the sliding door was still closed as thunder boomed loudly outside, reminding me with a jolt that I couldn't let my guard down.

I quickly worked to dry the rest of me as best I could, stepping toward the corner and away from the vicinity of the door to stay out of direct line of sight if it opened again. If anyone came inside, I'd have a moment or two to throw a towel over their head and dash back outside in the ensuing confusion. I surreptitiously stared around the room some more—a skill I had some experience in.

The counter, the kitchen, and the rest made it clear that the place was a restaurant. But I saw no bill of fare board or an à la carte or du jour menu—nothing visible about what they served or how much it cost. I had seen menus without prices before—always a big hint that I couldn't afford to eat there—but I had never been in an eatery with nothing of any kind. It was super weird.

My skin prickled as a stab of nervousness turned my insides. Something about this place was off.

The curtain partition moved, and a twenty-something guy—close to my age—then came out with a tray holding a tall, black ceramic teacup painted with several stalks of leafy bamboo, like the kind you'd find in a Japanese restaurant. He was about my height, which was too bad for him since, even with the blasted heels, I was considered short. Being vertically challenged came from my Latina roots—*Boricua* girls mostly came in small packages—but he looked to be a mix of some kind.

He was lean and compact like someone from Japan, but his slightly slanted eyes were the dark gray of a Scandinavian's. His black hair was styled in a smart cut that needed a trim. His black-rimmed eyeglasses had round lenses and were larger than usual, but suited him. The chef's outfit he wore was also black and appeared pristine, unlike the rest of the shop.

In my line of business, you learned to be observant and take cues from prospective targets. I didn't know if it was the fact that I was living on borrowed time or had been too damn close to the lightning strike or what, but nothing in this place was adding up.

The chef set the cup on the counter, gave a half nod in my direction and another at the cat, then silently returned to the kitchen.

My eyebrows bunched together. The guy hadn't said a word, moving with an economy of movement and silence that felt surreal. But hot steam rose from the cup, and that was all I needed to know before deciding to take it and bring it back to the corner.

Holding the mug was an almost carnal experience as glorious heat spread into my way-too-cold hands. I took a sip and shivered with delight as the heat ran down my throat and started thawing me from the inside. Being cold was not my thing. *Dios mío*, the warmth felt so good. I hugged the cup to my numb face and then finally took another sip. The flavor had a weird zing to it, so it wasn't green tea, but at the moment, I didn't care what kind it might be. All that mattered was that it was hot.

"Got the mop!" The woman called Ida shuffled back into view. "Got the robe too, like you wanted, Beauty." She held up and shook the mop in one hand, and waved a shiny, red, half-kimono robe with white flowers with the other. The long, unlit pipe still hung precariously from her lip.

Ida draped the robe over the back of the stool nearest me before she half-tried to trip me as she started mopping the floor. My feet hurt from all the standing and running, so I quickly kicked off my ruined shoes, which dropped me six inches. Even slouching, Ida towered over me. I sidled away, dropping off my empty cup on the counter and snatching the robe to put it on, before returning to my corner. My hands and feet felt alive again, tingling as they warmed up, and my core heated back toward normal.

"I'm really sorry about the mess," I said to no one in particular. My heart had calmed a little, though the flesh-rending fear still lurked close at hand, ready to take a bite at the slightest provocation. I might be out of the rain and dry, but no way was I safe. "I realize this will sound a little crazy, but with that storm outside and the lack of customers, would you mind locking up and turning off your sign and most of the lights for a bit? You'd truly be helping me out."

Gurgling like a five-year-old with amusement, Ida shuffled over to the entryway, turned the lock, and flipped a switch on the wall. The strips of frosted glass on the door turned dark on the other side. A trickle of relief had started to settle in my stomach when the lights outside came on again.

Shocked, my head swiveled back to the old woman. She looked at me over her shoulder, her face full of childish delight, her hand still on the switch. She turned it off, paused for a second or two for effect, then switched it on again, giggling under her breath the entire time.

The crazy vieja wasn't missing a few cards; she was missing half the deck! Flickering the lights off and on would only draw even more attention from anyone passing by. What was she playing at?

A flush of panic made me suddenly dizzy, and I started to reach out to drag her away from the switch if I had to. This addled woman would get me killed!

Ida, enough!

Like the lights, the old woman's face fell. Her lip stuck out like a petulant child's, but her hand dropped away from the switch.

As much as I dreaded going back out into the rain, staying here would be a major mistake. I reached for my emergency cash, which I kept tucked inside my strapless bra. "Can I buy one of the umbrellas?"

And why did they have so many? There was no one here besides the old woman, the cook, and the cat. So where had all the umbrellas come from? Was it some kind of marketing gimmick to make the place look busy and draw in customers, or something more sinister? Might I have unknowingly stumbled into some sort of human trafficking ring? My gaze was drawn to the odd-tasting cup of tea on the counter.

These people could have slipped anything into my drink, and I'd be none the wiser until much too late. And I had played right into their hands! *Dani, come on! What's the matter with you?*

If they'd drugged me, I wasn't feeling the effects yet. Well, this chica would not go down without a fight! The kitchen would have knives, and I could easily trip up the cook if he got in my way. Surely there was a back way out from there to the alley.

Calm yourself. You are safe here. The giant cat leaped from the padded shelf to the counter and sat, all in one graceful move. Her too-bright, alien green eyes never left my face. '*If you wish to leave, we will not stop you.*' The words didn't fall into my ears, which was why I hadn't known which direction they came from. Instead, they rang directly inside my head.

'*But be aware that if you do, you'll be rushing straight into death's embrace.*'

Loco or not, there was no longer any way for me to deny that the Maine Coon had been talking to me all along.

Chapter 02

"*¡No! No lo creo.* " I shook my head in utter denial. "It's not possible."

'*Not believing in something will not make it any less real, Daniela Maria Martinez Colón.*' The cat raised her right front paw and daintily licked her pink toe beans.

It took me a second to realize it, but when I did, all the warmth I had regained left me again. My name. It had said my *full name.* But I had never mentioned who I was. My right hand rose of its own volition and made the sign of the cross, something I hadn't done since my abuela passed when I was seven.

"I'm dead already, aren't I?" What else would explain all this craziness? But if I were dead, this was like no Heaven or Hell

I ever imagined. My legs turned suddenly into melting wax. If I'd still been wearing my heels, I would have toppled over and broken something. As it was, I had to brace my back against the corner to remain upright.

The cat sighed.

They could *do* that?

'*You are not dead, Daniela.*'

If *they* hadn't drugged me, maybe someone slipped me something at the party? But I didn't drink when I was working. Had somebody sneaked a designer drug skin patch on me? All this loco shit would suddenly make sense if they had.

'*You are not drugged, either.*'

I flinched. Was the freaking cat reading my mind? Its inhuman eyes seemed to grow bigger the longer I stared at them. The feline quit licking its toe beans and brought out its claws as if to check a manicure.

'*I also did not read your mind.*' It glanced my way, and I could have sworn it looked amused. '*I've done this a time or two, and the conversations usually run much the same as this one.*'

The room felt stiflingly hot, and my throat hurt as I struggled to get enough air.

'*My name is Beauty, by the way.*'

I scrunched down and put my head between my legs, dizzy and breathless, trying to calm myself before I passed out and made everything worse. A surreptitious glance toward the door showed me that Ida had moved on with her mop, leaving the way clear. The lock on the door was a simple deadbolt, so I could easily let myself out. So what "Beauty" had mentioned earlier seemed to be true. I could leave if I wanted to, but... "What did you mean when you said I would be 'rushing straight into death's embrace'?"

'*You're currently running for your life, are you not?*' Beauty asked.

How did she *know* that?

"Miss, your food is ready."

I almost jumped out of my skin, I was so startled by the voice coming from above me. It was the cook. I hadn't heard him come back in.

Rising shakily to my feet, I turned toward the counter to look. I hadn't ordered anything. The smell hit me first, almost as if someone had used a fan to send it to me: garlic and olive oil with a faint hint of banana. My mouth watered, recognizing what the scents meant, while my brain refused to process what it saw on the plate.

"*Mofongo*? You made *mofongo*?" Eyes wide, I glanced at the cook.

He flashed a faint smile before he nodded.

A yellow mound of fried, mashed, unripe plantains, garlic, olive oil, and—were those bits of *chicharron* mixed in as well? There was even a small cup of broth on the side and an open bottle of *malta* next to it. Since it was non-alcoholic, the malted barley drink was typically considered a child's drink, but I never had mofongo without it. It always reminded me of my abuela.

I took a shaky step toward the counter, still not believing what was there. My stomach growled at me to hurry on over, as I'd had little to eat before this mess started and I'd been running for who knew how long.

Still, there was no way on this Earth these people could know what I liked—yet there it sat. If I were ever asked what I wanted for a last meal before I died, this would be it. I reached for the fork with a trembling hand and took a bite. Tears instantly sprang to my eyes as the starchy, salty flavor flooded my tongue. I half-parked myself on the stool and took a sip of malta, and I was back at the worn Formica table in Abuela's kitchen.

A tear escaped to roll warmly down my cheek, the loss of my grandmother fresher than it had been in years. Yet the familiar flavors were also a balm for my fear-shredded nerves. A second bite clinched it—this was her recipe. But that was impossible!

My hungry, gurgling stomach didn't care. All it wanted was more food. So, after making the sign of the cross again, just in case, I blocked out everything around me and ate, drank, and enjoyed it. For all I knew, this *was* my last meal.

By the time I finished, my tears had dried, but my eyes prickled again when I saw what the cook brought me next.

"Are those what I think they are?" I asked, my voice not exactly steady.

He inclined his head as he switched my empty plate for a smaller one holding two pastries. "*Pastelitos de guayaba*," he said. The pronunciation was perfect.

I drank half the glass of water he had also brought, and using that as a distraction, placed my other arm on the counter so I could palm the knife that had come with the utensils. I hid it in the sleeve of the short kimono: if they pulled anything, I planned to be ready. Once it was safely tucked away, I reached out for the dessert: a puff pastry filled with guava paste and cream cheese, the top covered with powdered sugar—another Puerto Rican specialty.

I stuffed my face like a little pig, feeling calmer than I had since the moment before I'd spotted Pierson at the lucrative party. "Dios mío. You're a damn good cook."

The tiniest hint of a smile came and went again. "Glad you liked it." He refilled my water, then took charge of the first set of dirty dishes. His brow ticked up for half a second, but if he noticed that the knife was missing, he kept it to himself. No way to tell if that was good or bad. He headed back toward the kitchen.

'*If you're feeling better, I'd like to have a little chat.*'

Gooseflesh covered my arms and neck as the voice rang inside my head again.

¡Coño! The food had distracted me from the fact that this place had a telepathic cat.

Ida had also disappeared when I wasn't looking. But the front door still stood utterly unguarded. If I grabbed one of the umbrellas outside, I doubted they would ever realize it was gone. Yet I hesitated to leave all the same. I was good at reading people—it came with the job—and all that talk about running straight into death's embrace felt spot on. So what was the feline's angle? Everyone had one, even when they didn't realize it. I was positive they hadn't let me stay here and fed me out of the goodness of their hearts.

"Sure," I said, trying to sound more confident than I felt. I turned the stool so I could face the cat, though I would have preferred not to. "What did you want to talk about?"

'Did you perchance notice the "help wanted" sign outside?' Beauty asked. *'I would like to offer you the opportunity to work here.'*

"*¿Qué?*" My mouth fell open.

'I want you to work for me.'

My eye twitched. A telepathic cat was offering me a *job*? That lightning bolt earlier had to have hit me, and I was now burned and bleeding on the street, having a nightmare. Otherwise, how could any of this be real? "Um, what would that look like?"

And did that mean a cat was the boss here? How loco would that be?

Beauty ignored my question.

'*Room and board would be included, of course,*' Beauty said. '*And there are other perks. Staying alive would be but one of them.*'

Could a cat be smug? Because, at the moment, she sure looked like it—that jutting feline chin, the thrust-out fur-covered chest.

"So, I would need to stay in this place? Never go outside again?" I shook my head. "That would make this a *prison*. And eventually, some customer or other would rat me out, and then what? I would still wind up dead. And so would all of you."

I was arguing with a cat! Could this get any more insane?

'*I never said you couldn't go out,*' Beauty stated, blinking in slow motion. '*You'll be able to do so when the job calls for it and on your days off—if you've behaved yourself.*'

"But you said I would die if I went out," I countered. This chica wasn't born yesterday.

'*If you don't agree to work for me, that is correct.*' Beauty used a paw to sweep the fur over one ear.

How could taking the job make a difference? But then, how was this cat mentally talking to me in the first place? I shook my head. None of this was real. It couldn't be. I pinched myself, trying to see if it would wake me up or whatever—wasn't that how they always did it on TV?—but nothing changed.

"Let's say I believe you—which, to be honest, I'm not sure I can—what exactly would I be doing?" I asked. "You already have a fabulous cook and someone to clean the place. What do you need *me* for?"

Beauty got up on all fours and walked over on quiet feet, sashaying like some kind of feline supermodel. She rubbed up against me even as I tried to lean away, the urge to sneeze growing by the second. I loved cats, but my body didn't. As big as she was, I couldn't escape unless I were willing to fall over backward, stool and all.

But she sure was beautiful. Her white fur felt like the softest silk. This close, her green feline eyes glimmered like emeralds. She rubbed her head beneath my chin, and it was like being caressed by a lover.

My eyes started itching, and the sneeze was about to get the better of me when she pulled away. With a final swipe of her fluffy tail across my face, she moved down the counter and sat, coiling her tail around her in a circle.

I turned my face in the opposite direction, not able to hold back anymore. "Achoo!"

With her having put some distance between us, thankfully, the urge to sneeze didn't return. It would be a crime if I got snot on that gorgeous fur.

'*You have a unique set of talents, Daniela,*' Beauty said. '*Talents that I can use for a much loftier purpose.*' She gave me another of those slow, satisfied blinks.

Just how much did this cat know about me? And how? The food I'd eaten turned to rocks in my stomach. "And how exactly would you be using them?"

The smug look came back. '*To help troubled souls, of course,*' Beauty said. '*How else would they achieve peace and move on otherwise?*'

Then a loud knock came from the other side of the entry door.

Chapter 03

My heart leaped into my throat, fear rolling off in waves. I twisted off the stool, bringing out the dinner knife I'd tucked away, almost diving back to the corner. They'd found me! Instead of running and trying to find a hole to hide in until I might skip town, I had been lured in by the warmth, the food, and the offer of a job, and stayed here too long. Had that been the loco cat's true purpose? To keep me here until my killers could catch up to me?

The knock wasn't repeated; the sliding door pushed open instead.

But it had been locked, and the lights turned off! Had they picked the bolt somehow? These people still might not have had anything to do with my being found. Their deaths would be on my head! A cold sweat broke out all over me.

If I rushed past the intruder and made it outside, my pursuers would run after me and forget about the people here. I hunkered down, ready to make a break for it. *Please let me do this one last thing before I die!*

"Is it okay to come in again? Did you have enough time?"

I froze at the familiar-sounding boyish voice—one I'd been sure I would never hear again.

'*Your timing is perfect*,' Beauty said. '*Come on in*.'

I swallowed hard, hesitating so I could catch a glance of him instead of running off or forcing my way out the front door. *Mira*, I had to know!

A young man sheepishly stepped in through the open doorway. I couldn't breathe as I got a good look at him. There was no mistaking the side-swept fringe of his blond hair and the ever-present easy grin, which, with the open black shirt and creased pants, made him look like he'd just stepped off the cover of *GQ*. It was my best friend in the whole wide world.

"OMG! *Jay*!"

He turned my way, and our gazes met right before I plowed into him and squeezed him for all I was worth. "*Moron. ¡Pendejo!* I'm so happy to see you. I've been so worried!" Without my heels, he towered over me by a foot. I pulled back and shook him hard as if trying to shake fruit off a tree. "And now I'm going to *kill you*. You and your idiotic schemes!"

We might die at any second, but joy bubbled up and overflowed at the chance to see him again. After that night's debacle, I thought I'd lost him forever. My face hurt, I was smiling so hard.

But—

"Dani, I'm so, so sorry," Jay said, his eyes filling with tears. "They got you, too?"

All the happiness I'd felt at seeing him flowed out of me like water from a broken dam. "Wha—what are you talking about?" My hands dropped like heavy weights to my sides, and I took a trembling step back. "Di—didn't you escape like I did?"

I hadn't noticed it before, but Jay was dry, untouched by the heavy storm still raging loudly outside.

He shook his head, his hand rubbing the back of his neck as his ears turned beet red. "I got turned around. Took the wrong door," Jay said. "Got caught trying to find the right way again."

I could see it happening all too clearly in my mind. "Really, Jay?"

How many times had it been pounded into us to memorize the layout and always, always, *always* have a way out? And he'd gone and messed up the *one time* it really counted! It was so 'Jay' I would have laughed, except I might not be able to stop, even as it ripped me to shreds from the inside.

I was supposed to be the smart one. So why had I ever let him talk me into crashing that private party? But I knew why.

Because I wanted out, and he'd sounded so sure. If only I had pressed and questioned it more, he wouldn't be… wouldn't be…

"I've disappointed you again, haven't I?" Jay looked at me like a kid caught poking holes in the wrapping of his Christmas presents to sneak a peek at what was inside.

Suddenly, his expression brightened, his eyes shining. "But at least you made it out alive. And I'm super glad about that!" Then his smile dimmed, and he looked away, kicking at an invisible rock on the floor. "Still… this disaster was all my fault."

We had become best friends almost from the moment Pierson "recruited" us into his group. With my flash-powder temper and his easygoing surfer boy manner, we had balanced each other out—not that any of that was important anymore. "Naw. We're good, *hermano*."

I gave him another back-breaking hug to show him I meant it. But if he was dead, how was I able to do that? He was totally *here*. He was solid! His warm breath caressed my neck. I could hear his heartbeat. How could he feel this alive if he were dead? Could it all be some giant, drug-aided, elaborate prank?

'*Last Stop is a waypoint between the land of the living and the realm of the dead for those who aren't ready to move on, amongst other things.*' Beauty's voice rang in my head in the lightest of purrs. '*The normal laws of other worlds do not apply here. We have our own set of rules in this in-between.*'

"Dani, do you smell that?" Jay asked, excitement suddenly lacing his voice.

I let him go, Beauty's words still echoing between my ears as I struggled to make sense of it all. The cook came through the odd curtains again with a new tray filled with steaming food.

"No way!" Jay virtually jumped over to the counter. "Are those fried alligator bites? And *ceviche*? Freakin' awesome. Thanks, dude!"

I threw a glance at the cook. How had he known Jay's favorite dishes? How had he known *mine*? Was that part of how the laws worked here? Was he dead, too, like Jay? *Was I?*

My head started to pound. Surely I could take that as a sign that I hadn't died yet. And Beauty had implied as much.

But then why would the dead be hungry? Or be able to taste anything? My head throbbed harder, and I was swept with the sudden need to sit down before I fell down.

I grabbed the stool next to Jay's.

"These are so friggin' good!" Jay said. Half of his alligator bites were already gone. That boy could always put away his food. "You want some?"

My eyes prickled. "I already ate, but thanks anyway."

I felt someone's gaze on me, but when I looked up, the cook was already returning to the kitchen. Ida was still nowhere in sight, and Beauty had gone back to her perch on the shelf along the wall. So I swallowed hard, and tucked the knife still in my hand back up my sleeve. I watched Jay enjoy his last meal, trying to engrave his every move and sound into my memory, knowing that regardless of whatever was going on, this would be my last chance.

"Did I hear you say you had already been in here?" I asked him. This whole weird, crazy situation still made my head hurt, but he was the only one I trusted to tell it to me straight. Because deep inside, I knew darkness was coming. That this was but the briefest of reprieves before part of my soul got cut away.

Jay slipped me a sideways glance, as if he was acutely aware of the same thing. "Yeah. It was the weirdest thing," he said. "The place kind of called to me. And Beauty said she'd help."

"Help you do what?" I asked.

He stuffed his face rather than answer me. I couldn't gather the courage to repeat the question—at least not yet. When Jay was close to being finished, the cook showed up again. His timing was eerie. He had brought another tray, this one with two generous helpings of key lime pie.

"Key lime! *Yes*." Jay pumped his fist. "Dude, you are awesome!"

The almost non-existent smile made an appearance again. The cook set one plate before Jay and the other in front of me, then made off with the finished dishes.

Jay picked up his dessert fork and flashed an impish grin in my direction. I retrieved mine, and we crossed them like swords before a duel. Stuffed as I was already, my stomach churning and twisting with everything going on, I still ate the new dessert with relish because I was eating it with him.

"Holy moly!" Jay grinned, yellow filling showing on his teeth. "This isn't that condensed milk shit with a bucket of sugar thrown in. This is the real deal!"

I had to admit, the key lime was fabulous. Jay might be easygoing about most things, but he was a serious foodie about his pie. Whatever this place was, I was grateful they'd somehow managed to give him this before… whatever came next.

Jay bumped my shoulder with his. "I wouldn't have enjoyed this at all if I had gotten you killed, *hermana.* That wasn't what I wanted. You know that, right? I honestly thought I had good intel. That we'd clean house and finally get rid of your debt."

"I know." A forlorn sigh escaped before I could stop it. "You were pretty tight-lipped about where it came from. Was it Bobby?"

Jay glanced away. "Does it matter?"

I ground my teeth together. You would think being part of the same group *meant* something. The *cabrón* had only been with us for about a year, a "transfer" from out of state, from one of Pierson's friends' groups.

Not that I believed Pierson *had* friends. In his mind, everyone was a business associate, an asset, a mark, or beneath his notice. And though no one ever said, we were all pretty sure Bobby got into some deep shit with the law and had been dumped on us to get him out of the vicinity of the fire. The guy had skills, I'd give him that—which was the only reason they bothered to keep him from taking the heat, or why Pierson had taken him. Yeah, Bobby had been hot shit where he came from, but not here—and the prima donna hadn't liked that.

The pie turned to curdled lumps in my stomach.

The ungrateful ass had also put the moves on Jay to snag him off me. But though Jay had become smitten with the moron as planned, Bobby hadn't counted on Jay's deeply ingrained loyalty to me—he had remained my partner instead of switching. So I assumed this stunt had been Bobby's way of paying us back.

The flash of utter hatred at the *lambón* for having done this was so strong it left me gasping. I concentrated on the pain in my palms from the nails digging into them as my hands curled into tight fists on my lap. If I ever laid eyes on that cabrón again, he was a dead man.

"You warned me, and I knew better," Jay said, his voice barely above a whisper. "But I believed him anyway when he said he wanted to make up and play nice. He even helped with the research." He swallowed hard. "Bobby said that being in love was more important to him in the end than the pecking order."

He hung his head until I couldn't see his face. But there was no way to miss the wet drops falling on his legs. "I fucked up so hard, Dani. All I wanted was for you to be free of Pierson and get to live your life, be whoever you wanted. I would have helped Bobby fill in your spot and be number one. I'm really, really sorry."

I smacked my fiery loathing with the back of a shovel and buried it deep—for now. There were other things that needed to be taken care of before vengeance came into the picture. So I put Jay in a partial chokehold and rubbed a knuckle hard into his hair.

"Yeah, well, what else is new?" I shoved as much brightness into the words as I could. "Now, are you going to eat that pie or will I have to take it off your hands?"

He gave a half-hearted chuckle. "No way, man. That's mine."

Jay wiped his face on his sleeve and started eating again, his arm curled protectively around the plate. I pushed what was left of mine over so he could take it if he wanted. He chuckled again, this time sounding more like his usual joyful, carefree self before we got into a battle of elbows.

My eyes hurt and my throat closed tight, knowing this was the last time I would ever do this with him.

'Do you understand now?' Beauty's words trickled into my mind. I glanced over, and the glittering emerald gaze locked with mine. '*Your life was spared only because of him. So he could move on.* You *are his unfinished business.*'

Chapter 04

"What are you talking about?" I asked.

Beauty didn't reply.

Jay stopped shoving food into his pie hole. "I didn't say anything."

"Never you mind." I flicked his ear. "And no talking with your mouth full. So gross."

He opened his mouth wide and made loud chomping noises while making sure I could see everything in there. Jay was such a *child* sometimes. The itching in my eyes worsened, and it had nothing to do with my cat allergy.

'*Speaking aloud is not necessary when others are present,*' Beauty said inside my mind, seemingly for me alone. '*Just imagine what you would say out loud, but say it only in your head.'*

Didn't she say she couldn't read minds? How would this be any different?

'*No. I really* can't *read your mind—as I said. But speaking mind to mind is something else altogether.'* Beauty kneaded the air in front of her with her paws. '*Thoughts are too chaotic. But putting the words together in your mind as if you were speaking allows them to be heard. If you stay, you'll find this quite useful. So why not give it a try?*' Her alien feline eyes half closed as if daring me to do it.

Jay was still busy savoring his pie, so I gave it a shot.

'*What do you mean, my life was only spared because of Jay?*' I thought at her.

'*Oh, look at you, getting it right on your first try,*' Beauty said with a vibrating purr. She shifted onto her side like a pleased empress on a comfortable settee. '*This arrangement could work perfectly.*'

'*You're not answering the question.*' I was pretty sure she was doing it on purpose.

'*One of our jobs is to help the dead move on and put them at ease as much as possible before they go. You saw how upset he became at the thought he'd gotten you killed. But now that he knows you didn't die, his soul will be at peace and allow him to pass to the other side,*' Beauty said.

I was happy about that and all, but... '*But I'll still die if I leave unless I work for you.*'

'*Which would be unfortunate. Especially after we've gone to so much trouble to save you for your partner's sake,*' Beauty said. '*You wouldn't want to throw all that effort away and make him unhappy, now, would you?*'

¡Bruja! Using Jay's happiness and my life as bargaining chips to blackmail me into this? That was low. Though from a professional perspective, I had to admire her acumen.

Beauty's eyes closed to slits as if amused. '*If you prefer, you could stay until he transitions, then go out and meet your doom.*'

She was a slick one, that was for sure. '*If I take this gig, can I quit whenever I want?*'

Beauty dipped her head slightly. '*Absolutely. Though some advance notice would be nice.*'

I could read people pretty well, but how the heck was I supposed to read a *cat*? The offer seemed too good to be real—almost like I was making a deal with the Devil.

But Jay was dead. He'd confirmed it himself. And the party debacle meant my old life was over. I didn't have any prospects or any kind of a future out there to save. I was done no matter what.

Jay had finished off both pieces of pie and was now licking the plate.

'Fine.' My teeth ground into each other. *'I'll take the job.'* But if she thought I would just lie there and take it, I would prove her dead wrong. I would bide my time.

'Marvelous!'

"Bodacious!" Jay exclaimed, as if on cue, startling me. "That was totally and completely *bodacious!*"

He was so loud that the mysterious cook peeked toward us past his curtain.

"You, sir, are a god amongst men." A total surf-head when he could get away with it, Jay now gave the cook a double *shaka*, extending his thumb and pinkie with the rest of his fingers curled in.

A tiny grin tugged almost invisibly on the cook's lips as he returned the gesture before disappearing again.

"I wish we'd found this place sooner, Dani," Jay said, taking in the place now that the food was gone. "It's all sorts of awesome."

I nodded, not bothering to tell him that in order to come here, one had to die first, or come close to it. The kind of place no one should be in a hurry to get to, no matter how great the food was.

Jay turned his head toward the small hallway on the right as if he'd heard something, and stood up. A moment later, he turned to face me again, an odd eagerness shining on his face. "Dani, I've… I've got to go. They're calling for me."

I hadn't heard a thing. "Who's calling you, Jay?" My heart started beating faster. Somewhere deep down, I had an inkling of what this might be about. I slipped off the stool, tempted to grab onto him and never let go.

Couldn't he stay here with me? But even as I thought it, I knew it was a selfish wish.

Jay kept glancing over his shoulder, stepping backward into the hallway toward whoever or whatever was calling him, as if it were getting harder and harder to ignore. I followed him, not knowing what else to do—a fish after a shiny lure. The way his eyes lit up, it was obvious he wanted to go, but he was holding back because of me.

Tears threatened my eyes, claws of despair tearing at my insides. I was about to lose him. I would never see him again. How would I ever get along without Jay? He was all I had left. If the job had gone smoothly and been as lucrative as we hoped, I would never have left without him. Again, I was tempted to ask him to stay, and again, I held myself back, shaking.

We hadn't gone far before the hallway dead-ended at a black stone wall. The three-by-three stone blocks fitted together almost seamlessly, and they were so highly polished they acted like mirrors. Though it looked new, there was a weight about it that insisted it was ancient. Jay stopped right in front of it, as if the voices that were calling him came from the other side.

His gaze locked onto mine. "I'll miss you."

Then he came forward and hugged me.

I lost it. Crying out, I grabbed him back, burying my face against him. "¡*No puedes irte*! *Por favor*. ¡Jay, *no te vayas*! Don't leave me here all alone."

I was supposed to be the strong one. *I* was supposed to be the one watching out for him, the one setting an example of calm.

But I couldn't do it. My heart was cracking, splitting into a million pieces. I would never be able to put it back together if he left.

I had never known my parents, so their loss hadn't impacted me much, aside from the empty space they would have filled if they hadn't died. When Abuela passed, I was already in Pierson's group, learning the skills and doing errands for him that would help me pay back our growing debt. I had curled deep into myself and only gone through the motions until Jay's endless optimism pulled me back from the brink. But now he was leaving me, too. Please, Dios, let him stay with me!

"I love you, Dani," Jay said, his words as emotion-filled as mine. I heard the "goodbye" in them. He wasn't going to stay. Not even for me.

I cried that much harder. My grip on him tightened.

"Thank you for everything."

I pitched forward onto my knees, cracking them against the wooden floor because I suddenly had nothing to hold onto. Jay was still there, but he wasn't solid anymore. He half-floated, half-walked backward into the reflective black wall.

"We'll meet again someday. I'm sure of it," he said. "But don't be in a hurry to join me, hermana. Live for the both of us, and have awesome adventures to share with me when we meet again."

Then he was gone.

"*Jay*!" My voice cracked. The wail turned into a sob as I hid my face in my hands and leaned over my throbbing knees, my whole body shuddering so hard I felt it might fall apart, a horrid pain stabbing my chest repeatedly.

I felt Beauty's heavy gaze on me the entire time.

Chapter 05

How long I cried after Jay left, I had no idea. But never once did I stop feeling those alien green eyes watching me—whether as a witness to my loss or something else, I didn't know. She was getting off on my misery, for all I knew.

But it didn't matter. Nothing much mattered anymore—Jay was gone.

"What happens now?" I eventually asked the room in general. My voice sounded rough; every breath felt like sandpaper. My nose was clogged. I rose on wobbly legs, painful tingles zapping me here and there as blood flow returned.

'*A hot bath and sleep are in order.*' Beauty's words floated gently into my mind. '*You've had a long and draining night.*'

Ida appeared at the hall entrance from the eating area. Though she still wore the pink housedress and white apron, her back had straightened, and the capricious, little-girl look was absent from her lined face. Her entire presence felt different, but how or why, I couldn't say. "Please follow me," Ida said.

Throwing Beauty a veiled glance to make sure she was still there, I trailed after the older woman. Putting one foot in front of the other took most of my concentration. I couldn't remember the last time I had been this exhausted and wrung out.

Ida led me around to the U-counter's left hallway. The corridor seemed to go on forever. It was made of the same aged, reddish wood as the front.

Ida stopped before a doorway with frosted glass and a paneled sliding door. A half curtain, like the one before the kitchen, hung here. This one was red with a Japanese symbol on it. A second entrance, a few feet further, sported a blue drape with a different character over the same style door.

"This kanji means women, while the other is for men," Ida said. A shudder shook me, and the hackles at the back of my neck rose. The possibly addled woman didn't sound like she had before. The color of her eyes had changed, too. Hadn't they been brown? Now they were green.

Ida slid the door open and ventured inside. That was when I realized she also wasn't shuffling, but was walking normally.

An icy finger made its way up my back.

The new room had a wooden bench against the right wall, with a matching set of cubby holes on the left. Two steps led into a wider area done in dark slate tiles. Slim partitions separated multiple flexible showerheads into their own sections. Each had a small wooden stool, body brushes, soap, oils, shampoos, and conditioners.

Across from them was a bed-sized inset wooden tub with steam curling at the edges. An incense burner on a corner shelf by the bath scented the air with the woody, earthy creaminess of sandalwood. A gorgeous mural of Mt. Fuji and a tranquil beach filled the entire back wall.

"You undress here," Ida said, "then go wash over there." She pointed to the area with the stools. "Once you're clean, you can relax in the onsen and let your worries drain away."

Ida brought my attention to a cubby hole holding a small cooler. "After you finish and get dressed again, make sure to grab a drink. Nothing beats a cold fruit juice or coffee milk after a long soak."

I gave a nod, still totally creeped out.

"A first aid kit is in the cubby next to it, if you need it."

The bullet graze on my arm started hurting again, almost as if she'd woken it.

"Please take as much time as you like," Ida said. "Enjoy your bath."

She walked away and slid the door closed behind her.

I was alone.

Since there was nothing else I could do at the moment, I took advantage of the solitude and the unexpected chance to get cleaned up.

I took off the lovely red robe and folded it neatly before placing it into a cubby. I shimmied out of my wine-colored satin tube dress, which I was pretty sure was toast. My undies and strapless bra were next, along with my emergency cash and the recently liberated dinner knife. I had ditched my mini smartphone into the nearest dumpster after getting out of the building where the disastrous party had been held.

These few things were the only possessions I had left. Going anywhere near my apartment or contacting anyone I knew would be suicide, so everything else I owned was now gone. My eyes started stinging again, so I forced myself to move and not give in to the urge to wallow. There'd be no more tears.

I couldn't afford them.

I closed a second sliding door, which cut off the changing area from the rest of the bath, and sat on one of the stools. It was weird to get clean before bathing, but I'd seen enough yakuza movies to recognize the setup. Once I had scrubbed and rinsed every inch of me, blow-dried my hair, pinned it up, and cleaned and dressed the graze, I approached the sunken tub and got in.

The water was hot, but not overly so, and I sat on the built-in seat that ran all around the inside of the onsen. Sitting, the water level reached breastbone height.

¡Ay, Dios mío! This felt so good. I leaned my head back against the edge, letting the warmth sink into me. Bit by bit, I relaxed, allowing the water to work its magic. With my eyes half closed, I stared at the mural. I could have sworn a soft breeze came in from the bay to cool my heated face.

The sound of a far-off ship's horn had me blinking and sitting up straight. My eyes were heavy, so I reluctantly pulled myself out before I fell asleep again.

My body radiated waves of heat, so the water must have been hotter than I thought. I put everything back on except my ruined dress, tied the robe tight, and pulled out a milk coffee from the cooler. The bottle tab followed my still-damp duds into the trash.

I will admit that the first cold sip was true nirvana. The drink's coolness descended my throat and spread. Soon, the empty container joined its discarded lid. A pair of slippers had been set by the sliding door for me, pointing outward. I slipped them on before opening the door.

Neither Ida nor Beauty had mentioned where I should go when I was done, so I stepped out hesitantly. I was taken aback when I found the older woman waiting for me in the hallway like a patient statue.

"¡*Ay*!" My hand rose to my chest. "You startled me." All the sense of well-being and sleepiness I had managed to pull together took a quick step back.

"I'm *so* sorry." Ida didn't particularly look it. Her eyes were still green, and she seemed way too amused. "I was waiting to take you to your room."

"Oh. Sure."

Ida turned around and walked down the hallway. A set of stairs revealed itself to the right. Built-in shelves held more slippers and a pair of comfortable-looking black loafers.

"Shoes go here, or you can carry them up to your room with you," Ida said. "Only slippers or bare feet are worn upstairs."

An odd rule, but okay. Ida had on her bunny slippers, and I had the ones from the bath, so we didn't have to stop before going up.

"This place is larger than I expected," I said. Might as well gather what info I could. No telling how long I'd be here.

"Last Stop is quite versatile," Ida said. "It gives us what we need. However, I would suggest not getting on its bad side. That's never a good idea."

Without meaning to, I crossed myself. Was she saying this restaurant, waystop, whatever this place was, was *alive*? Did that mean it was constantly *watching* me? Goosebumps spread out in a wave all over my arms and legs.

The hallway at the top of the stairs was wider than the ones downstairs. The floor and walls were made of a lighter-colored wood and looked pristine, almost as if we'd entered somewhere new rather than still being in the same building. I spotted several doors with wooden plaques. On the left was one with a plain doorframe that matched its plaque, with black widow spiders carved at the corners. It had Ida's name on it.

On the right was a more elaborate door frame with angles and curves, giving it an oriental flair. A dragon and tiger were entangled together in a yin-yang symbol. The sign had a frame in the same style, the center black with white lettering. It was marked "Ryo/Ken" and the lettering looked as if it had been brushed on in slashes, like cuts from a sword.

A third door had an ornate baroque carved frame in a warm-colored wood. The plaque matched it, with "Dani" written on it in a flowing, curling font.

"Get some rest," Ida said. "In the morning, we can pick things up where we left." She threw me a wink, then walked back to the door with her name on it and went inside.

I stared after her, sure I had "left off" nothing with Ida, though I had with Beauty. I crossed myself again. Keeping my thoughts as far away from what that might mean as possible, I stepped into my assigned apartment.

Then I came to a dead stop.

My room *was* my room.

There sat the fancy iron rod bedframe in white and gold that I'd snatched at an estate sale. The frilly yellow and white bed cover—the posters of Puerto Rico in different art styles. Even the red and green lava lamp Jay got me for Christmas one year.

I stood rooted to the spot, knowing this wasn't possible. I pressed the palms of my hands against my eyes, a shot of vertigo making it feel like I was on a storm-tossed deck of a ship deep at sea. ¡*Dios, ayudame*! This was too much, too much!

Then my brain pointed out that not every detail was exactly the same. I was good with details, spotting what didn't fit—a long-studied survival skill. If I could figure out what was different, I might be able to keep from going *loca*. I racked my head trying to work it out from just the quick look I had taken.

The window. The window was missing. A large poster of a calm, black-sand beach had replaced it—*Playa Los Bohios*. I remembered the place from the only time I'd been to Puerto Rico since I was a baby. It had stuck with me because it was near the protected sea turtle beach. I shook my head, this not being the time to go traipsing down memory lane.

The second odd thing was the fact that there was no hint of mold or mildew in the air—one of the reasons rent was cheaper where I lived than in other nearby places. Keeping the stuff under control had been a constant battle since my meager cut of the day's take wasn't enough to run the A/C full-time. After Pierson's regular percentage, most of what I had left went against my debt for his help with my abuela, and housing and feeding me, along with several other kids, back when we'd first met.

So this *wasn't* my room—only a very close approximation.

My insides stopped roiling around. I opened one eye to make sure I could handle it and wasn't only fooling myself. Other minute differences jumped out at me—like the fact that the apartment was bigger than mine. All the furniture and other stuff were set farther apart from each other than normal. I could sit on the loveseat against the wall without smacking into my tiny coffee table. There was actually room on either side of the bed.

A sweet, vanilla-infused scent floated about. Someone had set a plate of freshly made sugar cookies on the coffee table. They were so fresh, I half burned my fingers picking one up. A bite proved they were still soft and chewy and had just come out of the oven—exactly the way I liked them. Jay had always rolled his eyes at me when I baked them because I devoured my share right away, while he waited for his to cool and become crunchy.

My eyes suddenly grew itchy again. I shoved a hot cookie in my mouth to distract myself.

Had the cook made these for me, or was it a gift from the house? But wait—buildings couldn't cook for you, right? *Right*?

I didn't grab another one; I'd had more than my fill of weirdness for the month. Leaving the light on, I crawled into bed. The pillows and sheets felt the same. ¡*Que extraño*! It only made my sense of disconnection flare. So I grabbed my blanket and threw it over me before hugging my knees to my chest and curling into a fetal position.

Much to my surprise and that of my oddity-drowned mind, I soon fell asleep.

Chapter 06

At first, I sat up and stretched, my eyes half closed. They were itchy and gooey. My sinuses felt congested. Then, I sneezed out of nowhere. ¿Qué?

That's when I noticed a few strands of stray white hair on the blanket—or rather, white fur.

I sneezed again, and everything that had happened the night before came back like a bucket of ice water dumped on my head.

Jay was gone. And I was trapped in some kind of freaky waystation for the dead.

With my stomach cramping, I stumbled out of bed and headed to my tiny bathroom. Except when I set foot inside, it wasn't. Unlike the bedroom area, which had been created to resemble my apartment in the real world, the "house" hadn't bothered to do the same with the restroom.

Gone was the cramped, low toilet made for children; the chipped off-white sink and cracked mirror; and the sad excuse for a shower. This bathroom was lavish, repeating the same warm wood and baroque styling of my door. The floor was tiled in white, black, and gold marble. A long vanity with a large sink held all my makeup, with room to spare. It also had a matching tucked-away stool. No more cheap, stackable Tupperware to keep all my things.

There was even a club-footed tub and a separate shower stall if I didn't want to use the Japanese-style setup downstairs.

I brushed my teeth (same toothbrush, same toothpaste), put on minimal makeup (all my regular brands plus a few more I hadn't ever been able to afford, and all of them brand new), and brushed my unruly hair in record time, the weirdness of having such a place making me twitch and freaking me out. It was like going to a Motel 6 and being transported to a five-star hotel penthouse. Relief washed over me as I crossed back into my replicated bedroom.

My closet door was in the familiar spot, though the inside had changed there, too. Rather than the squished coat closet where I had to literally fight to wedge my clean clothes in, it was now the size of something out of a fancy master bedroom. With all that space, my clothes only took up a small percentage of it. There was also a section where my shoes had been placed side by side in multiple rows rather than being stacked in their boxes to be pawed through.

I grabbed a pair of jeans, a blouse, a pair of sandals, and some hoop earrings before leaving the closet to get dressed in the bedroom. While I'd been in there, someone—or some*thing*—had made my bed, gotten rid of the cat hair, and set a fresh pair of undies and a matching bra on top of it. Cold sweat broke out in several places, and the hackles rose on my neck. I made super-short work of putting my clothes on and getting the heck out of the room.

Sandals in hand, I made my way downstairs barefoot, trying to make the least amount of noise possible. I didn't understand what this job I had been strong-armed into would cover, and I wasn't in a hurry to find out. Despite Last Stop being an eatery of sorts, I doubted they'd recruited me for my commerce acumen from the few online business classes I'd taken. Which only left my not-quite-legal skills—info gathering, scoping out locations for the boss, and, of course, my main talent. But what would the dead need a pickpocket for?

Once I made it to the bottom of the stairs, I slipped on my sandals and headed toward the restaurant part of the building. Gulping coffee of any kind was the first thing on my agenda.

I spotted the weirdo, Ida, sitting on one of the stools as I came in. Rather than the housedress and bunny slippers from before, today she wore a rather snazzy brown pantsuit, and fancy, expensive shoes. Her profile was all hard edges and angles, totally different from the child-like Ida I'd met when I first arrived, or the disturbing one who'd led me upstairs. She was also smoking a pricy, black-and-gold-wrapped cigarette brand set in a long jade cigarette holder, like in the old black-and-white films from the forties.

She saw me staring and turned her stool around to face me. Her ice-cold stare tried to pin me where I stood. "Who the *hell* are you?"

"Uh, hi. My name is Dani," I said, wondering what was happening. "We met last night?"

Her nose rose in the air, and she looked me up and down from her lofty position, her souring expressions making it clear she found me wanting. She blew a perfect ring of cigarette smoke in my direction before saying, "As if I'd waste my time talking to someone like you."

Cold shock turned into scathing heat. This kind of attitude always made my blood want to combust.

"Who do you think you are, talking to me like that, *bruja*?" This *Boricua* didn't take insults lying down.

Snooty Ida didn't reply, returning her stool to its original position, acting as if I'd ceased to exist.

My temper flared to erupting volcano levels. It took everything I had not to tromp over and yank her off her stool by the hair. My whole body shook with the need to teach her some manners via a healthy dose of violence.

I would have turned around and returned upstairs, but I didn't want to give her the satisfaction of having run me off. Instead, I took a couple of deep, calming breaths and sat in the stool beside hers. Her body tensed beside me, and she threw me a spite-filled glare. "Sit somewhere else, spic. Know your place."

"*No hablo inglés*. Sorry!" I flashed her the sweetest and brightest smile in my arsenal.

If looks could slice you into chunky pieces, I would have dropped dead right there and then. Luckily for me, I'd encountered enough of those over the years to make me immune.

When I still made no move to leave, the harpy slowly removed the cigarette holder from her mouth, switching her hold on it as if about to plunge it like a brand into my face.

"*Ida Rolls!*"

The older woman jumped in her seat, startled by the loud, unexpected voice. The jerky motion knocked the cigarette out of its fancy holder. Ida's corresponding glare in my direction grew sharp enough to draw blood. She turned away and masked her open hatred before glancing at the cook, acting as if nothing happened.

"Yes, Chef?" A tinge of tension and fear coated her voice, despite the act of innocence she put on. If she couldn't stand Latinos, I doubted she felt any different about Asians, or people of mixed races, but for whatever reason, she was loath to show it in front of him. Had they clashed before, and he'd come out on top? I wouldn't have expected it from someone as shy as him—but I would have paid good money to have seen it.

There sure were some odd interpersonal dynamics in this crazy place. And not just from Ida's bizarre set of personalities. Sadly, it did nothing to make me feel better about being here.

The cook drifted over from behind the kitchen curtain, his eyes never leaving Ida's—like a mongoose staring down a cobra. "You know Beauty doesn't like us being rude," he said. "And Daniela is one of us now."

Ida's entire face puckered as if tasting something sour. "I'll take breakfast in my room." She picked up the fallen cigarette and returned it to the holder, ignoring the ashes she left behind for someone else to clean up.

He watched her until she was gone. Then he turned his dark gray eyes in my direction, which were made prominent by his large, round-lensed glasses. "Sorry about that," he said. "This is one of her good days."

"*That* was a good day?" I couldn't keep the disbelief from my voice. "Does the bruja have Alzheimer's or something?"

The tiniest grin came and went on the cook's face. "Something like that."

At least I'd learned he could string words together. Jay had been a chatterbox. The cook seemed to aim for the exact opposite.

"What's your name, by the way?" I asked him. "You obviously already know mine." Might as well find out who I had to thank for that timely intervention.

His expression turned sheepish. "Ryo."

"Hi, Ryo. Sorry about all the drama last night," I said.

"Not your fault." He even looked like he meant it. And he'd recognized me despite my not looking like a drowned rat anymore. The fact that he didn't bring that up was a plus.

"Coffee?" he asked.

"*¿Con leche*?"

"Absolutely. Be right back." Ryo returned to the kitchen. The sounds of an espresso machine filtered over from the other side of the half-curtain. The scent of coffee and other delicious, tempting-smelling things wafted over as well, making my stomach rumble lightly in anticipation.

Glancing around, I noticed the front door was partially slid open to let in the fresh air. My pulse sped up with a tinge of fear, but looking out, I didn't see the warehouse district I'd run through in the storm. Instead, a beautiful green field with the sun rising on the horizon filled the view. I turned back around in a hurry, my heart pounding loudly in my ears.

Buildings didn't just get up and move. Right? *Right?*

I closed my eyes and forced myself to drag in long, deep breaths, the floor not exactly steady. My heart couldn't take much more of this strangeness.

"Here you go."

I half-flew out of my seat, my eyes popping open. I hadn't heard Ryo walk up. The cook was eerily quiet, coming *and* going. He set a nice-sized mug of *café con leche* in front of me, as well as a small plate with several cheddar cheese cubes and buttered pieces of toast. He then brought out a bottle of honey from beneath the counter.

Gooseflesh roamed all over my body. "Why did you bring that?" I pointed at the cheese cubes.

His gray eyes unfocused for a moment. "Because *Hokora*, our spirit house, asked me to," he said. "Was it wrong?" Ryo's brows raised minutely and bunched together, his voice sounding worried.

He did *not* just say the building told him to do this. Another round of goosebumps rolled pell-mell all over me.

"No," I said in a hurry, bringing my hands up to add weight to the denial. "I was just surprised. *Mi abuela* used to put cubes like these in her café to make the cheese get chewy and absorb some of the flavor. She used to dip her toast in her coffee, too. It's fun and nostalgic to do that every once in a while."

Now he looked confused. "Was she Swedish?"

"What? No!" It was my turn to be baffled, as if I hadn't had enough of that already. "It's just a thing she did."

"Oh." The tips of his ears turned red. "Sorry. I had heard that Swedes do something similar." He staunchly avoided eye contact. "Excuse me." The cook made his escape back to the kitchen.

Why did it feel like I had just kicked a puppy?

'*You might want to handle him with a light hand in the future.*' Beauty's voice rang in my head. She leaped up onto the U-shaped counter. '*His upbringing was... unusual. So his social skills and his ability to process emotions are sorely underdeveloped.*'

Ryo popped back out only long enough to settle a milk-filled saucer on the counter for Beauty. Her lush tail caressed his cheek like a hand in thanks before he disappeared again. He never once glanced my way. Beauty daintily lapped up the milk.

I was glad he couldn't overhear the conversation, especially if what she was saying was true. Her comments made questions bubble up, and then even more questions rose in response to those. But there might be an angle I could cultivate through the cook. If there was one thing I'd learned under Rob Pierson, it was to watch for opportunities and, once identified, exploit them. Survival of the fittest.

Needing a distraction, I put two cheddar cheese cubes in my coffee and added a little honey. After stirring my coffee, I dunked a buttered piece of toast in it and took a bite. Wistful flavors from my childhood of coffee, butter, and melting cheese exploded inside my mouth.

It had been too long since the last time I'd indulged in this. I was *so* going to pack on the pounds in this place.

Seeing Beauty drink reminded me of the stray strands of fur I found on my bed. "You were in my room last night," I stated boldly. "While I was in there, sleeping, and without my permission." What I couldn't figure out was how she had been able to lie there without a sneezing fit waking me up.

'*Perhaps.*' Beauty continued lapping her treat. '*This is my domain, and I will do what I like in it.*'

I guess that answered that. Though it irritated the hell out of me, I wasn't exactly sure what I could do about it. Jamming a chair against the doorknob might keep her out. Assuming there wasn't another way into the room I didn't know about, or that the place didn't move the impediment out of the way for her.

"What's the deal with Ida?" I asked, before I let myself follow that disturbing thorn-filled path. Besides, the more information I gathered, the faster I would get over all the weird stuff. Only then would I have my head on straight and be able to get the edge I needed.

Beauty turned slitted emerald eyes in my direction, blinking slowly as if she hadn't a care in the world and knew exactly what I was thinking. It was unnerving and made my palms sweat.

This chica wasn't going to back down, though. I kept my eyes locked on hers, demanding an answer.

'*Ida is something of a* special *case,*' Beauty finally said. '*She is here for punishment, to make amends, and to be my plaything.*' Beauty lapped at her milk some more.

The bruja was a cat's *toy*? The image of Ida showing me the bath last night rose before me—the obvious change in personality, the green tint that had appeared in her eyes. Cold shivers shook me where I sat. Was she using the old woman like a puppet? ¡Ay, Dios mío! Could she do that to me?

'Don't feel sorry for her.' Beauty lounged on the counter, having finished her treat. *'The Ida you first met is what she was becoming in the real world. Age regression due to Alzheimer's.'* She yawned. *'It's how she was finally caught. You see, Ida was a rather infamous Black Widow.'*

Claro. It fit the bruja to a T.

'After being convicted, she got shanked, thanks to her winning personality.' Something close to a purr swirled around in my head. *'I was in need of a helper at the time, and she wouldn't have lasted the night without interference. She was miffed that after agreeing to work for me, she couldn't get the upper hand over a mere feline.'*

I took a long sip of my coffee to hide what I could of my face. Typically, hiding my true feelings behind a pleasant mask was easy, but I was too freaked out to trust it was working right now. That last bit had hit a little too close to what I had been thinking a minute ago. Beauty kept insisting she couldn't read minds, but it was getting harder and harder to believe that. Sharp-toothed fear curled up at the bottom of my spine and settled in for an extended stay. *Jay, what did you get me into?*

'Dani, you've nothing to worry about. Unless you give me cause, of course.' Beauty's tail swished about in the air like a lure.

If she was trying to reassure me, it wasn't working. "Is Ryo being punished as well?" The last came out as a strangled squeak. *Get it together, chica*! *Do not show any weakness, or you're liable to become the one toyed with!*

'*No.*' Beauty gave me another of those slow blinks. '*He's here to atone for his sins—though they weren't exactly his own. And to have a chance to learn what living actually is. His skill set is rare, so we're fortunate to have him. I'm sure you'll find out about them soon enough.*'

Did everything she said have to sound like a threat? She had to be doing it on purpose. I spooned out one of the half-melted cheese cubes and ate it, my brain running at a thousand miles an hour. So the cook was more than a cook?

"I know I'm here thanks to Jay, but…" Let's rip that Band-Aid right off. "What will I be doing, exactly?"

'*You'll find that out soon enough, too.*' Beauty's emerald-green eyes sparkled with amusement.

Chapter 07

I asked no more questions and concentrated on finishing my food. Irritation at Beauty's evasions poked holes in my fear, and I let it, preferring that to drowning in terrorized uncertainty.

Ryo came by for Beauty's empty saucer and then headed to the back of the building with a covered tray. Beauty continued to lounge and stare at me as if enjoying my discomfort, eagerly awaiting what I might do next to entertain her. Ugh.

The sound of the restaurant's door sliding open sent me swirling around on my stool in a panic. If what I had seen in my quick glimpse earlier was real, there shouldn't have been anyone about to come inside.

The view outside the restaurant had changed again, though I hadn't felt a thing, making it more disturbing. I looked out into a quiet suburban neighborhood filled with two-story colonial-style houses and large trees. A light dusting of snow lay everywhere. This definitely wasn't Miami.

For the sake of my splitting head and sanity, I focused my attention on our unexpected visitor instead. She was a young Black girl with pigtails, wearing a red pinafore dress and a long-sleeved white shirt. The kid didn't have a coat, but the cold didn't appear to affect her. She gingerly stepped inside. "Hello?"

I was glad Ida had left the room in a huff. She would have probably snapped at the girl and sent her crying back to where she came from.

"*Chiquita*, are you lost?" I slipped off my stool, sure she wasn't supposed to be here.

Our visitor shyly shook her head.

'*This is exactly where she is meant to be*,' Beauty said silently in my mind.

It took a moment for my brain to connect the dots. The child couldn't be over six years old, and she was *dead*?

The girl ran forward, having caught sight of Beauty as she sauntered down the counter in our direction. "Kitty!"

Beauty jumped to the floor to meet her. '*Be gentle, child.*' Tail wrapped around her, Beauty assumed a stoic pose. '*Not everyone gets the privilege of stroking my fur.*'

Fighting to restrain her obvious excitement, the girl squatted and gingerly moved her hand to pet Beauty's back. "So soft." A barely repressed squeal followed.

How could this chiquita handle the reality of a cat talking into her mind as if it were an everyday thing? I had been exposed to it a lot longer, and I still couldn't wrap my head around it.

Her little face lit up with an enormous smile as purring and pleased trills filled the air. The girl gave another tiny squeal.

From the corner of my eye, I saw Ryo return in a rush and duck back into the kitchen, though he made no sound. How the heck did he do that? And what was he in a hurry about?

I got my answer less than a minute later. The cook came out from behind the half-curtain, bearing a tray with a super fancy strawberry parfait and a long spoon.

'*Beverly, look at what Ryo prepared especially for you,*' Beauty said.

The girl glanced up, her eyes growing wide upon seeing the towering concoction on the counter. "That's for me?"

'*Yes, sweetness.*'

This time, the squeal wasn't repressed at all and echoed with glee around the room.

'*Help her up, won't you, Dani?*' Beauty asked.

"Sure."

Before I could try to give her a hand, la chiquita had already clambered onto the stool on her own. She was bouncing in her seat as she reached for the long spoon. Ryo studied her intently as she dug in. Though a hint of a smile graced his lips at her wild abandon, the minutely furrowed brows over his warm gray eyes spoke of sadness and loss.

Beauty jumped on the counter and groomed herself while Beverly ate. The girl licked the inside rim of the parfait glass, having eaten every bite. She turned an admiring gaze in Ryo's direction. "That was so yummy. Thank you, Mr. Cook."

A bashful expression overtook Ryo's face as he brought out a cloth napkin for her to use. "I'm glad you liked it," he said.

I assumed they would now lead the child on through as they had with Jay, but no one moved to do that. Instead, Beauty inched a little closer to the girl. '*What unfinished business would you like us to take care of for you, Beverly Price?*'

That caught me by surprise. Could a child this young genuinely have unfinished business? I grabbed the seat next to hers.

The light dimmed in Beverly's face, and she hung her head, slumping her small shoulders. "Do I have to say?"

'*We can't help you if you don't, dear.*' Beauty's tone was remarkably gentle and kind.

"I, I took Mystic without permission and never got a chance to give her back," Beverly admitted. Her little legs started swinging to and fro.

Ryo quietly retrieved the used dishes and slunk to the emotional safety of the kitchen.

"Who's Mystic, Beverly?" I asked her, adopting the same tone as Beauty.

"She's a unicorn," Beverly said, with extra care on the last word as if she'd had to practice it to say it correctly. "A Beanie Baby unicorn." She looked up, tears shining in her young eyes. "She's Linda's favorite. She never let me play with her because she got her from her Gran, who went to Heaven."

Beanie Babies—a toy craze from the 90s that still had traction to this day. Might Linda's grandmother have gotten her one of the rare ones? Collectors had supposedly paid over half a million for some of those.

"Was it a 'special' Mystic, Beverly?" I asked.

Before the girl could answer, I got a flick of fluffy cat tail in the face, making me sneeze. Beauty's chiding voice rang in my head solely for my benefit. '*That isn't what we're after here.*'

'*We don't know that!*' I thought back to her, clenching my jaw. '*She could have taken the toy to sell it on eBay, for all we know,*' I snapped. '*And you haven't even told me a thing about this* job *you strong-armed me into, anyway.*'

The cat's insidious tail flicked at me again, forcing a second sneeze from me. ¡Coño!

"Bless you," Beverly said. Her little brow furrowed. "She's special to Linda. Is that what you mean?"

Beauty's tail was poised for another attack. "Never mind."

'*We can deliver Mystic back to Linda for you,*' Beauty told her.

Beverly's entire face lit up. "Really? Would you tell her I'm sorry, too?"

'*We should be able to manage that*,' Beauty said. '*Now, where might we find Linda's unicorn so we can fetch her?*'

"She's on my bed with my stuffed animals, behind my Wonder Woman teddy." Beverly leaned a little closer to Beauty. "'Cause Diana is keeping Mystic safe for me."

'*A sensible option*,' Beauty replied. '*Well done.*'

Beverly smiled from ear to ear.

'*We have a special room for girls your age to have fun in while they wait*,' Beauty said, half closing her eyes. '*But in order to get there, you have to play a game with Hokora. Are you up to the challenge?*'

The girl bounced excitedly in her seat. "I am! I am!"

'*Dani, please help her down so I can explain.*'

I helped Beverly as asked, curious about the game Beauty had mentioned.

La chiquita stared raptly at Beauty, waiting for instructions.

Before she said a word, one of the floorboards near the hallway entry on the left lit up a vibrant green. I froze, resisting a panicked urge to cross myself—again.

'*See the green board over there?*' Beauty asked. Beverly's head bobbed quickly, a small 'o' shaping her mouth. '*All you have to do is rush over to it and jump on it. Then watch for the next one and do it again. I'll warn you, though: Hokora is crafty. So, only hop on the green ones, or you'll have to start over. If you can't find the next board, make sure to peek around the corners of any nearby open doors. Can you do it?'*

In reply, Beverly squealed, ran for the lit floorboard, and jumped on it. The light went out, and Beverly let out another squeal as she spotted a newly ignited board further on. She took off after that one as well.

"How did she die?" I asked softly.

'*Brain aneurysm. Quite unusual for a child her age,*' Beauty said. '*She complained of a headache, and her mother had her lie on the couch for a nap while she finished dinner. When she checked in on her later, Beverly was already gone.*'

The poor little thing. Her family must be devastated.

An old ache poked at my ribs, but I ignored it.

"What happens now?" I asked. Sword-edged butterflies fluttered in my stomach.

The alien green eyes seemed to grow larger as they stared at me. '*Now, you and Ryo have work to do.*'

Chapter 08

Mira, I don't know what I was expecting, but what came next wasn't it. Ryo ventured out of the kitchen, carrying a slim laptop and a folding cell phone, and set them in front of me. I moved the phone to the side and opened the laptop. The default Google search page was already open.

My eyes widened. "You have internet?" I asked.

'Doesn't everyone?' Beauty's eyes shone with mirth. Even Ryo had minute crinkles at the edges of his.

Sure, pick on the new girl. Whatever. They wouldn't find my skills lacking. My nails were short and well-kept, a boon for typing on a keyboard *and* picking pockets. I put in Beverly's full name and the word "obituary." The results showed up immediately, proving that Last Stop didn't skimp on their bandwidth. Nice perk!

But it was still super weird. Why would ghosts need internet access? Not that I was one. At least not yet.

There were several hits, but I spotted her picture in the search's image section. Clicking it took me to the Shady Pines Funeral Home's website. Beverly's photo showed her in an adorable burgundy sundress, a smile shining brightly on her round face as she hugged a stuffed hippo with all her might.

A short obituary spoke of her effervescent nature and how badly she'd be missed. There were links for flowers, signing the guestbook, and sending sympathy cards. The footer gave Shady Pines' address and a contact number, but nowhere on the page did it mention the date or time of the funeral.

I scooped up the phone Ryo had brought and found it charged and ready to go. It was also the most current model. Dang, another perk! The clock showed it was past ten, so I dialed the funeral home. After a quick conversation, I hung up and then shared the results with the others.

"The viewing was last night, with the service scheduled for today. The procession will form at Shady Pines at ten thirty and head to the cemetery at ten fifty. There'll be a casual reception at twelve-thirty in the family home." I typed the Massachusetts address they had given me into Google Maps. "Which is here." I turned the laptop partially around with a flare so they could both see it.

If it was a test, I aced it. But Beauty and Ryo seemed neither pleased nor disappointed, as if they had expected nothing less from me than what I gave them. Tough crowd.

'*As this request is pretty straightforward, I doubt you need to attend the funeral,*' Beauty said. '*You should be able to create an opportunity to search for Mystic during the reception—a less risky option than breaking and entering.*' She blinked slowly in Ryo's direction. '*You should have time to make a casserole or two to take with you.*'

Ryo inclined his head, his expression grave as if she'd tasked him with a do-or-die top-secret mission. This guy took his cooking way too seriously.

'*The laptop and phone are yours to keep, Daniela.*' Beauty's eyes focused on me. '*Please make sure to put strong passwords on both.*'

Why would we need to guard our stuff? Better yet, from whom? "I'll do that. Gracias." ¡*Qué chulo*! At least the job came with some unexpectedly sweet benefits. It seemed Beauty wasn't as stingy as Pierson. But then again, it wasn't as if I was getting paid.

'*Let's swing by storage, then go upstairs to find you something suitable to wear,*' Beauty said.

Ryo was already heading back toward the kitchen.

"Sure." I picked up my shiny new toys.

Beauty led the way, her long tail raised behind her like a tour guide's flag. I kept several feet between us; the last thing I needed was for her to sweep that bushy fur across my face and give me an allergy attack.

She led me past the stairs and down a couple of corridors. The wooden walls turned into plain movable screens that made the new hallways as nondescript as those in a modern office building. Seemingly at random, Beauty stopped before one of them. It moved aside on its own, revealing a white plastered stone wall with a thick metal door. My eyes widened in surprise. This looked more like a structure you would find outside than one hidden away in the depths of a restaurant, even one as weird as Last Stop.

Loud metallic clicking sounds echoed in the empty corridor, originating from the iron locks of the thick door. It opened outward a couple of feet with a strange hiss.

Beauty glanced at me over her shoulder, emerald eyes twinkling. '*Come on in*,' she said before disappearing inside.

I bit my lip, still staring at the hefty door. Invisible fingers ran over my scalp. Was this getup to protect what was inside or to keep it in? I straightened my spine, not sure where these sudden, unsettling feelings were coming from.

I stepped around the partially open thick door and stepped inside.

The room was wide and deep, full of shelves and cabinets. Lacquered boxes of all shapes and sizes were everywhere. The place was immaculately clean, and a woody scent permeated the place. A weird undercurrent of energy played across my skin, making the hair on my arms stand on end.

Under no circumstances would I want to stay in this place alone, even if I couldn't say why I felt that way. Every instinct inside me insisted it would be a terrible idea. My traitorous fingers twitched with curiosity, though, wanting to open every box and see what was inside—like a junkie needing a fix thrust into the middle of a drug warehouse.

I noticed Beauty studying me, her furred head tilted at a slight angle. '*I would advise not giving in to any* curious *tendencies here,*' she said. '*Some of these items are considered dangerous.*'

My fingers twitched again. She wasn't making this easier by telling me that. "Why are we here?" I asked.

Beauty's head tilted in the opposite direction, her eyes half closing as if well aware I was trying to distract myself. ¡*Gata mala*!

'*I'm hoping we can find a suitable item for you,*' Beauty said. '*Life can be chaotic, as you're well aware. It never hurts to have an advantage.*'

That was clear as mud. It wasn't that I minded having an edge. But what in here could possibly do that? "Do you have something in mind?"

'*Not particularly,*' she said. '*Let's walk around and see if something presents itself, shall we?*'

What part of that sounded in any way okay? I wanted to stay in this place less and less by the second.

Cat allergy or not, I closed the distance between us—being accidentally left in here was the last thing I wanted. I felt weirdly hyper alert, and the sneaking suspicion that we weren't the only ones in here kept growing notch by notch. Which was totally *loco*, right?

"Has Ryo been in here?" I asked, not sure why I was doing it.

'*A couple of times*,' Beauty said, walking slowly past the shelves.

Would giving me a little more detail really be too much to ask? I was about to press the point when one of the lacquered boxes opened with a quiet pop.

'*Well, that's unexpected*.' Beauty sounded surprised.

"What is?" I asked, having already taken a hasty step back away from the box.

The lid closed, and the box floated from the shelf to hover before me. I froze.

This close, I saw that a blooming cherry tree was inlaid on the lid. It popped open again. Nestled within it was a delicate charm bracelet. It appeared to be made of silver, although the charms themselves were crafted from various materials—a sparkling pearl, an intricately corded knot, a copper shield, a crystal cube, a shiny selenite spiral horn, a jade comma-shaped bead, a golden gourd, and others I couldn't identify.

"It's lovely, but why give it to me?" I forced the words out through half-gritted teeth. Aside from all the woo-woo, it wasn't the type of accessory I would typically wear. The chain looked fragile. It would yank apart if it got caught on something, and the charms might give me away if I needed to pick a pocket.

The longer I looked at it, the shinier the silver seemed to become.

'*Why indeed?*' Beauty said, staring hard at the box. '*You won't be able to use it.*' The box closed and drifted back to the shelf. The moment it landed, however, the lid popped open again.

My hand moved through the sign of the cross before I could stop it. This was getting a little too freaky for me. Beauty continued to stare at the box for a long moment before finally sliding her emerald-green gaze in my direction.

'*I guess there's no help for it,*' she said, her voice echoing in my head with a sigh. '*Now that you've piqued its interest, none of the others will dare present themselves. What a bother.*'

I threw her a pointed look, not liking the sound of that one bit. Was she implying that the thing had a mind of its own? The gnawing need to be anywhere but in this room was quickly rising. Putting that bracelet on my wrist was not happening. "While I appreciate whatever we came in here to do, I'm good as is."

Beauty slid me a sideways glance, her feline face oddly amused. '*Perhaps*,' she said. With that, she turned around and led us out of the room. It was comforting to hear the iron locks click back into place as the thick door closed behind us.

Once we reached the stairs, Beauty sat and waited while I removed my sandals and donned slippers, then swept upstairs. I spotted the fancy pair Ida wore earlier already in the cubby. So even the *bruja* followed this rule. Good to know.

The entrance to my room opened as Beauty approached. Goosebumps rolled up and down my arms and sides. I kept forgetting this place had a mind of its own.

Once inside, I closed the door myself, not needing extra reminders of the fact.

'*Hokora-chan, would you please bring out what clothes she has in black?*' Beauty asked.

The closet opened, and several items of clothing floated out on their own. I half collapsed onto the loveseat, my heart pounding like a hammer as they bobbed along with exact precision for inspection. A floating box was bad enough, but a whole *procession* of floating objects was unnerving.

Beauty's emerald eyes glimmered at me with obvious delight. *¡Gata mala! She'd did that on purpose!*

'*These won't do at all*,' Beauty said, after turning her attention to the floating clothes.

Heat flushed my face, my jaw growing tight with irritation. "What's wrong with them?" Even as the words left my mouth,

I knew the reasons—too sexy, too short, too cute. One last garment appeared—a child's black empire dress with layered shoulders.

The moment I saw it, my breath hitched, and I had to blink back tears. I'd worn the fancy thing to Abuela's funeral all those years ago. One of the few times Pierson bought me something without thought of pinching pennies or adding to my debt. The time when the options for my future narrowed to only one lane.

A yawning emptiness tried to drag my heart into a hole. Thinking about my abuela reminded me that Jay was also gone.

I had no one left. No one at all. "Put that one away, *please*."

I was shocked when Last Stop did as I asked. The dress pivoted one hundred eighty degrees and floated back into the closet. I sent the house—her? him? it?—a mental thanks.

Had they found Jay's body yet? Without me there, would anyone claim him? Or would he be filed as a John Doe and buried in an unmarked grave? Assuming the men we'd tried to rob hadn't just dumped him in the Everglades to be disposed of by the alligators and crocodiles.

I put the bottom of my palms against my closed eyes, trying to hold back the tears. All of this should have poured out of me last night. I should be over it. Weaknesses made you into prey. Jay had been mine, and look where that had gotten me. You never showed your vulnerable spots when there were hunters nearby. And if there was one thing I knew for sure about this place, it was that Beauty was a predator.

I forced my hands from my eyes, only to realize the cat had silently gone. My dresses had also vanished, though one I had never seen before was draped on the bed. A pair of black flats, a small purse with a long strap, and an open round earring box showing two black coral studs had been set out on the little coffee table in front of me.

Grateful I didn't have to hold back anymore, I rushed to the bathroom and locked the door. I grabbed a towel to press over my face before sitting on the closed toilet and allowing my pain to pour out for a while.

After splashing water on my puffy, irritated eyes, I quickly retouched my makeup, staunchly trying to avoid eye contact with my reflection. That's when I realized there was something on the vanity that had not been there before—the lacquered box containing the silver bracelet. The lid was open, and the metal inside glinted as if trying to grab my attention.

When had that gotten there? I reached out just long enough to slap the lid closed. Wearing the thing was out of the question.

I left it behind and moved back into the bedroom, donning the black dress and accessories left for me. I had to admit the

V-notch neck and three-quarter-sleeved A-line dress looked good—flattering but still reserved. The hemline stopped below the knees as if it had been made for me. Since I was short, most dresses ran long on me.

A soft knock echoed from my bedroom door.

Taking a deep breath and slapping a pleasant expression on my face, I went to answer it. Beauty sat in the hallway, her tail wrapped around her feet. Cats could knock? But then again, she wasn't really a cat.

'*May I come in*?' Beauty asked.

Now she wanted my permission to enter the room? After barging in during the night and having walked into it like she owned it? ¡Gata loca!

"Sure." I moved out of the way. Maybe she was feeling bad about before? Yeah, right.

Beauty sauntered over to my coffee table and jumped to sit on it. With half-lidded eyes, she studied me up and down. '*The dress suits you. Hokora-san outdid herself.*'

"Gracias." I sat on the edge of my bed, staying well clear of her. If I was about to do a job, the last thing I wanted was white fur on the black dress, to say nothing of my allergies. Then the rest of what she said gradually trickled through. The spirit house—which was a "she," apparently—had fabricated the dress?

I was still reeling from that when Beauty continued. '*There are a couple of matters we need to discuss before you get started.*'

"Yes, like why you sent the bracelet anyway after agreeing I didn't need it?" I asked.

Beauty stared at me, green eyes wide and intent, her ears half-flattened on her head. '*What do you mean?*'

Her surprise sounded genuine, which only made my stomach roil faster. "The lacquered box from storage is sitting in the bathroom. Didn't you send it?"

She threw a glance in the restroom's direction. '*I did not,*' she said. '*Neither did Hokora-san. It's most irregular.*'

Mira, that's not what I would call it. "Are you saying the bracelet *brought* itself up here?" Shivers tap danced up and down my arms. "What exactly is that thing?"

'*It's an artifact,*' Beauty said, her tail swishing. '*Initially created and worn for protection. Though it evolved into something aware over time. But it tends to be finicky, and not everyone can meet the requirements to use it. Why it has become interested in you is hard to say. Perhaps it knows something we don't.*' Her tail continued to sweep back and forth, as if she were no happier about being in the dark than I was. '*However, I doubt there's anything to worry about. I'm sure it'll go back on its own sooner or later. Ignore it for now.*'

Why did I not feel reassured in the least?

'*Let's move on to what we need to discuss, shall we?*'

Something in her tone made me push everything back and focus. "Yes?"

'*You'll be in charge during this job,*' Beauty said, her mental voice serious. '*Ryo's social skills are yet developing, and he's likely to become flustered in a room full of people. So please keep it in mind.*'

"Claro." That should be easy enough. No worse than monitoring Jay and keeping him on task. My hermano was easily distracted despite his top abilities as a *stick,* the one who distracts a mark before he gets pick-pocketed. Or had been… I ignored the sharp stab to my heart. *Concentrate, Dani!*

'*However,*' Beauty continued, her alien gaze piercing through me, '*if Ryo removes his glasses* for any reason, *you are to follow his instructions to the letter. Do not question him. Do not hesitate to carry out whatever he asks. He will be the one in charge then.*'

¿Qué? What the heck was she saying? "That doesn't make any sense."

Beauty's smug look was back. '*It doesn't have to. Just please do as I ask.*'

I resisted the sudden urge to pull my hair out by the roots. I waved my hands around instead. "Yeah, sure. It's not like it's any more loco than everything else in this place!"

My flare of temper didn't seem to faze her in the least. '*Good. Glad to hear it,*' she said. '*As to the final topic…*' Here, she hesitated, which put me on alert. '*There's a slight possibility that you might encounter someone unexpected.*'

That sounded ominous. "Okay?"

'*A few individuals would like nothing more than to take my place here,*' Beauty continued. '*So there's always the possibility they might try to interfere with our regular business. Do keep a watch for trouble, won't you?*'

Oh, how wonderful. Now I had to watch my back as well. "Any info on who I should be looking out for?" I asked.

Beauty's ears dipped a little. '*You'll know them when you see them.*'

"Gee, that sounds swell," I replied, my words dripping with sarcasm. "Anything else you want to add to my plate while being as vague as possible?"

'*No. I think that covers everything.*' Her pleasant tone did nothing for my foul mood.

Beauty jumped to the floor and headed for the door. It opened for her without a word. '*Come along now.*'

I swiped my shoes off the coffee table and followed. At the threshold, I stopped and closed my eyes, forcing myself to take a couple of long, calming breaths, or I'd end up stomping my displeasure down the hall.

Jay, if you weren't dead already, I'd wring your stupid neck for doing this to me!

Chapter 09

When we arrived back at the restaurant counter, Bruja Ida was there. (I considered the bunny-slippered one *Niña* Ida, since she acted like a kid. The one who showed me to my room, I dubbed *Muñeca* or Doll Ida—whom I would be more than happy never to meet again. The whole possibility that Beauty had used her like a puppet would give anyone nightmares.)

She had switched cigarette holders, the new one a deep blood-red. The cancer stick was unlit, but she held the instrument as if it were, striking a pose like some diva from the 20s.

Ida had a fancy salad of some sort in front of her and a piece of still-steaming quiche. She was seated on the left-hand side of the U-shaped counter. On the opposite end, but right before the bend, was a covered plate, which I assumed was mine. Had it really been that long since breakfast? I must have spent more time being a *llorona* than I thought.

My inner critic decided to throw her two cents in. *Get your shit together, Dani! You won't survive at this rate.*

¡*Callate*! *I'm doing my best here, damn it. You try dealing with all this weird crap and see how well you handle it!*

Great, now I was yelling at myself. ¡Loca, loca, loca! I sat with a sigh. I didn't need to look over to know that Ida was glaring daggers in my direction. Why was she here, anyway? Couldn't the xenophobic bruja do us all a favor and take all her meals in her room? Niña Ida might not be all there, but she was way more pleasant than Bruja Ida.

Beauty jumped up on the counter. '*It would be nice if* all *of my employees learned to get along.*' She sent a pointed look in Ida's direction. The bruja shifted her death glare to the curtain separating the eating area from the kitchen.

I guess that answered that question—she was only here because the boss mandated it. Beauty then hopped to the shelf that ran across the wall and settled there to watch over us.

With another sigh, I removed the cover from the plate in front of me. A sandwich and plantain chips were nestled within. The crust had been cut away from the bread and cut diagonally, and the inside had a couple of square pieces of ham, sliced tomatoes, and mayo. My eyes started itching at the nostalgic sight. Why was everyone in this place so determined to make me cry?

I grabbed a half and took a bite, knowing that would dispel this attempt. No way did they know that as a little girl, I liked to eat these *only* after they sat a bit and everything melded together. But the moment I took a bite into it, I was forced to close my eyes to fight rising tears as the spot-on wistful taste inundated me with memories of picnics at the park or the beach with Abuela.

Honestly! What was the point of bringing all these recollections out from where I had buried them? Abuela and Jay, neither of them was *ever coming back.* So why torture me like this? It wouldn't help me get the job done!

A heavy thump close to me had me blinking my eyes open again. I found Ryo's dark gray ones gazing at me, a tiny frown creasing his forehead. He'd set a filled casserole carrier on the counter. He had also changed from his chef's outfit into a pair of slacks and a black turtleneck sweater.

Turning away from him, I used my napkin to quickly blot my face, just in case. When I turned back, I caught Ida sneering with delight in my direction, before pretending not to have done any such thing.

I'd had my fill of all of this. "Ryo, are you ready to go?" I asked.

His small frown grew more pronounced as he noted the unfinished food on my plate. "Did I get it wrong?"

That was what he was worried about? "No, it was exactly right. I'm just not feeling hungry. Pre-job jitters." That had never stopped me from eating before an assignment, though I never ate more than a few bites even then, but he didn't need to know that. I added a smile to support the lie.

He seemed to take me at my word, the frown disappearing completely. "Yes, I'm ready."

Might as well get this over with. I slipped the cover back over my plate and slid off my stool.

The coat rack with the built-in seat was no longer empty. A couple of heavy coats and other accouterments had been added. I recalled the sprinkling of snow I had spotted through the doors earlier, and my heart picked up speed.

Winter in Miami never got below sixty-three degrees. Snow was unknown there, though rumors persisted that it had snowed in the city once back in 1977. The only snow I had ever seen was in movies and on TV, or had been sprayed from a can.

Ryo came out and grabbed the burgundy coat with a faux fur-trimmed hood before holding it open for me to slip on. The thing was bulky but fit me perfectly, reaching almost to my ankles. Then he pulled out a weird pair of black boots. I sat on the coat rack seat to remove my flats, but he stopped me.

"These are overboots," he said. "You slip into them, shoes and all."

"Seriously?" I asked.

A hint of a grin came and went. "Let me show you." He grabbed one boot, then unhooked flaps and undid zippers until the awkward-looking thing was open and peeled back, showing a roomy, thickly lined interior. He set it next to my leg and had me slide my foot, shoe and all, inside. Then he re-zipped and tucked everything until it fit snugly.

By the time I had the overboots and thick gloves on and my bulky coat buttoned up, I felt like an Inuit or a wanna be Stay-Puft Marshmallow Man, but without the cute sailor hat. My small purse went into a pocket.

Ryo donned overboots, a black peacoat, gloves, and a beanie. It was a good look for him. I was pretty sure mine wasn't.

A nervous tingle rolled through me at the prospect of going outside. I still wasn't one hundred percent convinced that everything that had happened in the last twenty-four hours was real.

Ryo took command of the casserole carrier, then slid open the restaurant's entrance and waved me through. The immediate slap of icy fingers that then attempted to shimmy their way into my coat momentarily robbed me of my breath. I thought I had experienced cold before. Well, this chica had been *dead* wrong. Even my breath froze in front of my face. That was *not* normal!

I tried to look behind me, but all that did was expose my neck to the freezing temperatures. I literally had to turn my whole body to glance back. The door to Last Stop had already slid closed. Like it had in Miami, it seemed to be part of the buildings surrounding it. The weird statue of the pot-bellied, straw hat-wearing animal next to the entrance stared with its wizened laughing eyes. I turned back around, not wanting to think about it.

Beyond the restaurant's awning, people crowded the sidewalks, bundled up and moving to and fro, not giving us or Last Stop a second look. Dirty slush filled the street, but the snow falling and pooling in window ledges and on car roofs was so white it reflected the weak light that won through the overcast sky.

"The bus stop should be on our left," Ryo said, as if frozen water falling from the sky and the air being so cold it froze your insides with every breath were everyday experiences.

I'd been out here for less than a minute, and I already knew this Boricua did not belong here. Walking outside was dangerous! There were visible patches of ice here and there on the sidewalk. But then I realized what Ryo had said. We were going to a bus stop? Why? And where were the houses and trees I had spied when Beverly had first arrived? This looked like downtown.

I was about to say something when I accidentally stepped on an ice patch as we merged with other people trudging in the direction we wanted. My arms flailed wildly as my foot slipped despite all the grippy ridges on the overboot. Pure panic chilled my blood, driving all previous thoughts away. I was going to fall flat on my back, slide out into the street like a human hockey puck, and get run over by a car with chains on its wheels!

A muscular arm came out of nowhere and stopped my descent into icy doom. "I've got you."

Hearing Ryo's voice was a relief. My breath was coming in and out like a bellows, my insides already turning to ice cubes. I regained my balance despite my knees' continuous shaking. Passersby were sending me odd looks. *¡No me gusta, no me gusta, no me gusta!* Snow and ice were for penguins, not hot-blooded Latina girls!

Hanging onto Ryo's arm, I somehow survived long enough to make it to the bus stop. It was the longest five minutes of my life. My face had frozen solid, and the cold had worked its way through the gloves and into my fingers, but my torso was overheated from all the work to walk that far. How did people do this every day?

The sound of air brakes and the familiar stench of burned oil centered me a bit, reminding me of Miami's public transit system. Climbing into the bus with the bulky overboots and coat was a workout all on its own. Blessed heat blasted from vents on the floor, and I slumped into the nearest open seat, closing my eyes, already exhausted. Ryo sat next to me.

I felt his gaze studying me. When I opened them again, I saw that the small frown from before was back.

"*What*?" I admit the question came out sharper than I wanted.

His frown grew more pronounced. "Haven't you…" Color suddenly dusted his cheeks, and his gaze now avoided mine.

Ugh. "Spit it out." My patience might have become a *little* short by this point. When he still hesitated, I gave him a grumpy glare. "Just say it already!" Not my proudest moment, I admit.

His posture sagged a bit, and I could easily picture imaginary dog ears plastered to his head as his gray eyes blinked rapidly. The large black frames of his round glasses suddenly made him look years younger. "You've never been out in the ice and snow before?"

My cheeks grew hot. It wasn't like he'd had any way to know. "No," I whispered back, leaning forward to hide my face with my hood. I was so out of my depth that I had no choice but to clue him in. But no one else needed to find out. A weakness found was a weakness waiting to be exploited. This chica wasn't born yesterday.

"I'll do better," he said.

I raised my head, surprised by the conviction in his tone. It wasn't like it was *his* problem. He really was an emotional child. I looked out the window, not truly seeing what was out there. Why had I ever bothered getting out of bed this morning?

The bus crawled along, people climbing off and on at the different stops, a garbled automated voice calling the names of streets through staticky speakers. If I ignored the bulky coats and bone-snapping cold that shot inside every time the doors opened, I could almost pretend I was riding one of the MDT buses back home. It helped me relax a little.

Still, I had the nagging feeling I was forgetting something super important.

At one stop, an older man with a cane climbed on board. The rubber end hit a patch of half-melted ice in the aisle from someone who had boarded before him. The older man started to fall, making my heart speed up since I'd done the same not all that long ago. Faster than I would have expected of him, Ryo was out of his chair, leaving the casseroles behind. He caught the old man's arm and kept him from going all the way down.

Then it hit me—*this was my chance!*

I was back out in the real world. I could walk away. This wasn't Miami; it was another state. I could cut my hair, get colored contacts, glasses, and frumpy clothes, and no one would recognize me. I'd make some quick cash doing what I did best—any mall or area where a lot of people gather would do for that. My skills were good enough for "working single-o," meaning I didn't need someone with me to distract the targets while I picked their pockets.

The idea was beyond tempting. Sure, I'd be breaking my word, but I had been coerced into this in the first place.

I was up and sidling into the aisle to shuffle to the back exit when Ryo's sharp whisper cut through all the noise and chatter like it wasn't there. "Don't do it."

"Don't do what?" I asked with all the innocence I could muster. He didn't look or sound angry, but I couldn't take a chance on that. "Just stretching my legs for a second."

Ryo helped the man with the cane into a seat, never taking his attention off me. The bus jerked into motion again. I slinked back into my chair. There'd be other chances if I decided to bail.

Ryo's gray eyes locked hard with mine for a long moment, then skittered away as he sat. "Ken tried to run. It didn't go well."

Who the hell was Ken? Then I remembered the plaque I'd seen on the door at Last Stop. The weird one with the yin-yang symbol, marked as belonging to Ryo/Ken. Yet I hadn't met him. Was that because things "didn't go well?" "Is he your hermano, your brother?"

"Not, not exactly." He avoided my gaze and rubbed the back of his neck.

Could Ken be his lover, then? *Qué pena.* A part of me was disappointed at the thought. Mira, while I had no designs in that direction at the moment, he *was* rather fine to look at. I seemed to always get paired with partners who batted for the other team.

Wow, way to keep it professional, chica.

¡Callate! I'm working here. "So you're saying Beauty has a means of finding us? To bring us back?" I asked.

He nodded.

My "liar" radar was pretty good, and it said he believed what he said. Whether it was true was something else altogether. Then I realized this was the perfect opportunity to pump him for information away from where the boss cat or Last Stop might overhear. "How long have you been working for Beauty?"

Ryo's entire demeanor relaxed, minute signs of tension leaving his body. Ken was a sore subject; got it.

"A couple of years?" he said. "I don't pay much attention to dates."

"Huh." That was a weird response, right? "So what is she exactly? Do you know?" I asked.

He bobbed his head quickly, eyes suddenly shining. "She's a *bakeneko*."

"A bake-what now?" I hadn't run across that word before.

"A bakeneko," Ryo said. "A monster or ghost cat. Legends say they start as normal cats, but if they live long enough, they gain supernatural powers. The longer they exist, the stronger they become."

"¡*Embuste*!" I got a dirty look from a couple of the people around us and had to work hard to bring my volume under control. "No way! What does that even mean, anyway?"

"She can do things mortals typically can't," he whispered. "Like aiding the dead move on. Or helping us stay alive." His voice lowered another notch. "And she's not the only supernatural being out there."

I got a sudden chill that had nothing to do with the cold trying to claw in from the outside. First there were ghosts, magic restaurants, and monster cats. And now he was saying there was *more* to worry about? *Dang it, Jay! This is all your fault!*

"So… so why is she so set on helping the dead?" I asked.

He shrugged as if it made no difference to him. "She just does. I've gathered that it's a kind of important position. That she earned it somehow. Hokora is picky about who her caretaker is, too. There's been some mismanagement in the past."

Did I dare consider what that implied? That there was some kind of hierarchy to this whole crazy business? Mishandling of a spirit house also opened up all sorts of horrifying possibilities about the souls of the dead. It didn't bear thinking about! Not if I wanted to stay sane.

The automated stop-caller came on again.

"This one is ours," Ryo said.

I had totally missed it. So much for my being the one in charge. Why had Beauty bothered? Ryo seemed more than capable of doing this on his own so far. *I* was the bumbling newbie.

Ryo led the way off the bus, and I followed with a grimace, not looking forward to being exposed to the freezing temperatures again.

When he took the first downward step, I realized I could easily kick him out and force the door shut. But then what? If Beauty could find me as he suggested, it'd be a wasted effort, and would cut off whatever rapport I was building with the cook, who seemed fine with giving me information. At the moment, I had food, clothes, and a place to hide from the people who wanted me dead. My best bet was to bide my time and only try something when I was confident I could get away with it.

I followed Ryo off the bus.

Then I instantly regretted it as the frigid air sapped all the warmth from my body and made my face go numb again. How did people live like this? My teeth started chattering.

"You shouldn't do that," Ryo said. "You'll lose body heat."

I glared death at him. "And how… exactly… do I… stop?"

He blinked at me as if he couldn't understand how I didn't know that. ¡Coño! Now I regretted not having kicked him off the bus after all.

Ryo removed one of his gloves and reached into a coat pocket. He pulled out a folded black scarf. Then, before I realized what he was going to do, he partially unfolded it and tucked it inside my hood to cover my nose and mouth. A trail of heat branded my cheek where his thumb accidentally grazed it. The teeth-chattering stopped almost immediately.

"Better?" Ryo asked as he put his glove back on.

"Yes. Gracias."

His dark gray gaze passed over me as if to double-check before he gave me a curt nod. Taking hold of my arm to give me support, we began walking toward Beverly's home.

I recognized the neighborhood as the one I had seen outside the restaurant when Beverly first arrived. The snow had grown deeper, and large, fluffy flakes swayed in the air on their trek to join their compatriots. There was white everywhere I looked.

Now, hold on a minute.

If Last Stop had opened its doors here to let Beverly inside, why the hell had it dumped Ryo and me off in town to freeze our buns off as we trudged our way over here? What had been the point?

I jerked to a complete stop. Ryo halted as well and half turned to glance at me, the casserole carrier still firmly in hand. Snowflakes decorated his beanie and shoulders as if trying to claim him for their own. They could keep him forever for all I cared!

"Was that some kind of test?"

He gave me a blank look. "Was what?"

Did he honestly have no clue? That darn cat set me up! I trembled from head to toe, and it had nothing to do with the cold this time. She'd given me sufficient rope to hang myself! Testing me to see if I'd break my word. My teeth ground together, making my jaw hurt. What pissed me off the most was that I had almost fallen for it! *Twice*. Damn her!

"Daniela?"

I shook Ryo off and stomped on, not caring anymore if I fell. *My word wasn't good enough for you, gata? I'll show you what's what.*

Chapter 10

I was still steaming by the time we made it to 46 Otis Street. Cars were lined up in pairs along the long drive into the rear of the property. The sidewalk leading to the entrance of the two-story yellow house had been cleared of snow and liberally sprinkled with rock salt.

The yard was large, with full-grown trees close to the wide front porch, while the half closer to the street was bare aside from patches of dead grass barely visible in spots; the rest buried under a blanket of snow. Plots in Miami weren't anywhere near this big unless you had a lot of money to burn.

The handwritten sign on the door said to walk on in. I took a deep breath, pushing everything away except for the job that needed to be done. Ryo opened the door, and we went inside.

The foyer was packed with coats and boots, and we added ours to the bunch. A conveniently placed mirror let us adjust faces, clothes, and hair so we didn't look too disheveled after the trek. My eyes widened when I glanced at my reflection and didn't find an inch-thick coating of ice on my cheeks. Snug warmth surrounded us.

"Hi there." A woman in her mid-thirties approached. From her features, I could tell she was a relative of Beverly's. The fact that she looked sad rather than torn into tiny bits made it unlikely that she was the little girl's mom, not with as sudden a death as Beverly's had been. "I'm Lashonda, Tanya's sister," the woman said. "Thank you for coming."

She spotted the casserole carrier. "I can take those for you if you want," Lashonda offered.

Ryo glanced at me as if waiting for me to tell him what to do. "They're pretty heavy, to be honest," I said. "If you'll point us in the right direction, we'll take care of it."

"Sure, the kitchen is just past the living room," she said. "If you'll give me your names, I'll let Tanya, Darnell, and Burton know that you're here. It's nice of you to make the time."

There were three of them? Hopefully, it wouldn't be important. If I weren't so off my game, I would have done more research on the family when I'd had the chance.

"I'm Maria Gomez, and this is my friend, Johnny Sato." I purposely furrowed my brow and lowered my voice. "Though

I'm not sure Beverly's parents have heard of me. I'm new to the school."

"Oh, is that right?" Lashonda glanced over her shoulder for a moment. "I think Mrs. Whitmore is still here somewhere."

"Thanks. Good to know." I gave her a small smile. So someone from the school was here, possibly Beverly's primary teacher. I'd have to be careful. While getting ousted wouldn't be the end of the world, it would make future progress difficult, especially if there was a scene. "Though I didn't know her long, dear Beverly made a big impression on me. She was such a sweet girl, so full of energy. I was heartbroken to hear about what happened."

"Y-yes, it caught everyone off guard." Lashonda glanced away for a moment, a pinched look of grief overtaking her face. "Please excuse me." Beverly's aunt headed back toward the living room, which was filled with people.

Though the house was old, it appeared to be in good repair—no obvious cracks or peeling paint. The interior wasn't the original but looked to have been renovated once or twice and modernized, making it more of an open concept home.

The tasteful furniture had been moved around. Some pieces were obvious heirlooms, made of heavy wood and carved, while others fit more with the times, with soft tones and thicker padding. Folding chairs had been added wherever there was space to give visitors more places to sit.

Despite the number of people present, one couch set against a wall had an area clear of guests and seats, creating a buffer zone between the grieving parents and those who had come to comfort them, their pain too deep for anyone to withstand for long. Three people were seated on it—two men and a woman.

Beverly's mother leaned against the right arm of the sofa, her reddened eyes staring at nothing. Her face was slack, and she didn't seem aware of her surroundings. The handkerchief in her hands was twisted in a death grip. The man beside her sat close, his arm draped semi-protectively behind her. Rather than grief-stricken, he looked bored, though he at least made something of an effort to hide it. The second guy sat at the opposite side of the couch, a grave expression chiseled on his face, his fists opening and closing.

It was clear that those at each end were Beverly's parents. They were either estranged or, more likely, divorced. That would make the man next to the grieving woman her current lover or husband.

I was a little surprised not to see any *niños*. But then again, with the suddenness of Beverly's death, it would have been cruel to bring them—a constant reminder to Beverly's relatives of what had been so unexpectedly lost.

I wove through the crowd with Ryo in tow to reach the kitchen. With this many people and the lit fireplace, I'd already thawed out, *gracias a Dios*. I made eye contact with anyone so inclined, the easiest way to put people at ease.

Without slowing, I gave a slight wave to a woman sitting slightly off to the side. She had a pair of reading glasses resting on her chest, held around her neck by a colorful beaded string—the type of thing a bunch of kids might make for a teacher. She was dabbing at her eyes, so I doubt she saw me, but it would help sell the lie if Lashonda was looking.

Partially cut off from the living room and connecting to a breakfast nook and the dining room, the atmosphere in that part of the house was less somber, though those getting drinks or snacks from the laden tables in those rooms still kept their voices low.

Some covered casseroles were already on top of the stove, so Ryo removed ours from the carrier to leave them there. Looking around, I spotted what I hoped to find: a rear set of stairs leading up.

"Be right back."

Ryo gave a half nod. Without shifting his attention to my direction, he partially blocked the view in case someone was watching.

The thick carpet absorbed the sound of my footsteps as I headed upstairs.

Stopping a few steps short of the top, I listened for anyone who might be up there. Not hearing anything, I took a peek around the corner and verified the coast was clear before continuing.

Finding Beverly's room proved easy—the unicorn stickers on the door were a dead giveaway. The crystal knob would have also worked as a clue, as it didn't match those on the rest of the doors. For the first time, I wondered if Beverly was an only child. It would make her loss all the more tragic.

I opened the door enough to slip inside, then closed it quietly behind me.

As the ornate knob hinted, Beverly's bedroom was more than you would typically expect. All the obligatory furniture was there—a bed, a study desk, a chest of drawers, and bookshelves. But there were other, less common pieces, such as an armoire, twin bedside tables, a mirrored dressing table, and other bits. Every piece of furniture was painted off-white with silver trim. One corner of the large room had colorful fabric pinned up toward the ceiling to make it look like a circus or fairy-tale tent. A small round table with chairs and a baroque plastic tea set proclaimed it the location of many a tea party. And almost hidden by a fold was a rack with several Nerf swords and lightsabers—making Beverly a Warrior *Princesa.*

The kind of bedroom kids would kill for. I know I would have.

The bed was a four-poster canopy, of course, with a frilly cloth framing the top in purple, pink, and white, and a matching bed cover full of prancing unicorns. Nestled against the fluffy pillows was an army of stuffed animals and Beanie Babies.

As I came close, I noticed the covers were rumpled, as if someone had curled over them to sleep or weep. Sentimentality was something that Pierson had discouraged early in my training, but I thought even he might feel a twinge of humanity at seeing this.

Or not.

The Wonder Woman teddy bear sat in the middle of the stuffed animal horde as if keeping them pinned behind her so as not to drown the world with cuteness overload. "Thank you for your service, Princess Diana," I said, reverently shifting her to the side.

But the hidden space behind her was unicorn-free.

I quickly verified that Mystic hadn't slipped off the bed or been put behind any of the other members of the stuffed menagerie. She hadn't. I placed Diana back in her slot, trying not to glare at her for not taking better care of the unicorn. *Sí*, it was silly to blame the bear, but I didn't have anyone else to pin it on, did I?

It looked like someone had beat us to the prize.

Chapter 11

I listened at the door, then gingerly opened it to glance up and down the hallway before slipping out of Beverly's bedroom and making my silent way back downstairs. Ryo was still in the kitchen—cutting up vegetables, of all things. He looked to be replenishing a round glass tray split into sections with a bowl of dip in the middle. Though he never faltered in what he was doing, I knew he was aware of me as he slipped me a sideways look.

I washed my hands at the sink, then helped fill in the platter's gaps with the carrots, broccoli, and cucumbers he had already sliced and diced. "We have a slight problem," I whispered.

Ryo glanced at me with a raised eyebrow.

"Mystic wasn't there. Someone took her."

The brow rose higher. "Could it have been Linda?" he asked.

I shook my head. "I don't see how she could have. There's been no sign of any kids since we got here." I thought about it some more. "I'm pretty sure the mother spent time in the room, but if she took it, she'd be twisting it instead of the handkerchief. She could have put it down somewhere, but that doesn't feel right. Beverly was hiding it, after all. So I doubt her mom would have thought of it as her favorite. It must be someone else."

Beauty's mention of a third party who would not have Beverly's interests at heart rose for attention, but it was much too early to think that was the case.

Though Ryo didn't ask, I saw the questions in his gray eyes clearly enough: Who did I think it could be then, and what were we going to do about it?

I bit the side of my lower lip, not having the faintest idea. I had plenty of experience stealing, conning a mark, and talking my way in and out of things, but investigating stuff was new. Everything I had achieved before had been under someone else's direction, and aside from fleecing random tourists in crowds, there had always been a plan prepared and already in place.

Still, this time, I was the chica in charge, and by one means or another, I *would* get this done. I pulled out my phone and checked eBay, in case it had been put up for sale. Something else I should have checked before now. I got thirty-four hundred results, which I then sorted by newly listed and filtered for the US. Sadly, none of them were in the right date range or location. So much for the easy way.

"We need more intel," I said. "And the best method to get that is to mingle and fish or eavesdrop for what we want." So I grabbed the restocked snack tray and headed for the tables and those lingering there. Ryo trailed silently behind me.

Rather than set the dish on the table, I presented it personally to each person so they didn't have to leave their seat. Ryo had at some point picked up a carafe of coffee and refilled cups as we went.

None of the surrounding conversations was informative. So when Ryo returned to the kitchen to refill the decanter, I perched on an empty chair. Time to steer these people in the right direction.

"Forgive me for asking, but how was the funeral?" I asked quietly. "Unfortunately, we weren't able to attend."

"You didn't miss much, aside from a sea of tears." This came from a matronly lady wearing a veiled hat, sitting next to an older woman. "Pastor George is a dear, but something gets into him for funerals. If he doesn't have the entire congregation sobbing by the end, it's like he thinks he hasn't done a proper job of it."

"Nina, don't be that way," her companion said, slapping her hand lightly. "Crying is what they're for. It's therapeutic."

"That Darnell didn't shed a single tear," Nina said with a soft sigh. "I guess he didn't need any of the pastor's therapy."

Now we were getting somewhere. "That's Beverly's father?" I asked.

"No, honey." Nina shook her head. "That would be Burton. Darnell is Tanya's second husband." Her mouth grew pinched for a moment. But whether this was directed at Darnell or the fact that Tanya had another husband, I didn't know her well enough to tell.

"Do they get along?" I held out the tray so they could grab something if they wanted. "My father and stepfather did, but that's not the case for everyone."

The two women exchanged a look. Nina spoke first. "They… rub each other the wrong way. Best to leave it at that."

That explained the seating arrangement on the sofa *and* Darnell's arm around Tanya's shoulders. Half protection, half claim of ownership.

Her companion tsked. "Honestly, Nina, after saying something like that, who would be able to stop wondering about it?"

I raised a hand to my face to hide a grin. "I'll admit, you've piqued my curiosity."

"See! What did I tell you?" The older lady sat back, looking smug.

Nina sent her friend a glare.

A light touch on my shoulder made me glance up in surprise. Ryo had returned. I hadn't heard or sensed him until he touched me. He was silent as a ghost, that one. Gooseflesh ran back and forth across my shoulders.

Another woman joined us, the sounds of possible gossip having drawn her in like a moth to a flame. "James said he overheard the two of them arguing after the service in the men's room." She glanced around as if fearing being overheard. Looking for others to share this with was more likely. From the way her eyes glittered, she had a juicy tidbit she'd been holding onto, and now she was ready to dish it out. "Something about Darnell sniffing after the poor child's college fund."

Nina's eyes grew round, her mouth partially opening in shock, but her older companion nodded slowly as if not surprised.

This might be what I was looking for. Time to prod for a little more. "Surely he doesn't need the money?"

The newcomer leaned in as if to lower her voice, but did no such thing. It was only a tactic to draw us in closer to her web of self-importance. The perfect type to do the hard work for me. Sad how some people adored slandering others.

"He's got a decent job and a big salary, but he's always searching for more cash. He loves to dabble in real estate." She leaned in a bit more. "James said that the few times he's come to poker night, Darnell lost a lot, but never seemed able to call it quits, and did nothing but talk about properties he's picked up as "awesome deals" and seeing if any of them might be interested in investing. Good thing they only play for pennies, or who knows how bad it might get."

"I'm not sure this is something we should be discussing." Nina's brows drew together. "We're supposed to be here to support Tanya, not air out her dirty laundry." From her wavering tone and the way her companion suddenly reached out to take her hand, I had a feeling she'd dealt with someone who'd had a gambling addiction or similar before.

A tiny twinge of guilt rose at the fact that I'd turned the topic in that direction, but I shoved it to the back. What mattered were results and survival. Something I could never pound all the way into Jay's thick skull. *El tonto*. He'd still be by my side if he'd listened to me.

"You're right," I said, standing up, keeping my gaze lowered as if contrite for having started this. "We should go pay our respects. It's been nice meeting all of you."

I placed the vegetable tray on the table and steered Ryo back to the kitchen just long enough to grab a couple of clean mugs and paper napkins.

"You think the stepfather is the one who took it?" Ryo asked.

"It seems likely, but since it hasn't shown up on eBay, he either hasn't posted it yet, or he did something else with it." If it were a truly rare beanie, it would give him plenty of cash to gamble with. "I know how we can narrow things down a bit."

Time to show off this chica's superior skills.

Chapter 12

I took over carafe duty and led the way into the living room. A few people had cups, and I topped them off. The trio on the couch was much as we left them, though Darnell looked to be having a harder time hiding his monotony at the whole affair. Lashonda flitted here and there, passing a word or two with each guest. As cold as it was outsidc, no onc was in a hurry to leave the warm house, despite the pall of grief hanging over the place, and who could blame them? I wasn't looking forward to turning into an icicle again, either.

Positioning my phone's camera lens in the space between the carafe's main body and handle, I took several pictures of Darnell; I had already set the phone to silent so there would be no telltale click. Quickly palming through them, I made sure I got a clear one of his face. I snapped some of the other people at large in case my hunch didn't work out.

Plastering on a sad expression—not that it required a lot of effort when I looked at the empty, numb devastation covering Tanya's face—I crossed the void to the couch. Darnell's eyes lit up, though neither Burton nor Tanya seemed to register we were there.

"Would either of you like some coffee?" I asked softly.

Tanya didn't react at all, the handkerchief still twisted in a death grip as if it were the only thing tying her to the world. Darnell threw out a charming half smile, his gaze checking my face and other attributes. "Yes, please."

Ryo handed him a mug. I was surprised to note that he was studying Tanya's features rather intently, which was a little odd. I tucked the info away and then shut him out so I could concentrate. As I started to pour the coffee, I inched it over a bit and splashed a drop or two onto Darnell's hand. The effect was immediate.

He yelped in pain, dropping the cup and leaping to his feet, splashing his shoes and pants. Expecting the reaction, I had sidled out of the way, rather than have him bump into me and accidentally throw me to the floor. Then I stepped forward with wide eyes and a panicked voice. "Oh! I'm so sorry!"

Blocking the view with my body as everyone's attention lasered in our direction, I snatched his phone from his pocket as I brushed away at the spill with the napkins. "I'll go get some paper towels. It'll only take a sec!"

Signs of life returned to Tanya's face, her head flinching back slightly as her eyes blinked in confusion. Burton had sprung to his feet but hesitated to step any closer. Lashonda was already making a beeline in our direction.

"Don't bother," Darnell snapped. "I'll just go upstairs and change." He stomped off toward the main stairs.

How ungrateful. After all the trouble I went through to make him less bored.

"I really am sorry," I repeated for Tanya's and Lashonda's benefit. Lashonda sat at her sister's side, taking her hands in her own, now that Darnell's monopoly on her had ended. I tugged at Ryo's sleeve and slinked off in pretend shame back to the kitchen again.

Curious faces looked our way from the dining room. "Did something happen?" the nearest of them asked.

I made sure not to make eye contact. "My bad. I spilled coffee on someone." I dipped my head and went deeper into the kitchen. Luckily, no one decided to follow.

"You took something, didn't you?" Ryo's tone was curious rather than condemning. For no reason I could name, it came as a relief.

"I did." I showed him my prize—Darnell's cell phone. "Now to pry out his secrets." I stepped into the back stairwell, out of direct view, and pulled out my own device. I called up the best photo I'd taken of Beverly's stepfather and enlarged it until only his head fit the screen. Then, I held his phone in front of it and swiped up with my thumb. Boom! Gracias, face recognition!

I opened his album folder and peeked at his pics. And looky, looky, who was in there but the elusive and coveted unicorn, Mystic. From the care he had taken with some of the pictures of the Beanie Baby's heart tag, horn, and mane, he knew what he had.

His text history showed that he had sent the same photos to someone who wasn't in his contacts, as all it displayed was a phone number. Scrolling up, I saw that Darnell and whoever this was had shared sporadic conversations for years. They looked friendly enough, but reading between the lines told a different story. Our *muchacho* super sucked at gambling. And his emails showed that he wasn't all that good at the real estate game either. He hadn't done his due diligence and had been taken in by one or two scam artists with forged titles. Getting loans from the people you gambled with to pull yourself out wasn't too smart either.

He'd dug himself further and further into debt. Beverly's stepfather owed somebody some big moolah and had been scrambling to find a way to pay it, even offloading some of his legit properties for cheap. Finding Mystic must have seemed like manna from Heaven.

Addiction of any kind was dangerous. Not letting your wife know about it, not fighting to control it, or even admitting you had a problem, was a fast track to making sure your marriage wouldn't last. From the dates of some of the conversations, Darnell's gambling addiction wasn't a recent thing.

The pressing question at the moment, though, was whether he still had Mystic or if he had already passed her along. From his texts, the person he was in contact with regarding his debt had been highly interested in taking her off his hands.

I glanced over at Ryo. "We need to have a private talk with our errant stepdad."

"Now?" he asked.

"If we can manage it." I led the way up the back stairs, and he followed without comment.

I quietly made my way down the hall, looking for the primary bedroom while wiping my prints off the phone as I went. Ryo was so silent behind me that I would have sworn he wasn't there.

As bored as Darnell had seemed, I expected him to be taking his sweet time changing, in no hurry to reenter all the raw pain downstairs—a factor that would work in our favor. When I found the likely door, I knocked softly.

Moments later, it was yanked open, a frown and tightened lips marring Darnell's broad face as he spotted me. "Followed me to throw more coffee on me?"

"Not exactly," I said, throwing him a small, coy smile as I came in close and put my hand on his chest before he thought of shutting the door in my face. "That was just a way to get you alone." I let my smile grow warmer, locking my gaze with his. "I was hoping we could have a few private moments together."

Darnell's eyes lit up and grew slightly dilated as he lightly shook his head in confusion. He took a step back from the doorway, and I stepped forward, staying close.

He shook his head again, his Adam's apple bobbing. "What?"

Placing my other hand on his chest as well, I playfully pushed him back, and he was too startled to resist. I was now all the way in the room.

"We were hoping to ask you a few questions."

"*We?*" His head jerked back as Ryo stepped silently into the doorway. I *really* needed to ask him how he did that. "What's this about?"

I slipped past Darnell, glad to end the amorous charade. As he half turned after me, Ryo stepped inside and closed the door, blocking the exit.

"You took something that didn't belong to you," I said. "We want it back."

His gaze turned pointed, and he wouldn't make eye contact. "I have no idea what you're talking about."

"Sorry, but your photos tell a different story." I tossed his phone onto the bed. "Where is the unicorn?"

His eyes widened for a telltale moment, then narrowed again. He crossed his arms and straightened, trying to loom over me, then pointed toward the bedroom door. "Get the *hell* out of my house."

I grinned. "Maybe you'd rather have this conversation downstairs in front of your wife, Burton, and all your guests?" I said. "I'm sure they would find your out-of-control gambling habit, your bad real estate investments, your growing debts, and the fact that you stole a little girl's stuffed animal quite endearing." I tilted my head slightly to the side. "Don't you agree?"

His gaze suddenly bounced around as if looking for a way out or somewhere to hide. "You, you would do that? You'd hurt Tanya like that?"

"*I'm* not the one lying and stealing from a dead girl." I locked eyes with him, wanting to make sure he knew I was serious. "Hand Mystic over now or face the consequences."

Did I sound like a badass or what?

Darnell glanced over my shoulder at Ryo, and I could almost hear the cogs in his brain moving as he tried to estimate his chances of making a run for it. He was taller and outweighed Ryo by twenty pounds or more, but the cook's easy yet ready stance screamed that Darnell didn't stand a chance. When he looked at me, however, he saw no such impediment.

Darnell lunged at me, his fingers skidding off my skin as I evaded him. I was about to kick him in the jewels when Ryo beat me to him. He grabbed Darnell's arm and twisted it high on his back. Darnell let out a gasp of pain before Ryo released him, half-throwing him onto the bed.

Darnell cradled his abused arm, glaring daggers at the two of us, but remained seated.

"Maria?"

I glanced over at Ryo's gathered eyebrows and concerned gray eyes. He was worried about me? ¡*Qué precioso*! He had even remembered to use my alias. "I'm fine." I turned my attention back to Darnell. "I wouldn't try that again if I were you. The visitors downstairs might grow curious and come looking."

Darnell flinched, knowing that if that happened, his secret would get out. He'd have no way to keep us from blabbing.

"How do you *know* about the Beanie Baby?" His left eye twitched.

"No can do," I said. "You're the one answering questions here, not us. And stalling is not going to help you out of this." I gave him another smile. "The sooner you tell us what we want to know, the sooner we get out of your hair."

Darnell glanced at Ryo again. "I don't have it anymore."

Not good news, but it didn't surprise me. "Who does, then?"

He shook his head. "You don't want to mess with them. Lady Luck sent that special toy to me, knowing I needed it. My entire debt was erased in exchange for the thing because of his spoiled niece." His voice rose in pitch. "I can't have you screwing up this deal for me! Plus, you have no idea who you'd be dealing with."

"That's not your problem, though, is it? It's ours," I said.

His face drooped, nostrils flaring. "Not if you get caught! And you would be. They'll torture you until you tell them where the information came from, and then come after me! *So I'm not telling you jack.*"

The tendons standing out on his neck and the worsening twitching of his eye told me that we wouldn't be getting the answers we wanted from him. He was more afraid of them than of us. And though hanging him out the window like Batman and threatening to drop him might have a slight chance of changing his mind, it was too darn cold outside to try it. But the stench of fear coming off him was its own kind of answer. We were dealing with some heavy hitters—a gang, or more likely the mob.

This supposed milk run had gotten even more complicated.

Chapter 13

"Stay up here for at least ten minutes. ¿ *Comprende*?" I threw Darnell a glare for good measure. "And you might want to consider facing up to the fact that you have problems and do something about them. Tanya's suffered enough."

He puffed up to make some kind of denial, but then made the smart decision to keep his mouth shut. I had seen, dealt with, and preyed on plenty of addicts of all types to know that admitting you had a problem was the hardest thing to do. No one liked to acknowledge they were "that guy." But until you faced the fact that you had an illness, you couldn't hope to control it.

"Not much more we can do here," I told Ryo. "We might as well go back."

We went back down by the main stairs to put us closer to the foyer. Several of the visitors noticed us coming from the second floor, but didn't seem to think anything about it. They were way too trusting. I hoped they wouldn't need to learn that lesson the hard way.

Lashonda had moved to her sister's other side, forcing Tanya toward the middle of the couch. Burton had scooted over close enough to take his ex-wife's hand in his. At least those two had a better chance of comforting Beverly's mom than the man upstairs.

Ryo found our coats and other bits, and as we put them on, it dawned on me what we were about to do. My brain had been thoroughly distracted from the bad news until that moment. "Do we *really* have to go out there again?" I asked.

His eyes danced for a second behind his glasses. "Sorry."

¡*Pero no me gusta el frio*! The cold sucked! And if Ryo was part Scandinavian, as I suspected, he probably didn't mind the freezing temps at all, so I'd get no pity from that quarter. But this chica wasn't built for that! So I stole his muffler to put around my face like before. That he appeared not to care only made me want to kick him.

The moment he opened the door, however, I forgot all about the impulse, hunkering down as the freezing wind caressed the top of my cheeks and sent a chill all the way to my toes. I grabbed Ryo's arm, not looking forward to the slippery surfaces outside.

Though my hood cut off my view when I looked back as we walked away, I couldn't help but mourn the warmth we were leaving behind. Snow suddenly swirled around us as if making fun of me. Ugh.

As we headed toward the street corner, I came to a sudden stop. I blinked several times, not sure of what I was seeing.

"Ryo—over there!" I pointed between a couple of trees several houses down. A woman in a white dress or shift was dancing in several feet of snow. Aside from the dress, she had nothing else on—no coat, no gloves, no protection of any kind. "Is that woman *loca*?"

He looked in the direction I was pointing. "Oh. That's a winter spirit."

My jaw dropped. Was he yanking my chain? I could *not* be seeing spirits. "¡*Mentiroso*!"

His shoulders drooped, a hurt look flashing momentarily across his face. "I'm not lying to you. Why would I?"

I was kicking a helpless puppy again. I could find none of the usual flags that meant he was trying to pull one over on me. My gaze flitted over to the woman again. "Then why can I *see* her?"

His head tilted to the side as if not understanding the question. "You've been seeing them ever since you entered Last Stop. It's a gift from Hokora."

I blinked several more times as the meaning of what he said slowly seeped into my mind. *¡Ay, Dios mío!* Could what he was saying be true? But it was, wasn't it? I'd seen Jay; I'd seen Beverly. I suppose somewhere inside me, I had assumed I'd seen them because of where we were, not because I'd been given some new kind of woo-woo ability. *Dammit, Jay!*

Laughter drifted over from the dancing woman. It was proving hard not to believe that she was laughing at me. "So she's a ghost? A woman with unfinished business?"

Ryo started walking again. Since I was still attached to his arm, I had no choice but to go along. "No, not exactly."

I had the sudden urge again to whack him in the shins, but reined it in. "Explain. Use words. *Now*."

He stopped at the street corner and glanced at me. "She may have been a ghost once, or she may not have. Spirits are different from ghosts. They can come into being from a ghost, from accumulated feelings, or even from unknown sets of conditions—evolving from one thing into something else. Like Beauty. Or she could be a natural manifestation of an element."

I'd had my fill of this. I threw my hands up in the air. "That doesn't make any sense!"

Ryo flinched and took a step back as if I'd thrown scalding water on his face. His dark gray eyes looked lost as he glanced everywhere but at me. Beauty's comments about his lack of social skills and uncertainty in dealing with people came back to me.

"Sorry. I didn't mean to yell," I said. "This is all a bit much."

He gave a nod but still wouldn't make eye contact. *Way to go, Dani. And on your first day on the job.* A sigh rolled out of me and turned into cold mist once it got past the scarf.

Loud giggling rang just behind me, which made me turn around too quickly, and I slipped. Ryo mercifully caught me before I splattered all over the sidewalk. Once I was standing again, he stood in front of me, half blocking me from the giggler. That was when I realized our intruder was the woman we'd been discussing. Except, this close, it was clear she wasn't a woman at all.

She was humanoid in shape and wore a long, simple, white shift, but other details made it clear she was far from human. The hair I'd originally thought was covered in snow wasn't, but was a dazzling white as if formed from the purest snow. Her pupils were ice-blue dots surrounded by silver-colored eyes. The thing's facial features were full of angles, and her teeth were jagged like sharpened icicles. Her skin tone was icy blue.

"I don't know you. Should I know you?" She swayed from side to side like a snowflake caught in a swirling wind. Her feet were bare, and her toenails were hooked like talons. So were her fingernails. Was this the person Beauty had warned me about? "Why are you on my land making ugly noises? Hm?" she asked.

A different kind of cold now poured through my veins. Dios mío, had it come over here because I yelled at Ryo? *Dani, you and that nasty temper of yours might get us killed today.*

¡*Mierda*! How could I fix this? "I'm so sorry," I said. "It's my fault. I meant no offense."

She, if she could still be called that, turned her icy silver eyes to me. "I'll allow you to make it up to me." She giggled with renewed glee. Whatever she had come up with, it would clearly somehow be at my expense. I was sure of it. "Dance," she said.

"Excuse me?"

She smiled, clearly showing her sharp, icicle-like teeth. "You are of fire. Strip and dance with me. Show me how long you can burn. Then all shall be forgiven."

I'd last five seconds, if even that. And I had the horrible feeling she very well knew it. This was a whole lot more than I signed up for. I had no skills to deal with things like this.

Snow lifted from the ground all around, creating a swirling barrier to keep us there.

Ryo shifted, cutting off the creature's view of me again. "She is not yours to have, Cold One." The cook's voice held an edge I'd not heard from him before. "She is under Beauty's and Last Stop's protection." He took a step forward, crowding the creature. "She has the mark, as do I."

Mark? I had a mark? What in the world was he talking about?

The Cold One twirled where she stood, her laughter filling the air like the ringing of glass bells. "So you do. Yes. But why let that get in the way of having a bit of fun?"

Making me dance naked in freezing temperatures so I could die from exposure was what this thing considered entertainment? My ire rose in indignation. I was no one's *toy*. At least the anger created some warmth to combat the chill in my veins. Self-preservation warned me to keep my mouth shut, though, and for once I was able to heed it. I was way out of my depth here.

"Drinking some gingerbread martinis would be better," Ryo said.

Gingerbread martinis? That had come out of nowhere. What in the world was Ryo thinking?

The Cold One went still, her eyes glittering brightly. "Libations?"

"Yes. At Last Stop."

Ryo was inviting this thing home? *¿Por qué*? It was utter madness. Had the low temperatures driven him loco? I tugged at his coat's sleeve. "Is that really a good idea?" I quickly whispered, having no clue how acute this creature's hearing might be.

He gave no sign he heard me, his full concentration on the Cold One.

"I accept," the creature said. The swirling snow barrier dissipated, its components returning to the ground. "Let us go there now!"

This was *mondo* insane! Ryo didn't expect this thing to ride the bus with us, did he? I grabbed the back of his coat and hid my face against it, suddenly woozy. *Jay, you* ass*! This is all your fault!*

"It's just across the street." How could Ryo sound so calm? "We'll meet you there."

Wait. What did he say? I let go of his coat and turned around slowly. On the other side of the thoroughfare, the house that had sat on the corner had been replaced by the Japanese restaurant façade that had drawn me out of the rain less than a day ago, its neon sign beckoning brightly even in daylight.

If I needed any more proof that Beauty had set me up to test me when we'd first arrived in Boston, this was it. It also neatly explained how I'd found Last Stop in that warehouse district back in Miami. But how the building could displace and/or replace another structure, I didn't have the faintest idea. It stuck out in this suburban setting. Did no one else see it unless they were meant to? Was it somehow slightly out of phase? Unable to be seen unless the building wanted you to?

And now, monsters were part of the mix. I shivered. What more would be coming my way?

"We should go inside," Ryo suggested. "I'll make you something warm."

The promise should have been comforting, but it wasn't. He'd also be making something for whatever that creature was. It had already gone through the entrance into the restaurant, and I would need to do the same. And while this chica could take care of herself, I was ill-prepared to take on whatever *she* was.

"You'll be safe," he said when I just continued to stand there. "Last Stop has rules. It's a waystation, so the elemental will behave herself."

"A waystation for what?" I asked, dread pooling at my feet by the second.

"Creatures, spirits, the dead, the living. Those traveling through, to, or from another plane of existence or those needing a safe haven for a while."

And that was what I was afraid of. That every creepy, scary thing that went bump in the night was welcome inside.

Chapter 14

Ryo waited patiently beside me until I gathered enough gumption to move again. Standing still only allowed the surrounding cold to seep deeper into my bones. I wasn't a *pequeña* niña anymore, but it was proving harder than I would have imagined to make myself return to Last Stop willingly.

I would be crossing a line if I went. Onc I wouldn't be able to come back from—if it wasn't too late already. I could see ghosts and monsters! How did you come back from that? Even if I gave Beauty the finger and hauled ass away from here, and she wasn't able to track me as Ryo suggested, how did you stop seeing things nobody else knew were there?

A shiver rattled my insides as something else occurred to me. What if I ran across a monster worse than the Cold One? How would I protect myself then?

Yet, beneath all the fear and my mounting concerns also sang a familiar zing of excitement. The burgeoning thrill of stepping into uncharted territory—of pushing boundaries, pitting myself against others, of proving to anyone and everyone that I was the best.

My right foot inched forward of its own accord. Then came my left. When I stepped off onto the street, my stride grew wider and more assured. By the time I got to the other side, it was a march. My steps didn't slow as I glanced up when I came under Last Stop's awning and felt eyes on me.

Two crows watched me from a tight-knit nest wedged into the far corner. Had that been there before? It didn't matter! I even ignored the still-creepy pot-bellied statue with its straw hat next to the entryway. I reached for the sliding door as if I owned the place, and nothing would keep me from it.

I was Daniela Maria Martinez Colón! And no matter who or what you were, you would *not* intimidate me. I had a job to do, and I would do it!

Inside, heat wrapped me in a welcoming embrace. The moment Ryo closed the door, I couldn't wait to shed my coat and overboots.

Bruja Ida stood nearby with a mop, glaring death in my direction as the bits of snow that had flown in or clung to our clothes fell to melt on the floor. Her expression screamed that she knew this was an orchestrated and personal affront—as if I would waste my time concocting something like this. I was sure she felt our roles should be reversed; that was how things worked in her narrow world. Watching her clean up after us was rather enjoyable.

'*There you both are.*' Beauty's voice echoed inside my head. '*I was starting to worry that something might have happened to you.*' She was sitting on a stool beside the Cold One. The creature glanced our way and giggled. Snow swirled around her as if protecting her from Last Stop's warm interior. Would she melt without it?

I sauntered to the counter and sat, pretending the creature's presence meant nothing. Ryo had already padded silently away to enter the kitchen. As soon as she finished mopping the floor, Bruja Ida also disappeared from sight. I guess she didn't think much of our unusual guest. Surprise, surprise.

"I was promised gingerbread martinis," the Cold One said. A subtle edge of impatience tainted her voice.

'*And you shall have them,*' Beauty told her. '*But they take a bit of time to prepare, and we weren't expecting you.*' She lifted a paw and summoned her claws. '*However, I was disappointed to hear you were picking on my employees.*'

Had Ryo mentally contacted Beauty, or had someone else been keeping an eye on us? I resisted the urge to bite my lip.

The creature's bell-like laugh filled the room. "Her temper flares like fire. I couldn't help myself."

Beauty's forepaw moved like lightning. Three narrow cuts were now carved on the Cold One's arm. The creature hissed in pain and pulled back, almost falling from her stool. I froze, unsure of how Beauty had managed to hurt it or what the thing's response would be. I might have been safer staying outside and risking frostbite after all.

'*You* will *do better, or you'll never be a guest here again,*' Beauty said, her mental voice at sub-zero. '*My people are* not *to be messed with. They're under* my *protection.*'

Rather than erupt with violence, the Cold One shrugged, then giggled. "As long as there are libations to be had, what do I care about your pets?" The three furrows were already disappearing from her blue-tinted flesh.

'*I'll hold you to that.*' Beauty's tail wrapped around her feet. '*Now for introductions.*'

No, no, no, no! She couldn't be serious! But apparently, Beauty was because she turned her emerald eyes in my direction. '*Dani, this is Akasha, a winter elemental. Akasha, this is Daniela, my latest recruit.*'

"Hola." I gave her a canned smile, as I would have been way happier never to have met the creature at all.

Akasha dipped her head toward me, showing me her spikey teeth.

Just as the silence started to become awkward, Ryo came through the kitchen curtain carrying a filled tray. "I apologize for the wait."

'*Akasha, this is Ryo,*' Beauty said. '*Ryo, this is Akasha.*'

"Pleased to meet you, ma'am."

Akasha leaned forward, her icicled smile growing. "I was too distracted by the fire to notice it before. You're the sheathed weapon, aren't you?"

¿Qué? What did she mean by that? I waited for him to ask or make a comment, but he ignored it altogether. Instead, he partially unloaded his tray.

"Here is your gingerbread martini, as promised," he said.

I set aside the question about Ryo for the moment, curious about the drink that spared me from having to dance naked in the snow. I eyed it over. The glass looked similar to one you'd use for a margarita rather than the traditional triangle version. Gingerbread crumbs covered the rim. The drink itself was thick, like a milkshake, topped with whipped cream and a man-shaped cookie.

Despite her taloned hands, Akasha appeared to have no trouble grasping the glass and raising it to her eager blue lips. A contented sigh whispered through the air. "Humans are good for something, after all."

Everyone staunchly overlooked her comment.

Ryo filled a shallow bowl from a decanter I recognized as typical for warmed sake. Beauty daintily licked at the bowl's contents. So she enjoyed drinking alcohol as well?

Then Ryo came over to where I sat. He set a tall glass in front of me, one screaming of decadence with its topping of whipped cream and strings of caramel. Luckily, he had put a straw in it, or I wouldn't have been able to drink it without making a mess of my face. The first sip was hot, creamy goodness with a tang of rum. The double shot of warmth made my toes curl. ¡*Qué rico*!

"I brought you some of these as well," Ryo said, putting a small plate of gingerbread cookies on the counter.

I might not be much of a cook, but even I knew there was no way he could have prepared all this in the few minutes since we'd been back. Yet none of that mattered right now—the white hot chocolate, the caramel, the rum, and I were having a moment.

"Feeling better?" he asked in a whisper a few seconds later.

Amazingly, I did. "Yes, thank you." That's when I noted his tray was empty. "You're not having anything?"

A flicker of a pleased grin came and went. Was he that happy I noticed?

"I drank some hot tea while prepping things," he said. "Once the drinking starts, it's likely to go on for a while."

My eyebrows shot up. "They love it that much?"

He dipped his head. "They can never get enough. I have to keep everything alcoholic under double lock and key."

As if to emphasize the point, Akasha called out, "More libations!" while raising her empty glass. She dropped the decorative man-shaped cookie into her maw like a sacrifice or a threat.

"Gotta go." Ryo swung past to retrieve Akasha's glass and poured more sake for Beauty before disappearing into the kitchen once again.

I tucked the info about alcohol away, sure it might come in handy somewhere down the road.

'*Was your mission successful?*' Beauty's voice bounced into my head. Since she was still lapping at her bowl, I assumed this was a private conversation.

'*Only partially*,' I sent back.

'*Do tell*.' The last came with a partial purr. Was Beauty a lightweight?

I sipped my drink as I gave a mental report, with certain bits edited out. I hadn't yet decided whether I should bring up her lousy test and what I thought about it, or not.

'*That does complicate matters*,' Beauty mused when I finished. Ryo returned from the kitchen with two drinks for Akasha and refilled Beauty's bowl yet again. Could cats get drunk?

'*Yeah, before we go into that*,' I said. '*Explain why you didn't bother to tell me about being "gifted" with the ability to see spirits and* other *things,*' I demanded. '*A heads-up would have been nice.*'

'*Didn't I mention that?*' She looked over at me, her alien emerald eyes glittering with amusement. '*It must have slipped my mind.*'

'*That happens to you* a lot,' I lobbed back.

She blinked at me slowly, completely unperturbed. '*Sometimes it's better to tear off the Band-Aid than to coddle it and extend the pain.*'

'*Easing into things can have perks, too, you know.*' It was stupid to press the point, but I wanted my voice and displeasure heard.

'*I believe I mentioned that I have done this before.*' There was no heat behind the soft admonishment.

I nibbled on one of my gingerbread men. '*Is there anything else I* should *know?*'

'*There's plenty,*' Beauty said. '*But for now, just be aware that since you've been seen, word about you will spread quickly. We're likely to have a lot of visitors at some point.*'

Claro. Let's all go and have a look at the human newbie. Can it do any tricks for us? I fought the urge to pull my hair.

'*There's nothing to worry about.*' Beauty flicked her tail as if sweeping away something unimportant. '*Most of them are harmless. And you'll need to become used to them in any case. Sending the souls of mortals to the next plane is but one of the paths that can be taken from here. And there are other services we're occasionally called on to perform.'*

None of that sounded good at all.

'*As for the complications with Beverly's request,*' Beauty added, '*I'll put feelers out for more information. Since most spirits can't be seen by humans, they can typically infiltrate places and gather intel when needed. They've got short attention spans, which can be a hassle, but they get there in the end.*'

'*So why can't they just grab Mystic for us, then?*' I asked her. '*Wouldn't that be easier?*' If the ones holding Darnell's debt were a gang or part of organized crime, as I suspected, keeping out of harm's way would be the smart play here.

Beauty's ear twitched in my direction. '*Most of the supernatural creatures in the human realm can't affect it directly. They exist in a dimension that overlays ours. Very few of them have the power to directly influence your reality. And most of those that can, can only move things for short distances or to perform harmless effects. There's also the risk that if we ask for help from any entities powerful enough to take it, they might decide to keep it on a whim.*'

Why did that not surprise me? So much for doing stuff the easy way.

It made a crazy type of sense that most of these phantoms, monsters, or whatever they were, couldn't do a lot. Otherwise, there would be more proof of the existence of ghosts and other supernatural beings. Stronger creatures, like Akasha, might be seen if they allowed it, and then disappear just as quickly. A simple answer that would explain the origin of much of the weirdness talked about in ghost stories and urban legends.

So I would stick with doing things the old-fashioned way, then—I'd use the internet. Hopefully, I could find some chatter about the local players.

But there was one more thing I needed to ask Beauty about. '*Ryo mentioned that both he and I have some kind of mark. What's that about?*'

'*Look in the mirror. It will show you what cannot normally be seen.*'

That sounded rather ominous. I had wondered why there was a mirror in the restaurant area. Was it a security measure of some sort? Did that mean spirits could hide their normal appearance? *Dani, quit stalling.*

I turned my head and saw that the reflective glass had moved to face my direction. I barely held back a gasp as I noticed a soft green glow emanating from between my eyebrows. The image magnified on its own, showing me the outline of a butterfly on my forehead. The wings suddenly fluttered as if they were alive.

My trembling fingers rose to touch it, but I could feel nothing. Might this be a trick? Like the ghosts who would ride with you on Disney's Haunted Mansion ride?

One glance at Akasha was all I needed to know that it wasn't. But how had the mark gotten there? Was Ryo's in the same place? And did it appear when I had taken the job, or was that the reason Beauty had been in my bedroom last night?

Positive that I couldn't handle the answers to any of that right now, I gulped the rest of my rum-spiced hot cocoa and slipped away.

Chapter 15

Since Akasha and Beauty were taking up the area by the hallway I had used before, I escaped through the other one. Gooseflesh crawled on my arms as I neared it; it was the last place I had been with Jay before he'd turned insubstantial and floated through the mirror-like, black stone wall, leaving me behind.

A shaky breath rattled through me when I only found an open hallway, much like the one on the left side of the counter, and no obstruction in sight. The ancient wall that blocked the way was gone. How could a solid barrier just vanish like that? I hadn't imagined the thing. So where was it? Where had Jay gone?

I shook my head, knowing that getting on that particular merry-go-round would take me nowhere. Jay was dead, and nothing would change that. I smothered the pang of pain that rode shotgun with the thought.

Several feet farther on, I spotted a sliding door on the right. It wasn't quite closed, so I risked a peek, hoping it was a way into the kitchen. I couldn't see deep enough into the room to tell, which seemed odd, so I decided to go in and find out.

The entry led into a wide-open space. A large island sat to my left, and the side facing the curtains that led to the restaurant seating area was full of built-in stoves, ovens, fryers, and more. That was what I had seen hints of from the front counter—except the island was wider than the opening. The side facing me looked to be used for general prep.

The layout screamed "ergonomic kitchen." They hadn't skimped on amenities either. The zone was well-lit; sections of the floors were covered in anti-fatigue mats; and all the cookware was top-of-the-line and restaurant-grade. Gadgets of all kinds were hung along the right wall, like tools in a mechanic's garage.

On the opposite side of the room, I could see a huge walk-in cooler with a commercial freezer beside it. There was also a sizeable pantry for dry goods. In the corner nearest to me was a small changing area and bathroom. A round table with two comfortable-looking padded chairs sat nearby.

Overall, it was the type of setup any top chef would give his right arm and left leg for—and they could have it. Cooking wasn't one of my skills.

"Daniela?" Ryo walked out of the cooler, holding a half-head of cabbage. He'd changed out of the turtleneck and back into his black chef's uniform. The bright overhead lighting glinted off his large, round spectacles.

"Um, hi," I said. "I hope you don't mind my intruding into your kitchen. I was curious about the place where you make the magic happen."

His brow furrowed slightly. "Magic?"

"Sure. How else would you describe taking a bunch of random ingredients and creating something incredibly delicious out of them?"

He blinked a couple of times, his brow furrowing further. "I've never thought about it like that."

"*Seriously*?" I had seen the pleasure he took from people enjoying his culinary delights. If he didn't consider his creations magical, which they totally were, how *did* he view them?

He appeared staggered by my shocked reaction. I needed to work harder at remembering what Beauty had said, and handle him gently. But in my defense, I had zero experience dealing with someone who seemed to have spent most of his life living under a rock. "Sorry. Forget I mentioned it. It's been a truly long and tiring day."

He gave a half nod, his expression clearing, taking me at my word. I marveled again at his seeming innocence. They would have eaten him alive in Miami.

"Maybe a late lunch would help?" he suggested. "You didn't eat earlier."

My stomach chose that moment to gurgle and make demands despite the cookies, sinful white chocolate, and caramel hot cocoa I had just imbibed. I remembered his troubled look when I didn't finish my sandwich before. "That's a great idea."

One of his tiny smiles came and went. I swear, he really was like a little puppy—very easy to please.

"It'll just take a minute," he said. "You can sit here, or I can bring it out to the counter."

I was sure Akasha and Beauty were still there, so hard pass on going back. "Here would be great."

A metaphorical tail wagged behind him as he nodded and hurried to the prep side of the island. Sitting in one of the comfy chairs after turning it to face in his general direction, I watched him work. It was more pleasant than thinking about all the supernatural weirdness.

He shredded the cabbage half in record time, after cutting it in half again and removing the core. Grabbing two oval-shaped plates, he swept most of the cabbage strips onto the left section of both dishes before liberally squirting a pre-made dressing over them. A fresh loaf of bread was pulled from a warmer, and he cut several thick slices.

The rising scent of the warm bread started my mouth watering. Ryo zipped around to the other side of the island and soon returned with a covered plate. Inside were a handful of golden fried cutlets on a mesh set over paper towels. He nestled a couple of them on the slices of bread, added what remained of the shredded cabbage, and a different kind of sauce. Then he topped them off with more bread, making a sandwich, and sliced them in half before transferring them to the oval plates.

I swear, all this happened in less than three minutes.

He set one of the prepped dishes in front of me. The gorgeous katsu sandwich begged me to eat it, so I happily granted its wish. Ryo's dark gray eyes danced as he brought over napkins and forks.

The soft, fresh bread; the crunch of the fried chicken cutlet; the tangy sweetness of the tonkatsu sauce—my mouth was in heaven. I swallowed and forcibly held back from taking another bite, pointing at my plate. "See? Magic. Pure—culinary—magic." I chomped a second mouthful.

The small frown returned as Ryo lifted what he'd made and took a tentative bite. He closed his eyes and chewed slowly, his furrowed brow smoothing out bit by bit. He finally reopened them, and they locked with mine. "I… think I understand now."

A goofy grin split my face. "Good. No point in creating magic like this and not enjoying it." You had to take joy wherever you found it, or you would rot from the inside.

We spent the next several minutes eating in companionable silence. Once done, I sat back with a contented sigh. "All this awesome food is going to make me fat," I said. "Any chance Last Stop has a gym? Or better yet, an indoor running track?"

Ryo stood to gather our dishes. Did this *chico* ever quit moving?

"If she likes you, there can be," he said. "She was nice enough to make a specialized training room for me." He placed a hand gently on the nearest wall after wiping it clean on his apron. "She also modernized the kitchen on my behalf."

I resisted the urge to cross myself. It was unnatural to think of a building as alive, despite all the proof I had already seen. "How… how do you make a place like you?" I asked. It wasn't a question I had ever expected to be asking.

"Show her respect. Acknowledge her. Protect her." His gaze caressed the walls and ceiling as he spoke.

"Talk to her?" I added.

He nodded.

I suppose that would be no weirder than the way guys talked to their cars. Though automobiles weren't able to make things float around or create unique rooms for you if they liked you. "Thanks for the info," I said, meaning it. "Do you mind if I ask you something else?"

"No," he said. "Go ahead." Ryo pushed up his sleeves and turned on the sprayer at the sink.

I fidgeted for a second, trying to figure out the best way to broach the topic. "You have some experience with the supernatural stuff out there, right? Can you tell me more about them? Like things I should know? I assume we'll be running into more of them." Whether I wanted to or not.

Ryo nodded but didn't speak for several moments, as if gathering his thoughts. His hands never slowed as he continued to clean the dishes. "There are different types of spirits. We mainly deal with the newly dead—animal or human—who have unfinished business. Those who don't have anything holding them back can pass through here invisibly; they use the gateways that take them onto the higher or lower realms, depending on where they are headed. But some who've died will refuse to move on, and never come through here. They remain in the world as ghosts or lost souls, some eventually turning into malignant spirits, or monsters."

That did *not* sound good at all. I went ahead and crossed myself, regretting having asked. "Do we have to deal with them?"

He threw me a look over his shoulder. "No. Those fall under the purview of priests and exorcists, not us."

A wave of relief swept through me upon hearing that, though it added more weird questions to my ever-growing list.

"You mentioned that Akasha might be an evolved spirit. Can you tell me more about that?"

Ryo grabbed a towel to dry his hands and came back over. He hesitated, his eyes moving as if internally searching for words. I had a feeling he rarely talked this much. "Objects, places, animals, and even concepts can sometimes evolve into a supernatural creature or spirit. Mountains, rivers, lakes, the elements, man-made things, or creatures like Beauty. Some are tied to where they came into existence; others migrate from place to place."

I would have said he'd been reading too many fantasy books, except I'd seen them for myself. I doubted Akasha had ever been human, though I had nothing to support that suspicion. She just seemed too feral for that.

"Then there are those who come here from the spirit realm."

My poor *cabeza*. This was getting too complicated. "You mean like angels from Heaven?"

"I... I don't think so," Ryo said. "Beauty would be the one to ask about that."

Yeah, no. That was a headache for another day. I tried a different question. "Where does the food come from, and the other goodies?" If they had a permanent supply chain, that might be an angle I could exploit or turn to my advantage.

Ryo sat down, setting the towel on the table. "It depends," he said. "Donations and gifts account for some of it. But Hokora is for the most part self-sufficient. She draws and pools energy from the different dimensions she connects to. She transforms the energy into whatever is needed."

That sounded complicated, but it did a lot to explain how she had recreated my old apartment. Governments would go to war to gain control over something like that. "And how does she connect to those places exactly? I mean, how does she know where to go?"

He didn't hesitate. "Instinct. She goes where she is needed."

Yeah, right. It might have been too early to ask that one. I'd had more than my fill of woo-woo stuff already. But I decided to make mental room for one more, because this might be my best chance to ask it. "By the way, why did Akasha refer to you as the 'sheathed weapon'?"

Ryo became stock-still and stared only at his hands. Was it a taboo subject? He hadn't appeared to care when Akasha used the term.

"It… it has to do with Ken," he said. "And the fact that I help keep him in line." His gray gaze flickered my way to see how I took his reply. It was obvious there were things he wasn't saying. This Ken guy honestly sounded like a handful.

"That makes sense… I guess." It wasn't like I was putting all my dirty laundry out for him to look at, so why should he show me his? I decided to let it go for now. "Thanks for the late lunch—and the explanations. I really appreciate it." I gave him a smile, turning on a flash of charm so he would know I meant it.

He looked away, color touching his cheeks, and as I left, I could swear he was wagging a tail again.

Chapter 16

Back out in the hallway, Akasha's bell-like laughter echoed from the eatery area of Last Stop. Snippets of music whispered through, as if her visit had now turned into a party. I shook my head, wondering how anyone could think that feeding alcohol to a winter spirit was a good idea.

Did Beauty think of our visitor as the "mostly harmless" type? If so, I didn't want to see what she considered dangerous—I might not survive it. Despite how they downplayed it, I was pretty sure Akasha would have been okay with me freezing to death just to put out my "fire." Mark or no mark.

I rubbed my forehead again, still feeling nothing there. I had decided I was more or less fine with being "marked," as they called it, I guess, as long as it could be removed once my time here was done. At least they hadn't branded me like cattle. The last thing I wanted was to be thought of as someone's property.

A floorboard by my left foot began pulsing with light as if it were a prompt on a computer screen. I stared at it, having no idea what it meant. Surely Last Stop wasn't inviting me into the same game it had created for Beverly. I was debating what to do when the pulse ran down the hallway. A moment later, it lit up next to my foot again. Was the spirit house trying to get me to follow it? I mustered my courage, glancing at the walls and ceiling.

"You want me to go that way?" I asked. It didn't feel as stupid to voice the question as I had thought it might. It probably helped that nobody else was there.

The board by me lit once more and moved from one plank to another slowly, as if to encourage me. I shrugged and followed it, pretty positive that the day couldn't get any weirder than it already had been.

The glowing boards led me to a sliding door of wood and frosted glass, similar to the one for the women's bathing area. Not sure what to expect, I opened it and stepped inside.

Then my eyes threatened to pop right out of my head.

The room wasn't a room at all. The sun shone above me! And clouds! I saw no trace of a ceiling, only a vast open sky. I stared at it, my heart slamming against my ribs, a cold sweat gathering in my pits. A jogging track wound off in both directions. Lush grass, manicured shrubs, and tall trees of different varieties were everywhere. I smelled the greenery and heard birds playing in the foliage. The ambient temperature was cool, not freezing, and the color of the leaves and the thick canopies clearly stated that winter had touched nothing here.

I was forced to sit down before I fell down. It was becoming a habit.

Then a familiar squeal sounded, heading in my direction. I looked up in time to see Beverly skid to a stop in front of me.

"Dani! Isn't this place *great*?" she said, hopping from foot to foot as if overfilled with energy and needing an outlet. "There's a swing set, a fort, a duck pond, and even cool places to hide!"

I plastered a smile on my face for her benefit, despite the sudden desire to dig a hole and bury myself in it. "It sure is."

"And I made a friend! His name is Loaf!"

As if having been waiting for his cue, a Pembroke Welsh corgi padded over from behind a bush on its short little legs. With his tall ears pricked and an inquisitive expression on his face, he started sniffing around me. How had a dog gotten in here? Surely, he wasn't one of the dead?

Out of habit, I held out my hand so he could sniff it, then reached over and scratched his ears. He was solid. He felt alive. But Jay had been the same way, too, before he left, so I had no real way to tell. The physical laws ruling this place were not the same as those I grew up with.

The corgi's white and gold fur was neat and brushed, so someone had been taking care of him. After he finished cataloging the smells, he lay next to Beverly, facing the park. It was easy to figure out why they'd named him Loaf—his body looked like freshly baked bread when his head was down.

"He's short, but he runs super fast!" Beverly said, scrunching to pet him. "I love him."

To my surprise, Loaf turned and licked her arm as if to say he loved her, too. I'd heard corgis were quite intelligent, but surely not to this degree! Though if cats who lived extremely long lives could become higher beings, might that not apply to dogs as well?

"Did you find Mystic?" Beverly kept petting the dog, not looking at me directly as she spoke.

"Not yet, but we're working on it." I stood, brushing off my black dress. My limbs no longer felt like rubber bands, and held me upright.

She flashed me and then Loaf a big smile. "That means we can play some more!"

The corgi gave a soft bark as if happy about the development and sprang to his stubby legs. They both took off toward a playground area I hadn't noticed in my earlier shock.

Despite the impossibility of this place, Last Stop had shared it with me, and it was perfect for jogging. Weird or not, impossible or not, it would be a shame not to use it. Or so I kept telling myself.

I left and hurried upstairs to change.

Armed with my old (recreated) iPod and wireless headphones, my hair in a ponytail, and wearing shorts, a sports bra, and a t-shirt, I returned to the miraculous park area. I was prepared for what awaited me on the other side of the sliding door now, so it wasn't as big a shock to the senses the second time. I could even pretend to ignore the fact that this open space was an impossible room inside a bizarre, supernatural restaurant.

I worked through my stretching routine, then set off on the path in front of me. Jogging this soon after a meal was not typically recommended, but I needed it and needed it *badly*. Running and endurance were necessary skills in my particular trade, and maintaining them was something I had come to enjoy.

It was also routine, normal, and all my own. The rhythmic movements, the loosening muscles, the air caressing my face as I ran. The deep beats of reggaeton, saucy jazz, disco, alternative music—whatever the random algorithm picked from my library—but all played at a low volume, so I was still aware of sounds around me in case of trouble.

The familiar regimen was comforting—as long as I didn't think about *how* I had my playlist back. The real thing had probably already been wiped clean and the iPod sold, with the rest of my belongings stolen or redistributed to the members of the wire mob, assuming they hadn't destroyed everything looking for clues as to where I might have run off to.

Tears pricked at the corners of my eyes, and I violently blinked them away. My llorona phase was over. This wasn't the first time my life had been turned on its head, and I doubted it would be the last. I would get over it and make the most of what had been offered to me. At least until I figured out how best to come out on top.

Bobby Shoeman's face rose unbidden before me, wearing his usual smug, I-know-things-you-don't expression. My fist launched out to smash it in, though he wasn't really there. The cabrón had to pay for what he did. Maybe I could talk Akasha into paying him a visit. She could make *him* dance, then perhaps eat him afterward.

I felt a nasty smile pulling at my face. If matters went sour here, I would list him as *my* unfinished business. Have him punished for getting Jay killed. It gave me something to look forward to.

A bark snapped my attention to the left. The large playground sat there, and I spotted Beverly waving at me from the top of the colorful fort full of tubes, monkey bars, and rope swings. Loaf came sprinting right for me and barked again as he matched my speed to run beside me. His tongue lolled out the side of his mouth, and he had little trouble keeping up.

I let my acid-filled thoughts fall away and waved at Beverly. Loaf stayed with me for an entire lap as if to make sure I wasn't going to quit halfway. The thought made me laugh. And I didn't mind the company. After the full lap, he peeled off to check on Beverly, who took the fort's slide to meet him halfway.

When I'd had enough, I slowed and did more stretches, my head clearer than when I had come in. Supernatural or not, people had things they coveted or other motivations. Finding what they were was how you gained an edge. No matter how mind-blowing, this chica needed to discover everything she could and then figure out how to use it. To do that, I had to earn Beauty's, Hokora's, and Ryo's trust. And the fastest way to that was by completing this messed-up job.

Helping a little girl find peace would be a bonus.

I soon left to head upstairs to shower and begin my research. That was when I noticed the stairwell on the other side of the hall—one that hadn't been there when I'd first found the place. *¡Ay bendito!* I bit the inside of my cheek, reminding myself sternly that I had promised to take everything in, no matter how weird or crazy.

So after taking a deep, calming breath and removing my shoes to put inside one of the cubbies, I took the stairs. I even congratulated myself because my hands weren't shaking, proving everything was under control. Yes, this was a decent plan. I had this! Boricua for the win!

Feeling pretty good thanks to the jogging-released endorphins and looking forward to a well-earned shower, I bopped on over to my door. Unfortunately, that was when life decided to punch me in the guts.

I was reaching for the knob when I was suddenly yanked halfway around and pushed back hard against the wall.

Chapter 17

My heart leapt into my throat, a shot of adrenaline spiking in my veins at the rough treatment. But I forgot all about the ache in my back from hitting the wall when a hand clamped onto my neck to pin me against it.

Then I got a look at my attacker's face. Ryo! But my brain dismissed this almost before the thought was born. He physically looked like the cook, but there was no way it was him. The cold, emotionless gray gaze was nothing like Ryo's. These unspectacled eyes were dark holes sucking the warmth directly from my soul. Instinctively, I knew the blank stare was that of a killer. With a sinking feeling, I realized this must be his roommate, Ken.

Terror flooded my mind, trying to cripple my brain, but I clamped on it hard. If he were what I thought he was, my fear would make me less than nothing to him. Some killers fed on that.

I grabbed his wrist to force him to let go, but it was like trying to twist iron. This Boricua was no pushover, though. I tried to grab and bend his pinkie to force him to release me, but he swatted my hand away before I could take hold.

"What do you want?" I asked. "Why are you doing this?"

His grip tightened, cutting off my air. Unable to breathe, staring at that dead face, it got harder and harder not to give in to a wave of panic. I tried to knee his groin, but he blocked me again.

"This will be your one and only warning," he said. His voice was as stripped of emotion as his expression, and he brought his body close to mine. "Do not look at, speak to, or interact with Ryo in any way unless it is *absolutely* necessary. Or the next time we meet, I will *end* you. Understand?"

I didn't doubt him. Not with those empty eyes staring back at me.

He let go. I slid down the wall, gasping and choking, trying to get air into my tortured lungs. Ken never looked back as he silently walked away and entered his room, leaving me to pick up my own pieces.

After a minute or so, I was able to grab my shoes, rise unsteadily to my feet, and escape into my apartment. I locked the door. Unbidden, my entire body started shaking, my throat on fire. I've had people grab me and threaten me before, but this was on a whole other level. The bastard could have killed me right then and there if he'd wanted, and there wasn't a damn thing I could have done to stop him. The self-defense courses I had taken never accounted for someone like him.

¡Carajo! Last Stop was supposed to be a safe space! But now I had a psycho killer living next door to contend with. This was not what I signed on for!

Grabbing random bits of clothes, I wove my way to the bathroom and the shower. I locked that door as well, for all the good it would do me if he came at me in earnest. Flimsy things like locks wouldn't keep someone like him out if he wanted in. But it was all I had.

I turned on the shower, and as I stripped, my gaze landed on the reopened lacquered jewelry box and the charm bracelet nestled in there. It had yet to get bored and return itself to the storage room, it seemed. Another factor proving this place wasn't safe at all!

"Go back where you came from already!" I slapped the lid of the thing closed, not wanting to look at it. Just something else sticking its face in my business that I could do without. I jumped into the cascading water.

I barely felt the scalding temperature, the chilled horror still clinging inside me making me numb. It disgusted me and made me feel dirty that I would need to cave in to his demands, but what else could I do? *¡Pendejo!* My skin was already bruising where he'd grabbed my throat. I sat on the shower's seat, and let the water pummel me.

I could tattle on him, force him to become Beauty's problem, but that would set a bad precedent. Brand me as weak. Someone who couldn't handle their own problems.

Besides, the threat itself didn't make any sense. Was Ken somehow afraid I would steal Ryo from him? I'd just met the guy! He was cute, sure. But I wasn't planning to elope with him. *¡Problemas, problemas, y mas problemas!*

I shut the shower off with a hard twist, annoyance and anger finally chipping away at my fear. My hands were mostly steady by the time I blow-dried my hair and got dressed.

I ignored the fact that the lid of the lacquered jewelry box had popped open on its own again. I had bigger things to worry about, like putting on my makeup and hiding my ripening bruises. It would be a total pain to cover them for the couple of weeks or more it might take them to heal, but it wasn't like I had a lot of choices. Leaving my hair loose would help as well.

I spoke several phrases out loud, and my voice sounded fine, so that was one less thing to worry about. But I still had no idea how I would deal with this.

"Last Stop—or do you prefer Hokora?—would you mind letting Ryo know that I'll be eating in my room tonight?" I asked. I didn't have the faintest idea if the place could understand me, let alone deliver a message, but I had nothing to lose by trying. I'd had my fill of drama for the day.

It chafed hard that Ken was making these ridiculous demands, especially as Ryo had proven decent to work with so far. And he was my only source of direct information. The painful bruises on my throat, however, told me what I could expect if I didn't follow through. I'd need to find a weapon, just in case. If Ken was this pissed about me just *talking* to Ryo, I was sure almost anything else might set him off. I needed to be prepared for that. I couldn't allow him to catch me unawares again.

I'd go to the kitchen after hours to see what kinds of knives were available. A couple of ceramic knives would be perfect. I might not be physically strong, but stabbing his wrist would make the cabrón let go if he grabbed me again. He'd rue underestimating *this* Boricua.

Feeling marginally better, I grabbed my laptop and curled up on my couch to do some research. Anything to distract me from that ugly confrontation.

Licensed sports gambling was legal in Massachusetts. They had a ton of casinos, too. So it didn't look to be the best place to help you stave off addiction. Too much temptation everywhere. And there were likely a ton of unlicensed gambling places as well. No wonder Darnell had gotten in trouble.

Narrowing down whom he'd given Mystic to would be a nightmare. Too many loan sharks and street gangs in Boston. A long sigh escaped me. I would have to hope Beauty's contacts came through. Pierson had always been the one to worry about gathering intel. We just carried out his plans unless we were working at some public venue. I guess it wasn't as easy as he'd always made it look.

Knuckling down, I searched the Boston PD website, trying to see how deep the public statistics went, then moved on from there. The city had plenty of gangs—the Lenox Street Cardinals, the H Block Street Gang—and sixty or more were considered active. There wasn't enough information floating on the internet to narrow down which of them were into illegal gambling or loan sharking.

The list of organized crime families was shorter, with most of them long gone or still barely hanging on—the Patriarca crime family, Winter Hill Gang, and the Charlestown Mob. And while illegal loan sharking was a problem in the city, specifics weren't online, supposedly due to legal and safety ramifications.

¡Coño! They weren't making this easy at all!

On a whim, I tried looking up Ida Rolls. While I didn't think Beauty had any reason to lie about the bruja, I also knew better than to take her solely at her word. Results popped up almost immediately. Ida had been quite a busy beaver. She'd had five husbands, each of whom had met with an "accident" not long into their marriage. I held back a shudder.

Why would anyone do that? Was it just for the cash? But further reading revealed that *she* was the one who was rich. Her husbands were the ones marrying *her* for her money! She'd been a looker, too, in her younger days. So why turn yourself into a honey trap? Did she just have terrible luck with men? Or was it something else?

A couple of articles had dug deeper into her life. She had lost her father while she was still very young, and her mother had soon remarried. Though Ida refused to talk about it at trial, her lawyers still tried to paint a picture of repressed childhood trauma from abuse at the hands of her stepfather and the societal norms in that era of keeping dirty laundry in-house, as the underlying cause of her penchant for murder. Yikes!

Not that it had done Ida any good in the end. She'd been sentenced to life in prison with no option for parole. She was also now listed as a wanted fugitive. Details were sketchy, only stating that she'd arranged for her escape once placed in the prison infirmary.

Having learned more than I really wanted to about the bruja, I decided to try my luck at getting info on Ryo. I got nowhere fast. No famous chefs with Ryo as a first name, and none with a psycho twin brother.

Since my whole aim had been to distract myself, I switched my searches to the supernatural. Maybe I would have better luck there. *No bueno.* The amount of lore on the web was staggering—with no way to tell what was legit, what came from anime, or what was embellished fiction. Some bits and pieces fit what I'd been told, but others, not at all. And now I had been denied access to my easiest source of information in my new reality. My hands curled into fists as I got mad at Ken all over again.

A knock at my door shocked me to my feet. I grabbed hold of my metal nail file, the closest thing I owned to a possible weapon. Now I really wanted those ceramic knives. If I could somehow manage it, a stun gun would be even better, as it would let me hit him from across the room.

I palmed the nail file so it rested against my inner arm and kept it out of view. My breathing started to speed up, but I consciously brought it back under control. I stood behind my door and opened it a crack, pulse pounding, hoping to be able to slam it closed if it was *El Coco* Ken on the other side.

Despite the tingling shot of panic at the familiar form, I almost flopped with relief when I caught sight of the telltale glasses and realized it was Ryo carrying a laden tray. I should have known he'd be the one bringing the food. I should have asked Last Stop to float it to me, or have Ida bring it. Assuming la bruja could be bothered with such a menial task—or that I could trust her not to spit all over it.

"Where should I put this?" Ryo asked. The two covered dishes gave no hints as to their contents.

I hadn't opened the door any further than the original crack. "Leave it out there. I'll grab it in a minute."

"I don't mind bringing it in for you," he said earnestly. That thing he did with the micro frowns started to form.

"I appreciate that, but I don't need you to," I insisted quickly. "Just set the tray on the floor and go. All right?" The last came out sharper than I'd meant it to.

"Did I do something wrong?" he asked. Confusion marred his entire face.

"No," I said, trying to keep my tone low and not take my frustrations out on him. "You're fine. But life will be simpler if we don't talk to each other for anything other than business."

Now he looked like a kicked puppy. *Curse you, Ken!* "I don't understand."

"You should go have a talk with your brother, then." I moved to close the door, but his hand flew out, and suddenly it wouldn't go anywhere, despite my having the better leverage.

"*What did he do?*" Where his twin's eyes had been cold and bottomless, Ryo's were filled with fire and fury. I was stunned that he was this incensed on my behalf, and that he immediately suspected Ken of having done something.

I swallowed hard, which made me inadvertently grimace as it poked at my bruised throat.

Ryo's eyes widened as he noticed. His face suddenly lost color as he made connections from the evidence and took a half-stumbling step back, almost dropping the tray. His chest heaved in and out as if he couldn't get enough air.

Rather than take this opportunity to shut my door, like any *sensible* person would have done, I opened it wide instead. I grabbed the food before he dropped it and set it on the floor. He barely seemed to register that, critically studying me from head to toe as if looking for further signs of injury. He was still having problems catching his breath.

"You're going to pass out," I said. "You need to calm down and breathe."

He waved that aside. "Did he—did he *hurt* you?"

The utter horror reflected on his face as he waited for an answer made me hesitate. I felt suddenly shaky inside as I began to realize that perhaps Ken had let me off easy. "Not really," I said, fighting to keep my voice steady. "He gifted me with a bruise or two and an ultimatum, but that was it."

Ryo didn't look reassured in the least, but his breathing eased off a bit. "I swear I won't allow him to do anything like that to you, ever again."

His set jaw and tightening fists told me he was serious, but unless he planned to stick by his brother's side twenty-four/seven, he was promising the impossible. But I nevertheless appreciated the sentiment.

"You don't believe me."

The hurt in his voice took me by surprise—that he had figured it out, even more so. I held up my hands. "No. That isn't it," I said. "I'm sure you'll try. But it's not that easy."

He straightened where he stood, the fire back in his eyes. "I *won't* allow it. You'll see."

Ryo stormed off toward his apartment like a knight about to enter the dragon's den. I just hoped I wouldn't end up becoming collateral damage.

Keeping my door propped open with my foot, I grabbed the filled tray off the floor and locked myself in my room.

The soundproofing at Last Stop was phenomenal, unlike the paper-thin walls of my old place, where you could eavesdrop on everybody else's business whether you wanted to or not. So sitting in a replica of my room and hearing nothing coming from next door was a little unnerving, especially as I was pretty sure Ryo and Ken's confrontation was likely to be loud.

Instead, it was so quiet that I clearly heard my stomach gurgle.

I sat with a sigh and took the covers off my dinner. I had learned early that you never ignored an opportunity to eat. Depending on what went down with the brothers, there was a chance Beauty would boot me out into the street. Ryo and Ken had been here a lot longer than I had. Last in, first out.

My stomach grumbled again as the savory scent of a hearty meat stew wafted from beneath the dish as I removed the lid. The second cover revealed a generous slice of cinnamon-topped apple pie. After my long run and all the unwanted extra stress, I salivated at the wondrous smells and sights. Ignoring the slight twinge of guilt at the pathetic thanks I had given Ryo for his efforts, I dug in.

My taste buds were instantly flooded with a harmony of glorious flavors. The potatoes almost melted in my mouth, and the meat was so tender it fell apart all on its own. How could one man make so much culinary magic? My twinge of guilt enlarged into a throb. I mentally punched it back. Why should I spoil my dinner over them? They were complete strangers. And if their drama got me thrown out, that was even more of a reason to enjoy this as much as possible.

At least we were in another state, which would give me more breathing room to figure things out and stay off the radar of the people who were looking for me. If Beauty did kick me out, I hoped I'd be able to keep the coat and other winter gear—otherwise, I wouldn't stand a chance out there. And if Akasha somehow found me again when I was no longer under Beauty's protection…? Brrr, that wasn't worth thinking about.

By the time I ate the last delicious bite of apple pie, I still had heard nothing from next door. No one had come to take their ire out on me or to tell me to leave. There was no way to know if these were good signs or not.

I carefully cracked my door open and peeked up and down the hallway before opening it further to place my tray out. The corridor was as silent as a grave.

Rather than close the door, I stood there, my ears primed to catch the slightest sound as the seconds ticked by. What the hell was I doing? *What was I expecting?* This wasn't any of my business!

Yet, instead of retreating and locking the door again, I picked up the tray and quietly made my way toward the kitchen.

The entire building was quiet—*too* quiet. It felt queerly empty, abandoned. I was sure Last Stop had witnessed everything that happened—that it might know what had occurred during Ryo's confrontation with Ken. As attentive and kind as the cook treated the place, was it upset for him? Could buildings have feelings?

The kitchen was deserted when I stepped inside. From what I could see of the counter past the half-curtains, the restaurant area was also empty, and the lights were off. Either Beauty and Akasha had moved their drinking to another room, or the winter spirit had finally gone home.

I set the tray by the sink and, on a whim, decided to wash my dirty plates. Don't get me wrong, I wasn't feeling responsible in any manner, shape, or form—I was just paying Ryo back for having brought it to me. The sound of running water was rather soothing as it fractured the all-encompassing quiet.

Once the dishes were clean and I'd dried my hands, I reached out to touch the wall as Ryo had done hours before. For a moment, I thought the dark wood felt warmer than it should have. But I had no time to think about it, because just then I saw the door to the kitchen slide open from the corner of my eye. I stood absolutely still, my heart picking up speed—sure of who it had to be, yet half hoping it wasn't.

Ryo drifted in like a ghost, making no sound. He headed toward the walk-in freezer, so he didn't see me. I was rapidly weighing the odds of trying to slip past into the hall or hiding behind the island, not positive he'd appreciate finding me on his turf without permission.

But before I could decide or he could open the freezer door, he snapped around in my direction, a knife appearing in his hand out of nowhere. For a frozen moment, I thought Ken had stolen Ryo's glasses, the expression behind them was so emotionless and cold. I gasped before I could stop myself, my hands flying up to cover my mouth.

He palmed the blade back to wherever it came from—a trick I wasn't sure even *I*, with my super nimble fingers, could reproduce. His whole body relaxed as if releasing tightly coiled tension, though until that moment, he had shown no signs of it.

That was when I finally noticed that he'd been punched multiple times in the eye and the side of his face. He'd been hit so hard that the swelling had already started. My guts twisted inside, and before I realized it, I was running over rather than trying to make my escape.

"¡Dios mío! Did that *cabrón* do this to you?" Scalding heat tainted with a touch of fear flashed through me—if Ken would do this to his own brother, who knew what he might do to *me*.

Ryo's gaze skittered away. "It wasn't him."

"Are you *mental*?" I demanded. "Why would you defend him after he's done this to you?"

His dark gray eyes met mine head-on. "Because he didn't do it," Ryo said. "I did."

I knew the cues to look for, how to tell if someone was lying. But none of them were there. "Why in the world would you do such a thing?" I hugged myself and took a wobbly step back.

Ryo's brows drew together as he stared at the floor. "Because it was the only way to force him to listen to me. He hates it when I get hurt."

I took a shaky breath, suddenly nauseous, as goosebumps ran chaotically across my skin. The cook was all kinds of loco. Even more than his psycho brother. Because who in their right mind would do that kind of damage to themselves for a veritable stranger? "That's nuts! You know that, right?"

He hung his head as if I had smacked his nose with a rolled-up newspaper. What *was* it with this guy?

I forced my arms to my sides. "Go sit," I ordered, pointing at the small table we had used for our late lunch. "I'll grab some ice for your face. The longer we take to treat it, the worse it will look in the end."

Not waiting to see if he'd do as I asked, I grabbed a kitchen towel and searched for an ice maker rather than opening the freezer. A bag of frozen vegetables would have done the trick, but I had a feeling there might not be any of those around. Ryo's culinary integrity probably demanded that he use only fresh ingredients.

Wrapping the towel around the noisily escaping ice cubes, I joined him at the table. Ryo had taken a seat as instructed. "Put this on it," I said, holding out the wrapped ice.

He took the bundle and gingerly placed it over the right side of his face. I sat across from him, chewing at my lip.

"Did you break anything?" I asked him. "Should we go to the emergency room?"

"No. I was careful."

That sounded wrong for so many reasons. My temper flared. "So why isn't *Ken* helping you with this?"

Ryo carefully shifted the bundle of ice against his skin. "We couldn't both do it."

Yeah, that didn't sound *strange* at all. Curiosity bubbled insistently inside me. I tried to rope it in and tie it down. I didn't know these people—I didn't *have* to. They had "trouble" written all over them. But how else was I to get any leverage to use on them when I needed it?

I bit the side of my bottom lip again, trying to work it out. The idiot cook had hurt himself on my behalf. Maybe I should cut him some slack. It was obvious that the two brothers had some kind of toxic relationship.

Then a worse thought formed in my head. "Even with the ice, that's still liable to swell pretty badly and bruise. No way Beauty won't notice it. Will it get you guys in trouble?" I asked.

Beauty could put Ken on a spit like a *lechon,* roast his ass, and serve him to Akasha as an hors d'oeuvres for all I cared, but what Ken had done wasn't Ryo's fault. Nor mine, for that matter.

He seemed to give it some deep consideration before replying. "No. I don't think so," he said, a flush suddenly creeping up his neck to the tip of his ears. "But she'll be disappointed, which is worse."

This guy did *not* have his head on straight. Why would he care that much about what our feline employer thought of him? People disillusioned others all the time—whether they wanted to or not.

"Does Last Stop have any creams or medicines you can use? The sooner you start with anti-inflammatories, the better," I said. Jay and the rest of us in the wire mob had plenty of cause to know all about them. Pierson had never been the most patient of teachers or bosses.

"I have remedies in my room," Ryo said. "But thank you for thinking of me. And for bringing and cleaning your dishes. You didn't have to."

I glanced away, knowing I hadn't exactly done any of it for altruistic reasons. "No biggie."

"You can borrow some of the ointments if you like," he volunteered. "I have plenty."

That was sweet of him. He was too nice for his own good. Unlike his twin. "I appreciate the offer," I said as I rose to my feet and gave him a warm smile. "If I decide to, I'll let you know. See you tomorrow."

What I could see of his expression looked pleased, as if pummeling his own face to hear the phrase had been worth it. His nonexistent tail wagged behind him as I left.

Ryo was the strangest guy I'd ever met. And that was saying something.

Chapter 18

A violent sneeze brought me rudely awake. I rose to a sitting position, rubbing my suddenly itchy eyes.

A glance at the clock showed it was almost seven, so I dragged myself out of bed. From the cat hair left on my blankets, Beauty had used me as a pillow again. But why was my allergy only reacting to her *now*? How did it not bother me while she was actually here? That feline had an awful lot of tricks up her sleeve.

With no idea of what the day would bring, I decided to go for a jog while I had the chance. I'd share what little I'd learned about the Boston crime scene with Beauty mentally before going to bed, so she'd know I was working on it and trying to do my share despite the resulting lack of usable info. Keeping her happy and on my side as much as possible was paramount. I would get nowhere without her trust.

My sneakers were still in the shoe cubby at the bottom of the stairs, so I sat to slip them on. Out of habit, I turned them upside down and thumped them against the corner to dislodge any unwanted visitors. Sadly, parts of Miami were notorious for their large roach populations, and you did *not* want to put shoes on without checking them first. The suckers didn't bleed, but finding their bodily remains stuck to your sock—or worse, your bare feet—was revolting.

So, I was surprised when something fell from the shoe. Several somethings. The metal tacks made soft clinking sounds as they dropped to the wooden floor. *WTF?* Why would anyone bother to put those there? My initial thought was that it was Ken, trying to get back at me, but even as the notion formed, I dismissed it. After our rough first meeting, it didn't seem like something he'd pull. Punishment would be a face-to-face affair, so there would be no doubt where it had come from.

Another name rose before me, though, and this one fit perfectly—*Ida*. Nasty, cowardly, and so juvenile. There weren't that many of us here. Did she think I was too stupid to figure it out? Odious *bruja*. She might well deserve to be Beauty's plaything. Feeling any pity for someone like her was a waste of time.

I placed the thumbtacks on top of the cubby so she would know I had found them, and for the others to see. I wouldn't tell on her, but I wasn't going to hide this either. And if anyone asked me why tacks were sitting there, I wouldn't lie about it. If Ida tried anything else, she would rue the day we'd ever met. I'd make sure of it.

A grin tugged at my face at the thought of that.

Putting her out of my thoughts, I went on to the indoor (?) park. All the extra carbs I'd been ingesting lately needed to go. I also wanted to stay fit to deal with whatever this new, odd life of mine might throw my way.

I took a deep breath as I reached for the sliding door.

Despite knowing what would be on the other side of it, when the entryway opened to what my brain emphatically insisted was an outdoor space, while I simultaneously knew I was still inside Last Stop—ugh. The disconnect kept trying to curl my brain cells into knots.

The sun stared at me from the same position as the last time I'd been here. But the puffy clouds moved along unimpeded. *Qué extraño.*

Fighting the urge to cross myself, I focused on doing my stretching exercises instead. A joyous bark made me glance in the direction of the playground. No sign of Beverly, but Loaf was careening toward me like a speeding bullet.

I wondered where she was. Did ghosts need sleep? I'd seen them eat. But was that necessary, or only something to bring them comfort?

"Morning, Loaf." I bent down when he arrived so he could sniff my hand, then scratched him behind the ear. He gave me a lick in return, which made me smile. With my cat allergy and Pierson's rules against having pets, I'd never had one. If I ever got out of this, I might adopt a rescue. I would need to study how to care for one, as I didn't currently have much of a clue, but it was something nice to look forward to.

Tongue lolling, Loaf rolled onto his back for a belly rub. I indulged him a bit, surprised at how soft his fur was. Watching him squirm with delight was rather therapeutic. "Do you want to come on a run with me?"

He gave a bark as he rolled over again, his tiny bobtail wagging enthusiastically.

Smiling, sure he hadn't understood me, but was only responding to the tone of my voice, I turned on my music and set off. Loaf caught up and ran beside me for a full circuit like he'd done previously, before peeling off to lie on the grass and watch me continue. I had yet to catch any sign of Beverly.

I wasn't worried about her, was I? The chiquita was dead. Surely nothing else could happen to her now.

Loaf rejoined me on the next pass, then sat out the one after.

I was about to leave, finally having done enough, when a *thing* came out of the bushes. My heart rate shot instantly upward. Instead of a squirrel or chipmunk as I had seen elsewhere in the park, what tumbled out now was something else entirely—a furry orb about the size of a soccer ball with long, wavy strands of hair and a pair of enormous, red-rimmed, deep purple eyes.

I didn't have the foggiest idea what the unnatural thing was, but it stared dead at me. Then a second one rolled out, identical to the first, except this one had a giant mouth full of jagged teeth rather than eyes. It smiled, and there was something oozingly unpleasant about it.

Though moments ago I had been hot and sweaty, I now felt cold all over. How had these things gotten in here? But more importantly, would I be able to make it to the sliding door before they could bring me down?

I was about to turn and make a run for it when I found I couldn't look away from the odd purple eyes, which were pulsating. I tried to step backward, not sure what the heck was happening, but my muscles wouldn't move. The furball with the ugly teeth rolled slowly forward in my direction.

Heat flushed through me from head to toe, terror nibbling at me, the thing's intent horribly obvious. *¡Madre de Dios!* It was going to *eat* me!

Loaf was suddenly there, barking as he sprinted to encircle them. The thing blinked, startled, allowing me to look away. I could move again! This was my chance to escape. But what would these things do to the brave little guy if I left? *¡Estas loca! Move!*

The two creatures orbited each other as if unsure what to make of the dog. The eyes on the first had shrunk, though they didn't let Loaf leave its sight, while the other gnashed its crooked teeth together, the mouth growing wider.

After running a last hemming circle, Loaf used barks and nipping movements to herd the two creatures toward the sliding door rather than away.

"Loaf, what are you *doing*?" I backed on to the side to steer clear of the lot of them, not thrilled in the least that he was cutting off my only way out—even as my insides continued to churn with worry for him. If he cornered them, surely they'd attack.

But as he jumped from side to side, barking and snapping to keep them moving, the door slid open on its own. Had Last Stop done that, or had they? All three disappeared inside.

Internally, I cussed up a storm, as I found myself going after them.

Loaf stood only a few feet down the middle of the hall on the left, his tongue lolling, cutting off the only avenue of retreat for the two unexpected intruders. Both furballs had also stopped—because the way forward was blocked by Beauty. Though she sat regally, her long tail coiled neatly around her paws, palpable displeasure radiated from her. She grew in size as her emerald eyes glared at the pair before her.

The furballs quivered as if squished by her mere presence.

'*I thought I'd been quite clear in my instructions*,' Beauty said, her tone harsh, as she loomed over them. '*You were to wait in the assigned room and not go wandering about*.'

As she continued to grow, she started looking less and less like a cat and more like a giant-sized feral lion. Her canines had become thicker and longer, her mane bushier, and the tips of her ears and head rounder. A master predator.

A subconscious, primal fear sang in my veins, despite not being the object of her ire. Loaf appeared to take it all in stride.

The two round creatures tried to flatten themselves further. Twin reedy voices finally answered her. "We're sorry."

'*See that you don't forget again*.' A giant paw lashed out and whacked them like a racket, sending the dual furballs bouncing against the walls and ceiling, until a hole appeared and sucked them in, then closed behind them.

I blinked, and Beauty was back to normal size; all her antagonism and anger had evaporated as if it had never existed. Now that it was over, exhaustion washed over me. Why had I ever bothered to get up this morning? I wanted nothing more than to crawl back into bed and pretend none of this had ever happened.

'*I hope they didn't disturb you unduly*,' Beauty said. She made it sound as if all the furballs could have done was interrupt my day like a couple of rowdy kids. What *bullshit*!

"You said I'd be safe here!" I yelled. My whole body shook in a delayed reaction. "Those things were going to *eat* me! If not for Loaf, they would have. And you'd never have known!"

Her impassive emerald eyes met my gaze straight on. '*You were never in any real danger, Daniela. Even if Loaf hadn't intervened on your behalf, I wouldn't have allowed it to go that far.*'

"¡Mentirosa! If that were true, where were you when Ken tried choking me to death?" As soon as the words were out of my mouth, I realized I had said too much.

Beauty's head tilted to the side, seemingly unsurprised. '*He only threatened you. If he'd meant to kill you, you wouldn't have known it had been done until it was much too late.*'

Was that supposed to reassure me somehow? Well, it wasn't working! "So, not mentioning that you're housing a lunatic assassin was just another way you're keeping me *safe*?" My hands flew into the air. "*¡Qué mierda!*"

Beauty's furry ears turned away for a second, as if offended by either my volume or my words, then she tilted her head in the other direction. '*You're my employees, not newborn kittens with their eyes closed. You can solve your problems among yourselves. As long as it doesn't interfere with your work and you don't go too far, I don't see why it requires my involvement. You're adults, after all, are you not? And there's always the option to call out to me mentally for aid,* if *it's required.*'

My hands clenched and unclenched as I tried to get my breathing and raging temper under control. She wasn't wrong, but that didn't mean I had to like it. And the idea of mentally reaching out to her had never once crossed my mind. Why would it? And mira, that heavy subtext proclaiming, I'd better have a darned good reason if I ever did so—that didn't help either.

Those damn alien eyes kept staring at me, waiting to see what the crazy mouse would do next.

Loaf padded over and lay beside my leg, then added a soft whine. What he was trying to tell me, I had no idea, but I appreciated his support all the same. It gave me something to latch on to.

"*Fine.*" The acknowledgement came out through gritted teeth. I had the fervent desire to punch something.

Beauty got up to all fours, her tail at full mast. '*Glad to hear it.*' She raised her head, simultaneously wrinkling her nose. '*I'd advise you to clean up and then come back for breakfast. But do hurry; I've a roomful of beings waiting to impart information, and I need both you and Ryo to be there.*' She turned away, the end of her tail flicking as she went.

My cheeks flushed with embarrassment, cooling my anger, sure that I reeked to high heaven. I doubted sweat and fear made for a lovely bouquet. I headed for the stairs with Loaf bounding behind me.

Only as I sat and removed my sneakers did I realize the staircase had changed. There was now a foot-wide ramp with a rough surface on the left side of the steps. I found out what it was for as I started up. Loaf followed me, his toenails making soft clicking sounds against the wood as he climbed. The new gradient was easier for him to navigate than the stairs. Did he have a room, too?

But evidently that wasn't the case, because the moment I opened my door, Loaf shot between my legs to get inside. "Um, Loaf. You're a cute *perrito* and all, but I'm not sure I'm ready for a roomie."

The corgi ignored me, his nose working a mile a minute as he sniffed around the place. A sigh ran through me. *First, a cat decides I'm a fun sleeping pillow, and now a dog has latched on to me. And neither one cares for my opinion on the matter.*

I sighed again.

Remembering Beauty's request for speed, I left Loaf to his own devices, grabbed some clean clothes, and jumped in the shower. By the time I got dressed and half blow-dried my hair, the corgi had made himself comfortable on my couch and was chewing on a tennis ball. Where he'd found *that* I didn't have the faintest idea.

Sighing yet a third time, I hurried from the room and down to the restaurant area. If Loaf wanted out, I was sure Last Stop would accommodate him. But the same question as before rose in my head—if the dog was there, then where was Beverly? Had the chiquita given up on her unfinished business and moved on? But if that were the case, surely Beauty would have mentioned it, and why would I need to meet a roomful of beings who might have information?

My steps slowed as I realized what I'd just thought. Beings? As in *not* human? Surely not! My squirming guts told another story, however. I really and truly should have stayed in bed this morning.

When I entered the restaurant section, no one else was there, though a steaming cup of café con leche and a covered dish were waiting in the last place I'd sat at the counter. Assuming they were for me, I took the lid off to find an omelet filled to bursting with strawberries, topped with powdered sugar, and a side cup of whipped cream. I had never heard of such a thing, but it looked scrumptious. So I attacked it with wild abandon, hoping the carbs and calories would help me survive the day.

I'd just finished the delightful feast when Ryo poked his head through the curtain from the kitchen. "Good morning," he said. "Are you finished?"

I gulped what was left of my café. "Yes, I'm done." I hoped I sounded as pleased as I felt. "It was great. Thanks for making it."

His tiny smile came and went, and the imaginary tail wagging was in evidence. The swelling from the beating he'd given himself was barely noticeable, though that side of his face was now black and blue, bordered by a yellowish green. The bruises looked terribly painful. I'd made sure to cover mine with makeup, but he left his out in full view.

"Do you know where we need to go?" I asked him.

He gave a quick nod. "Let me set these in the sink, and we can make our way there. Meet me at the kitchen door?"

"Sounds good." Ryo seemed all right other than the bruises. Had he settled things with Ken? Not that I'd be asking. The less I thought of the psycho, and the farther away from him I could stay, the better.

Ryo exited the kitchen at about the same time I reached the entry. "This way," he said, indicating I should precede him if I wanted. Side by side was good enough for me. I wasn't eagerly anticipating what would be coming next.

A flood of giggles washed out of the room as Ryo slid open the door to the right. Beverly sat on a cushion by a low table, surrounded by *things* out of an ugly nightmare.

The two long-haired furballs were there. So were stylized cloud-looking things that floated about and gave off sparks. Several large, folded umbrellas were hopping around. Their handles were literally trousered legs with loafers, and their folded canopies had a giant eye like a cyclops. A few sported different types of hats at their points. Orange traffic cones kept trying to bite them at the ankles by tipping sideways to reveal a sharp-toothed mouth hidden underneath.

Others present appeared as deformed or mutated animals, stood upright, and wore clothes from past eras. Some were metamorphosed amoebas with multiple eyes or mouths. There were so many of them that the large tatami room felt crowded.

But rather than being terrified by the ghastly sight, Beverly laughed and clapped her hands in pure delight, as they kept vying for her attention and performing tricks. Platters of cookies and other treats were spread around the table along with servings of tea. All appeared to have been well received.

Ryo removed his shoes and stepped inside. Several of the creatures quickly hopped, crawled, or hovered out of his way so he might sit. I slipped my feet out of my shoes, but my legs refused to take me past the threshold. Then something soft grazed my leg, and I had to choke back a scream as I flinched away. Startled, I looked down only to find Beauty's emerald gaze staring at me.

'*Go on in. They will not harm you.*' Her eyes narrowed. '*You need to get used to dealing with them. So why not start now?*' She sauntered into the room.

A shiver crawled up my spine with spiked talons. Was she saying this wasn't a one-time thing? *Dios protéjame.* I crossed myself *twice.* Ryo and some of the "guests" kept glancing my way. The longer I stood there, the more obvious my reluctance became.

¡Coño! When had I turned so spineless? This chica once dared to walk into a *police station* and plant evidence against a cop. If I could do *that*, then I could do *this*. Gritting my teeth and plastering on a neutral expression, I stepped into the room.

Chapter 19

"Dani!" Beverly jumped to her feet, finally noticing me, and waded through her new friends to come grab my hand and drag me over to sit by her.

I tried hard not to flinch or screech as I bumped into or inadvertently touched some of the twenty-odd "things" in the room. She pulled me onto a vacated cushion. The nearby creatures swarmed around us, hemming me in. Facing the table left my back exposed, which made me more nervous and caused my fingers to twitch.

I heard sniffing close behind me and felt my hair move as it was handled lightly by claws, tentacles, and who knew what else. One of the cloud-looking things hovered right over me. Whispers passed back and forth, but I couldn't make out the words. I would have given almost anything to be anywhere else.

"Aren't they great?" Beverly asked, beaming at her new friends. "And they're helping us find Mystic!"

I nodded, not trusting myself to speak coherently at the moment. My brain was babbling to itself as I struggled not to freak out and run screaming from the room. But they were helping us look for the missing Beanie Baby… so I needed to put up with it.

Beauty stepped onto the low table somewhere in the middle and sat. "I apologize for the wait," she said.

My eyes almost popped out of my head as I realized she had spoken *out loud* rather than in our minds. '*You can talk!*'

Beauty slipped me a sideways glance. '*I've been talking to you ever since we met.*'

'*That's not what I meant, and you know it. You can speak aloud!*' Either she liked keeping her cards hidden, or she enjoyed toying with people. I was pretty damn sure it was the latter.

'*Now, now, Dani. Let's stick to the present business, shall we?*'

Oh, she liked playing all right.

"Before we start, I want to introduce you to the newest member of Last Stop," she said, raising a paw to point in my direction. "Everyone, this is Dani. Dani, everyone." She raked the myriad clusters of strange beings with a pointed stare. "Do try to remember what she looks like and behave yourselves. I will *not* take kindly to those who don't." She sent a sharpened glare toward the double fuzzball, who again tried to make itself as flat as possible.

Giggles, a few guffaws, various animal calls, and rapid murmurs filled the air.

"Now that you've had your snacks and introductions have been made, it's time to get to business," Beauty said. "What have you found out for us?"

Chaos reigned for the next several minutes as the different minor spirits and creatures tried to share what they knew. Not that much of it sounded useful. Beauty seemed able to hear them all clearly, rather than the maelstrom of jumbled sound their diverse voices were making. It gave me a pounding headache.

A giant sheet of paper wafted into the room and settled on the back wall. It began filling with lines that turned into a city map of central Boston. Tiny icons showed where each of the creatures typically haunted.

"Did any of you actually *see* the unicorn?" Beauty eventually asked.

Beverly slipped her small hand in mine and squeezed my fingers as she looked around. Tears gathered in her eyes as the seconds ticked by, and none of her new friends spoke up.

"Well, I wasn't gonna say nothin' in case someone else saw it, but I mighta done." The soft, reserved voice piped up from

Ryo's side of the table. A tiny black fedora, sporting a bright green and red feather that was larger than the hat, waved at them from the end of a black and gold pinstripe-suited arm to grab their attention.

The surrounding creatures near the hat pulled back so the one waving it could be seen.

A cinnamon-colored ferret-like creature returned the hat to his furry head, then straightened his pinstripe suit. "Name's Cyrano, and I don't believe in snitches, see, so I didn't want to set my tongue to wagging if I didn't have to. But as this here is a special case..." He sent a sharp-toothed smile in Beverly's direction.

"I didn't spot it with my own two peepers, mind ya," Cyrano added, "but I heard the wannabes talkin' about it and how it's locked away in the safe in the upstairs office of the club. The boss has it earmarked for one of his nieces."

A tiny fedora icon got added to the wall map on a street near the Boston Logan International Airport.

Then a cacophony of voices blared, calling the ferret's words into question, or others jumping in to say they'd heard of it first. It devolved into complete pandemonium.

An ear-splitting roar tore through the room, shocking everybody into silence. "Enough!" Beauty's ears had flattened against her head, the thick, luscious tail lashing back and forth on the table top. "I thank you all for coming, but everyone except for Cyrano and my people can now leave. And *no* detours. Am I understood?" Her sharp gaze raked the area.

The door out of the room opened on its own.

Every last one of the guests bade Beverly goodbye before they left. I wasn't sure what she'd done, or if it was that uncommon for niños to have unfinished business, but they all seemed captivated by her.

I was more surprised to hear a few whispers of "glad to meet you" sent my way as they filed out.

Beauty fluffed out her ruff and ears with a soft shake of her head and shoulders. Cyrano took the vacated cushion closest to her, sitting on his hind legs, his small arms resting on the tabletop. He removed his hat and set it on the table, making sure the large feather didn't impede the view of those remaining. His black, beady eyes never left Beauty, as if drinking in the sight of her and committing every detail to memory. Could supernatural creatures fall in love? These two weren't even the same species. A rather perplexing thought to contemplate.

"Beverly," Beauty said, "Loaf was wandering about the halls not long ago. Would you help him make sure everyone made it out?"

The girl squeezed my fingers one last time before hopping to her feet. "Okay."

As she ran out, she filched a few of the leftover snacks, probably to give to Loaf since he'd missed out. It was a real tragedy that this sweet child had died. But life was unfair that way.

A second large piece of paper flew into the room as Beverly left, and then the door closed behind her. Ryo had said nothing throughout all the mayhem, though I doubted his gray eyes and his ears had overlooked a thing.

Cyrano spoke as lines began appearing on the new sheet. "I took the liberty of casing the joint, since I was there." He swept a five-fingered claw over the fur on his head as if to smooth it out. "The place is called Wise Guys Lounge, see. It's one of those whatchamacallits, themed bars? Made to look and feel like a speakeasy. My kinda place," he said. "They have a back door through a neighboring business, and they also have a secret entrance and exit in case of trouble, though that one isn't common knowledge for the customers."

Miami had some of those—Red Phone Booth, Room 55, and Dante's HiFi, to name a few. Pretending to buy drinks illicitly had a certain allure, as if they were somehow getting one over on the law without actually breaking it. They were great places for Jay and me to work through to meet our daily quotas.

"The place is legit, in its way, see," Cyrano continued. "It's owned by what remains of the Patriarca mob family. The old guard is gone now, so what's left are just flunkies with titles and old shoes they can never fill, and wannabes. Their real racket is sports betting, which is still illegal here nowadays, unlike just about all other kinds of gambling."

Darnell was even more of an idiot than I gave him credit for. If Cyrano was right, these mobsters were coasting on the old reputations of others and were nothing like those who had come before them. Not that I would underestimate them. Armed posers could still get you killed.

Chapter 20

Cyrano wasn't flighty and didn't seem to have ADD, unlike a bunch of the other *things* I had met that day. He provided us with a lot of good intel and had done a thorough job checking out the three-story building, and specifically the lounge itself.

Last Stop added every detail to the multi-floor map. Like having an architect on call or unrestricted access to the city archives.

"You've been very helpful, Cyrano," Beauty said. "Thank you." A light purr rang in his direction.

The ferret's eyes glittered at the praise. He had a thing for the cat, all right. *Qué mono*. Though if the attraction had been from some of the other ghastlier-looking visitors, it wouldn't have been cute at all.

"My pleasure, see," he said, grabbing his hat and setting it on his triangular head with a flourish. "I'll keep an eye on things in case something changes."

Beauty tickled his chin with her tail. "That would be lovely. Thanks again."

The moment Cyrano left, Ryo pulled some stacked trays from a hidden closet behind the tatami walls and started gathering the leftover cookies, brownies, and other sweet and salty snacks. Despite the number of creatures that had been present, they'd made less of a mess than I would have expected. Whether that was due to fear of Beauty's wrath or actual manners, it was hard to say.

I pitched in by collecting the ceramic teacups, the pent-up anxiety of being in a room of supernatural creatures flowing out of me now that they were gone.

Beauty jumped lightly off the squat table and sat by the wall where the maps were hung. "Thoughts?"

I couldn't tell if she was asking Ryo or me, so I threw my two cents out first. "Getting in shouldn't be a problem, though we might need to deal with security cameras," I said. While Cyrano hadn't mentioned any, since he likely couldn't be picked up by the video feeds, it might never have occurred to him to look for them. I would need to assume they had some. Were spirits and other supernatural creatures even tech-savvy? "Opening the safe holding Mystic might be a show-stopper." I shrugged. "I'm no safecracker."

Beauty nodded and turned her gaze to Ryo.

"It will depend on how old it is. If it's an antique, I should be able to manage it," he said.

He could crack safes? Just what kind of cook was he? "We have to do something about those bruises first, though," I added. "Anyone seeing them is going to remember you. I'm assuming we'd want to avoid that." Putting makeup over those would hurt—a lot!

He glanced at me, then looked away. "That won't be a problem," Ryo said. "You'll see."

There was a hint of a mischievous tone in the way he said it. His imaginary tail was wagging again. He sure was easy to please. The total opposite of his humorless twin.

I pulled out my phone and did a quick search for the lounge after taking a pic of the maps so I'd have them handy. "Their posted hours are from 4 pm to 2 am. But if they're also running a sports betting racket, someone would need to be there during the earlier part of the day. No way would they want to lose out on the cash to a different bookie," I said. "Gamblers are a superstitious lot—some want to bet as early as possible, while others like to wait to commit until the last possible moment.

"It's a good 'bet,' ha, that the people who want to do business during off hours are gaining entry by the back door Cyrano mentioned, so that could be one way in. Or we might use their secret escape route for our own purposes." From Last Stop's map, there was a decent chance it ran through tunnels from a forgotten subway or a dug-out passage created all the way back during Prohibition days.

"We should check what we can ourselves once the place opens for the day," I said. "Since alarms and cameras mean nothing to creatures that can't be seen or heard, there might be things we need to be wary of that Cyrano wouldn't have thought about."

"Good," Beauty said. "I'll leave it to you then. Don't forget to bundle up before you go."

¡Ay! I had forgotten about the cold! What little excitement had been building at the job froze over and cracked into pieces.

Ryo threw me a pitying look from behind his large, round-lensed glasses. "It won't be as bad this time. We'll be close to the lounge when we leave."

While I didn't think he'd lie to me, I still wouldn't believe it until I saw it. Beauty had played tricks on me before. "I'm sure you're right."

I grabbed one of the filled trays and headed for the door.

We had a few hours to kill before lunch, and some more after that before the lounge officially opened, so I went upstairs once Ryo and I had finished bringing all the leftover snacks and used dishes to the kitchen. Rather than leave my shoes in the cubby, I brought them with me, not wanting to give Bruja

Ida any opportunities for more mischief. The tacks I'd left out were gone.

As if summoned by my thoughts, Ida was coming out of her room as I reached the top of the stairs. With her coiffured hair and snazzy clothes, it was obvious her faculties were working today. I would have preferred Niña Ida instead.

From her startled expression, she'd no more expected to see me than I had her. Had she been the one who removed the tacks, or had it been one of the others?

I plastered a pleasant smile on my face, knowing it would annoy her. "Good morning, Ida." The familiar use of her first name by someone she deemed an inferior would also rankle her no end.

Her lips twitched once, then formed their own smile. "Good morning." The pleasant sentiment didn't reach her eyes, but at least she had made the effort. Working toward redemption was supposedly one of the reasons Beauty had snatched her from death's embrace.

Not that I was buying Ida's act for a second. No way her kind turned a new leaf overnight. But just in case, I bobbed my head at her encouragingly and beamed before heading to my door. "Have a great day!"

If it were an act rather than a genuine attempt, it would be fun to see how long she could maintain it.

Now armed with something to look forward to, I hunkered down to do more research and start getting ready.

According to the Wise Guys' website, there wasn't a particular dress code, which was a plus. Sweaters and lots of layers would be called for.

As I rummaged around for something appropriate, I realized Last Stop had added a few things to my closet again. I almost squealed in delight at the sight of a dark blue cashmere sweater. Cashmere was the warmest wool out there, and super soft. She'd also supplied me with a black set of thermal underwear. I'd only ever seen these on TV, as there wasn't much of a market for them in the tropical weather of Miami. Last was a cute pair of lined winter boots.

I might manage not to turn into a frozen popsicle after all! ¡Gracias a Dios! "Thank you, LS!"

With that taken care of, I spent some time using Google Maps to familiarize myself with the area around the lounge, seeing what buses or commuter lines were nearby, memorizing what I could, etc. Preparation had kept me alive this long. Just because I had changed employers was no reason to change my habits. You never knew what could go wrong. A point that had been proven yet again with the worst possible results for Jay.

My eyes burned even as I wished he were next to me so I could kick him. *¡Idiota! How dare you leave me all alone?* I punched my pillow a couple of times, then hugged it to my chest, struggling to keep myself together. I needed to stop being such a llorona!

Disgusted with myself, I left my room and went downstairs. It was still too early for lunch, and I was loath to bother Ryo in the kitchen. Maybe spending time in the park would help lift my spirits. I was about to turn in that direction when a loud wood-on-wood smacking sound reverberated from the front of the eatery.

Before I knew what I was doing, I was running full tilt toward it. When I got there, I saw that the sliding entry door had been shoved all the way open, with force—wood chips and cracks in the runners told the tale of the unnecessary violence that had occurred. A shimmering field of some sort covered the exposed entryway.

Ryo was there in his black chef's outfit, a cleaver half raised in one hand and a long, pointed knife held in the other, every muscle taut. If he'd been a dog, he would have been growling, hackles raised, ears plastered back to his head, and his teeth showing.

On the other side of the shimmering field stood one of the most gorgeous men I'd ever seen.

Chapter 21

The stranger wore a startlingly white three-piece suit, red alligator shoes, a matching crimson handkerchief folded with angled peaks in the pocket of the outfit, and a giant ruby gracing his neck where a tie would typically be. He had a square jaw and a Roman nose, and his eyes golden in color—seemed to almost glow. His perfectly disheveled thick brown hair had a reddish tint to it. His skin was a sunny tan.

A modern-day Adonis stood before us, if you could ignore the cruel twist of his lips and disdainful stance as he pounded an impatient fist against the field covering the entryway. I took an instant dislike to him, revulsion crawling over me despite the pretty packaging. I'd met way too many men like him before. Bad news all around.

His golden eyes shifted in my direction as he became aware of me.

I had to blink several times as everything about him shifted as if a switch had been thrown. His lips changed from a savage curl to a glowing smile in less than an instant. His arrogant stance transformed into a friendly, delighted one. "Well, hello there."

His voice was like pure honey—sweet and cloying. But no matter what the package or comportment, the whole package still screamed "predator" to me.

"Dani, stay back," Ryo said. He didn't spare me a glance, his entire concentration on the man before him. "He's dangerous."

The stranger gave no indication of having heard him. He was too busy dissecting me from head to toe with his golden stare. "You must be the new *pet*," he said, somehow making it sound condescending and wonderful at the same time. Our gazes locked, and his eyes glowed brighter, as if trying to suck me inside them. "Won't you invite me in? I would like us to become better acquainted."

My mouth opened of its own accord to do as he said, but I was able to snap it closed before any words escaped me. Why had I almost done what he wanted? Primal fear swept up my spine as pressure built behind my eyes.

"*Invite me in*. There's no need to be impolite."

Doubt wriggled in as the compulsion to say the words came at me again. There was nothing to fear from such a nice man, was there? Why not ask him inside? The tension inside my head increased. I bit the inside of my mouth, confused as to why I would be tempted to ignore what I had already intuited about the man. Was he doing something to me? Mentally nudging me to do as he wanted?

"Desmond, stop this at once!" Beauty sauntered over to stand between us. "Honestly, could you be any ruder?" she asked. "You're as aware of the house rules as I am."

He dismissively waved a hand. "I rather think of them as guidelines," Desmond said with a smirk, breaking eye contact with me.

The force inside my head snapped away like a rubber band, making me stagger.

'*Daniella, are you all right?*' Beauty's voice enquired in my mind.

'*Yeah, I'm okay,*' I thought back, my brain still throbbing from what I could only assume was a mental assault. '*Who the hell* is *that?*'

My fear transformed into flames as realization trickled in regarding what he had attempted to do to me. The cabrón had tried to mentally *manipulate* me! I shook where I stood, fighting to restrain myself, wanting nothing more at the moment than to claw the bastard's eyes out.

Beauty ignored my question. "Desmond, why are you here?" she asked, her voice razor sharp.

Our wanna-be intruder folded an arm across his chest as he rested the elbow of the other on it to tap his index finger against his cheek as if having trouble recollecting the reason and what he'd just tried to do to me meant nothing at all. ¡*Pendejo cabrón*!

"Gee, let me think," he said. He held up a manicured finger. "You've got a new pet." A second digit joined the first. "You invited a bunch of the minor rabble to a party." Then a third. "And you shared multiple drinks with a measly elemental."

His eyes hardened. "Yet I've not heard one word about any of it from you."

Beauty yawned, drawing it out longer than usual. "I don't work for you and am under no obligation to share anything." She yawned again. "The meetings you've referred to were related to our duties. *Not* that it's any of your business, even if they hadn't been. And you're quite capable of transporting yourself between realms, thus having no need to come here." Now her tone turned frosty. "Yet here you are, breaking things and harassing my employees, and you dare wonder why Hokora-chan would prefer to keep you out."

Movement at the corner of my eye vied for my attention. It was the mirror attached to one of the eatery's posts by the counter. It angled itself to show me Desmond's reflection. My throat clamped shut, and my temper froze at what I saw there.

The suit and shoes were the same, but the man who wore them no longer looked human. Desmond was now a person-shaped mound of seething flesh that oozed, rolled, and never stopped moving. A pair of crimson-colored spiraling horns rose from his head, a ring of flames endlessly turning between their tips like a crown.

I tore my gaze from the disturbing image. Who or whatever he was, I wanted nothing to do with him. Beyond the creature, the streets and people of Boston continued with their routine, utterly oblivious of what was happening or who stood amongst them.

Ryo's bristling stance had yet to ease one iota.

"What *it* feels is irrelevant," Desmond said testily. "It is but a tool to be used. As I will prove to you once I am given dominion over it." He snapped his fingers. "Now, call your dog to heel, drop this field, and allow me inside. My patience is wearing thin."

Beauty stepped daintily forward and, with a mere tap of her paw, closed the sliding door on its newly repaired grooves. Her bubbling laughter suddenly filled the air.

The loud, angry roar that originated from the other side shook the walls. Strangely enough, however, it lasted only for a few moments. It wouldn't have surprised me if he had stayed out there cursing and screaming at us all day to vent his frustration, but he seemed to have more self-control than I would have given him credit for. The whole thing left a smear of chilled fear rattling through my bones and a foul taste in my mouth.

I crossed myself, hoping I would never run across that "man" again.

"Who… what was that thing?" I asked for the second time. The sudden need to sit almost overwhelmed me.

"Just a powerful, blustering blowhard," Beauty said, turning her back to the entrance. Her emerald eyes glimmered.

Ryo finally relaxed, lowering the knife and cleaver as he backed away from the area near the door. He sent a quick, questioning glance my way before scurrying toward the kitchen.

Was he worried about me? It pushed the lingering dread back a touch. But I still wanted my questions answered.

"Can you be a little more specific? *Please*?" I was drowning standing there. I was so out of my depth.

Beauty jumped onto the lunch counter, then spread out as if she were Queen Cleopatra lounging on a chaise. "Desmond is a royal prince from the spirit realm, what some humans might refer to as a demon."

I stumbled over to one of the half-backed stools, sorry to have my terrible suspicions confirmed. With her partially closed eyes and relaxed pose, I was sure Beauty was laughing at me. Didn't she ever tire of these games?

"Don't let it worry you," Beauty said. "Just think of him as a tomcat trying to mark his territory." Her tail swished about. "Though it's been centuries, he's still sore about Hokora choosing me over him."

Ryo came through the kitchen curtain carrying a tray. On it were a shallow bowl of milk and two ceramic Japanese teacups. After setting the saucer in front of Beauty, he pulled a stool from beneath the counter on his side and sat, then placed a cup before me and kept the last for himself. I noticed the barest of tremors as he took a sip.

Clearly I hadn't been the only one rattled by all this.

So the "demon" was only a sore loser? Only another crazy thing to add to the growing list? That's not what Ryo's reaction to the guy told me. He hadn't batted an eye about Akasha. But his full-on response to Desmond spoke of a much higher threat level. The fact that the cabrón had tried to force me to his will didn't speak well for him either. His true form made him a creature from a nightmare.

Believing in ghosts and the supernatural was one thing, but there were demonic beings bopping around as well? Did that make Hell and souls getting punished for sins real? What about God? Heaven and angels? Did those exist as well? Or were these demons just powerful entities, like in the non-Christian faiths?

My hand shook worse than Ryo's as I took a gulp of the hot tea. I was just a pickpocket—how was someone like me supposed to deal with any kind of demonic being? My chest grew tight, and cold fingers closed around my throat as other possibilities rose for inspection.

"What's to stop him from attacking us when we're not here? From trying to make me do things I don't want?" I asked. My voice quivered a little. I didn't have any experience with guns, but I really wanted one right now. The higher the caliber, the better. There had to be a way to make all this weirdness quit rattling me every other minute.

"He won't," Beauty said. She switched to mental thoughts as she lapped at her milk. '*He'd risk too much in doing that. No spirit house would ever trust him if they sensed it or if the act came to light. His general attitude is already a black mark against him, though he seems oblivious to that fact.*' She snorted. '*He can't get it through his thick head that* this *is a partnership, not a master-slave relationship.*'

So, Last Stop had really picked Beauty to work with it? "I'm assuming the position holds some prestige or power? Is that why he wants it?" These were motivations I could wrap my head around.

'*That may be part of it.*' Beauty's tail twitched. '*But I doubt that's all there is to it. He's not typically this flamboyant either. It was a bit too theatrical, even for him. So I'm sure he's working up to something.*'

If that was supposed to make me feel better, she had totally botched it.

Chapter 22

Lunch was a subdued affair, thanks to Desmond's rowdy attempted intrusion. I barely tasted the chef's salad Ryo had put together, despite the luscious creamy Italian dressing and all the super fresh veggies, meats, and cheeses.

I kept mentally plucking at the threads of the dread-filled knot the demon prince had left in his wake, trying to figure out his angle, especially since Beauty had told me it wasn't his usual style. Not knowing what made the guy tick was a huge stumbling block in making sense of things, though. And demons were *real*? The thought alone made my skin crawl. My mind continuously flashing back to the image of what Desmond truly looked like didn't help matters, either.

There could be nastier entities out there that I had no idea about, let alone what their motivations or goals might be. But it didn't stop me from picking at the problem like an old scab, anyway.

Ida joined us at lunch, which was unexpected, but I assumed it was only thanks to Beauty's mandate that we get along. I had too much to handle as it was, so I paid her no attention aside from returning an acknowledging nod, and that seemed to suit both of us.

Trying to research demonic lore online only made me jumpier and more nervous, and didn't get me anywhere, so I dropped it. Instead, I switched over to studying the maps, street views, and floor plans of the lounge until my eyes crossed, then went upstairs and got changed for the afternoon's adventure.

A small cross-body purse was just big enough to hold my phone, a can of pepper spray, a set of lock picks, and my cherry Chapstick. Last Stop had recreated or somehow gotten hold of my tool set, as I'd found it in the same place I had stored it in my original room.

A fresh application of makeup and leaving my hair down ensured my neck bruises remained well hidden. There were techniques I could have used to alter my general appearance slightly, but I doubted we'd need to take such precautions here. We were only checking out the lay of the land, so I didn't bother.

When I got back downstairs, I found Ryo already waiting for me, wearing much the same as what he'd put on to go to Beverly's house—a black turtleneck but with jeans rather than slacks. But he'd worked some serious magic on his face. If I hadn't seen them myself, I would never have suspected he had bruises hiding there. Mira, I couldn't even tell he was wearing makeup! Who *was* this guy? And would he be willing to teach me his techniques?

He checked out my clothing and makeup choices and gave an approving nod. I was oddly pleased by his approval and would have preened, but I was a professional. This chica was no noob.

Donning our armor against the cold weather, which was hungrily waiting outside for a chance to pounce on us again, we got ready to go.

Ryo took the lead and gently slid the front door open, as if trying to compensate for the violence the entryway had received from our earlier scary, rude, and unwelcome guest. That reminded me that Desmond could easily be waiting for us outside, which sent a shiver through me that had nothing to do with the cold pouring in from outdoors.

A flood of sound crashed into us as we stepped out—loud, slow-moving traffic engine noise, blaring horns, tires splashing in the half-melted snow. The wind had died, so the stench of exhaust lazed around like a fog, trying to cover everything. But it wasn't all bad. There was no demonic prince in sight, first of all; second, the sun was shining brightly, wrestling back the cold and creating sparkles in the melting icicles and snow.

The two crows, cuddled together in their nest in the awning's inner corner, made subdued clicking and rattling sounds as if glad to see us again. We merged with the pedestrian traffic on the sidewalk.

This section of Boston was full of red and brown brick buildings, most rising to only five stories or so. A few had been polished to give them a more modern look and feel, while others appeared as they had since the day they were built. Glancing both ways down Congress Street, I saw contemporary glass structures that rose several floors higher than these, as if newer constructions were slowly trying to hem in their shorter, older relatives and choke them out.

Twisting to look behind me, I saw that Last Stop was currently nestled inside a red brick structure, as if it had always been part of the landscape. The pedestrians making up the busy foot traffic didn't even give it a glance as they walked past.

Ryo offered me his arm, and though the sidewalks looked a lot less treacherous than the day before, I took it gratefully anyway.

Now that I had been supernaturally marked and given the ability to see them, I saw minor spirits and beings everywhere. And not just the anthropomorphic or amoeba-like ones who'd been at the meeting, but also a few that looked like normal humans. I hadn't seen a single one of either on our last excursion, aside from Akasha. Had her presence kept the others away from the area of Beverly's home, or was something else attracting them here?

The more I looked, the more of them I saw. Mira, there were too damn many of them—they were *all* interested in watching us, which was worrying. It was almost as if they were waiting for something. That was loco, right?

I badly needed a distraction.

"Had you met Desmond before?" I asked Ryo. "Do you think he'll be back?" We humans needed to stick together, right?

It took a moment or two before he answered. "Briefly, before my welcome party." Ryo hesitated. "He smelled of death." His grey eyes turned to look at me before skidding shyly away. "It'd be best never to be alone with him."

"Oh, *that* won't be happening," I assured him. "He might have a pretty outer package, but he gave me the total creeps."

Ryo inclined his head, taking me at my word. He guided us to the nearest crosswalk, and we surged with other pedestrians to get to the other side. Once across, the human wave split off in different directions, like the sea crashing against the rocks. Our destination was on the block's far end. Though the walk was less unpleasant and bone-chilling than the last time we'd been outdoors, I was still glad Beauty had parked Last Stop close to the lounge.

A recessed entry faced both sides of the intersection and opened to a set of steps leading down to a thick metal door with a view slot. The two street-facing sides of the support column at the corner held black vertical signs with a thick, masculine font rendering the words "Wise Guys" in white.

The lounge's website had given instructions on how to get inside. I knocked on the metal gateway three times. The sliding peephole slid open. "Yeah? Whaddya want?"

"A bit of moxie," I said.

The slot closed, and a moment later, the door was pulled ajar. "Come on in, then."

The greeter was a human version of Cyrano—he wore a fedora, a pinstripe suit, and an attitude—except the craggy, hairless face was nowhere near as cute as the ferret's.

Our welcomer signaled for us to go further inside with a tilt of his head. "Sit yer ass wherever you like, doll."

"Thanks!" I wasn't surprised to see that he was wearing a concealed shoulder carry harness with something high caliber nestled inside it. Most patrons would assume it was all part of the speakeasy atmosphere rather than thinking him actually armed.

Ryo let me lead the way. A couple of pulled-taffy-looking spirits jiggled in behind us, and there were already several others hiding here and there inside. Had someone told them we were coming? But who? Beauty had sent the rest of the supernatural beings away before asking Cyrano for details. And he seemed like the type who was able to keep secrets.

Wannabes or not, the mobsters had outfitted the fake speakeasy well. Dim golden lighting, dark woods, with plenty of Art Déco touches and elaborate crown molding. Cozy, private wraparound booths with leather seats occupied the wall on the right, while a polished bar ran most of the length of the room on the left.

The wall behind the bar was bursting with shelves holding all manner of alcohol-filled bottles—even some that looked like they might contain homemade hooch because of their handwritten labels. From the details Cyrano had given us, I knew the entire set of shelves could be lowered, the top becoming a second counter. The bartender was known for activating it several times a night for effect. There was also a tucked-away scent sprayer which added a touch of gunpowder smell to the air. Big band music poured at a low volume from hidden speakers.

Framed newspaper clippings about Prohibition and bootleggers, as well as photos of famous gangsters—especially those belonging to the Patriarca Family—dotted the walls. A few crude open crates were nestled into corners, showing packing straw and what could be the necks of bottles, adding to the illusion of illegal dealings. That the owners actually *did* carry on illicit activities must have made the whole thing something of an in-joke to those in the know. Hiding in plain sight had worked for thousands of years, after all.

I chose a booth midway to the back, where the restroom and employee-only areas were located. I unzipped my coat but didn't take it off. Ryo shed his like a second skin. Laminated menus for both food and drinks, with the lounge's name done in gold, rested in wooden holders set in the middle of the tables.

"I spotted a couple of recessed cameras in the vestibule," Ryo said in a lowered voice. "At least one inside so far."

He had good eyes. I had noticed the ones outdoors, but none yet indoors. "We'll need to do something about the recordings then."

I scooched around the leather seat until I was sitting beside him, the better to sell the idea that we were on a date, with the added benefit of being able to have a conversation at a lower volume, thus reducing our chances of being overheard. "By the way, do spirits usually congregate this close together? There were an awful lot of them outside, and there are more than a few in here, too."

Ryo nodded, his spectacled gaze roaming about the room without being obvious about it. "This isn't normal."

I grabbed a menu and pretended to look at it. "Do you think Beauty put them up to it?"

"No. She wouldn't compromise the mission like that."

The wording made him sound military, but I was sure he had never been in the service. Their kind had a telltale walk and way of standing and moving about. With SOUTHCOM and HARB so close to Miami, I'd seen plenty of jarheads and other armed forces types. He wasn't a police officer either, as they, too, had a certain way about them that generally gave them away. I'd figure him out sooner or later. "So what is it then?"

His shoulder rose in a light shrug. Ryo might not believe Beauty was responsible, but the tiny wrinkling of his brow told me he didn't like it any more than I did. This kind of vibe would have had me and Jay call it quits and look elsewhere to ply our trade. But with the Beanie Baby being here and not knowing when they might give it to the niece, casing the place before breaking in later couldn't wait.

A waitress wearing the telltale short cocktail dress and pillbox hat of a cigarette girl came by to ask for our order. She gave Ryo an interested smile and flashed her blue eyes at him, but he didn't appear to notice. That was a first for her, I bet; she was a looker with rather significant assets. I ordered a couple of Shirley Temples and some nachos, and she left sending a slight pout in Ryo's direction, which likewise went unnoticed. I barely held back a grin.

"One of us should check what we can of the rear before the place starts filling up," I suggested. A couple of other guests had entered, and more would be coming as their workday came to an end.

"I'll go." Ryo slipped out of the booth. "And I'll see if I can find out why the spirits are here."

I was more than happy to leave that last part to him. "Good idea."

Since I was alone, it was time for some people-watching. You could learn a lot about a mark by observing them as they moved about, especially when they had no clue you were looking. Reflective surfaces were a big help in keeping targets unaware.

So I secretly observed the bartender as he deftly made our drinks. The burly man wore a long-sleeved white shirt with sleeve garters, along with a dark green vest and tie, as if he had been plucked straight out of a 1930s Hollywood movie. The door's guardian had settled onto a stool by the entrance to the lounge and was busy staring at his cell phone.

The waitress delivered our drinks and the nachos, and her eyes lit up when she noticed Ryo wasn't at the table. Since there weren't many options, she would assume he had gone to the restroom. I was sure she was thrilled at the chance to try her luck again without my being in the way. I'd seen this scenario play out several times with Jay. If being a chick-magnet had been a superpower, Jay'd had it in spades, despite not swinging that way.

"Listen, I wouldn't waste my time if I were you," I said. "He bats for the other team."

She looked at me in surprise, her cheeks coloring. "I don't know what you're talking about." She turned around in a huff and headed toward the back.

I couldn't help myself and called after her. "Good luck!"

A muffled giggle rang out beside me. I almost jumped out of my skin when I realized something inhuman sat coiled next to me. It was the size of a garter snake, but its scales were the color of pearls with a pair of thin stripes running down its length in black. It also had multicolored feathered wings, two near its head, and smaller twins by the tail. Most disturbing were its pair of miniature arms and hands, which it was using to stifle its giggles. Its brille-lidded eyes matched the hue of its scales.

A tiny, female voice rose to my ear. "My master wants you to have this."

Her tail prodded at a business card I hadn't noticed beside her.

"Your master?" My words came out in a squeak.

"Yes," she said, rising into the air with a single flap of her wings. "He also said you should be careful today."

My heart skipped a beat. "Careful of what?"

She didn't answer me, instead darting away through the nearest wall. If not for the business card still on the seat, I might have thought she had never been there at all.

Chapter 23

I didn't touch the card. I reached out for one of the nachos instead to act like everything was normal, even as my stomach clenched in nervousness. Surreptitiously, I glanced around the lounge again as I chewed, trying to catch a glimpse or hint of my visitor's supposed master. The doorman was still busy with his cellphone, and the bartender was checking some glasses for streaks. The reflection of the couple who had come in after us showed they were happily chatting. No one else had arrived.

So how had someone known I was here to send the flying snake to me? The security cameras? Or maybe the winged serpent had delivered the message to the wrong person? But how many people able to see spirits could there be? Might this be tied to the reason there was a crowd of supernatural beings in this place?

¡Coño! I was flying blind here!

I looked at the business card, still not touching it. In a small black font, two words were nestled on the white background—"Shaman Corps." I knew what shamans were, and corps was typically a military term, but both together? Scowling, I used a fork to flip it over. The back was as plain as the front, with an 800 number and an extension written on it. Neither the name nor the number rang any bells.

I grabbed another cheese- and meat-laden chip. It tasted like greasy sawdust. If they'd been from a three-star Michelin restaurant, they'd still have tasted the same.

Ryo soon returned, and I scooched over so he could sit, palming the business card and hiding it in a pocket as I did so. A deep frown marred his face.

"Is something wrong?" I asked. Had he seen the snake?

His troubled gaze slid in my direction for a moment. "The waitress..."

I barked a laugh of relief. *This* was something I could deal with. "Did she make a pass at you? I thought she might."

Ryo's brow furrowed further. "A pass?"

Surely he'd been flirted with before? "You know, hit on you? Come on to you?"

"I was her… target?" His whole body coiled tight, and he glanced back the way he'd come as if expecting a surprise attack. "I didn't sense any malice or weapons on her."

Was he serious? "No, tonto. That's not what it means at all." Well, yes, he had been her "target," but not in the way he meant. "She found you attractive, is what I'm saying. Someone she thought she might like to get better acquainted with. And she wanted you to know that, and hopefully find out if you felt the same."

The tension about him eased, but didn't entirely go away.

"Did she hand you a piece of paper or a cocktail napkin?" I asked.

He shifted all of his attention my way. "Yes."

"Is there a phone number written on it?" Despite all the unknowns at the moment, I felt amusement bubbling inside me.

Ryo pulled a folded napkin out of his pocket and straightened it on the table. Not only had the waitress given him her digits and her name, she'd taken the trouble of putting a heart over the 'I' in Shirley.

"How did you know?" he asked me. His brow had finally smoothed out, and his gray eyes widened slightly as he stared at me with a disturbingly large amount of wonder.

The better question was, how did he *not* know this? "It's a common way for women to show their interest in a guy, to say they'd like to get to know him better. Especially at bars. In the same way a man will send a girl a free drink to let her know he's interested."

His eyebrows went up. "Oh, I see. It's a seduction technique." Now he looked like an excited puppy. "Good to know."

Regular people did not talk or act this way. He *definitely* hadn't had a normal upbringing. My curiosity about him started percolating again. But that was when I noticed several new minor supernatural beings bouncing over the bar. Snooping about his background would have to wait. "Were you able to find out why there are so many spirits congregating here?"

"Yes." His expression instantly turned serious. "Someone spread a rumor saying there's going to be a drinking party somewhere around here. They were told to look for Last Stop employees, as the festivities would be wherever we were."

That sounded fishy as hell. "Has anyone done something like this before?" I asked.

"No. Not that I know of."

That was… interesting. Desmond sprang instantly to mind as the culprit, but what would he gain from pulling such a stunt? Was he hoping to distract us from our job, or was he building a big audience because he somehow knew we would fail and wanted it made public? Regardless of the reason, that clinched it for me. Enough was enough.

"Ryo, we should leave." I worked at keeping my voice and expression calm. "Something about all this doesn't feel right." I hated to turn tail, but this was only supposed to be a chance to get the lay of the land before the actual grab. If we were already compromised, we might need to rethink the whole business.

He dipped his head and was about to slip out of the booth when…

"Shit!" The bouncer jumped to his feet, his eyes glued to the phone. Dropping it into his pocket, he then jammed shut the bolt on the metal door before slapping down a brace, which he then locked in place. He slapped the open sign switch to off before taking off at speed toward the back of the lounge.

He'd effectively sealed us in. Or more likely, made it so no one else could get inside. Despite the fact that they were known to occasionally put on a show for their customers, the panicked look in his eyes and the beads of sweat on his brow told a different story. Something big was happening.

The bartender pulled a sawed-off shotgun from beneath the bar and threw a glance our way and at the other couple. "You'll want to hunker down beneath the table for a bit," he said, then hit a hidden button that dropped the booze bottles from view. "Can't have those Prohis messing with our customers."

Nice try on his part. Too bad his pale face and trembling lips gave away the fact that this wasn't part of the standard show for the patrons. We ducked beneath the table as suggested.

Trepidation flooded my veins and made my fingers twitch. The other couple let out some nervous laughter.

Then the echo of muffled gunshots bounced our way. Fear's cold fingers climbed my spine as adrenaline made my heart pound. Ryo's body became suddenly tense, the tendons standing out in his neck. He glanced at me, then off in the direction of the shots.

"Dani, I'm going to take my glasses off." His voice was barely above a whisper, and he watched me intently with puppy-dog eyes. "Please don't be afraid of me."

I recalled Beauty's words about how if he removed his eyeglasses, Ryo would be the one in charge. It made no more sense now than it had then. What difference did it make whether he had them on or off? Goosebumps traveled down my arms. "O… kay?"

He swallowed hard, no longer meeting my gaze, and took them off. In an instant, Ryo was gone. It was the same body, the same face, but Ryo no longer existed in it. The reserved shyness, the curious gaze, the light in his eyes—all were now absent. A stranger had taken his place. Except he wasn't exactly a stranger. I had met him before. There was no way I could ever forget those soul-sucking eyes, the emotionless stare.

This was Ken.

He and Ryo weren't twins. They were separate facets of the same person.

Chapter 24

My brain filled with a whirlwind of internal cursing. I had half a mind to think sharpened versions of them straight at Beauty, whether she could hear them or not. Ryo suffered from dissociative identity disorder, and she hadn't *told* me? And now Ken, poster child for psychopathy, was in charge? The guy who had threatened to *kill me* was the one with the job of keeping me alive? ¡Mierda!

A slight tic in his left eye said he was no happier about it than I was. Not that I cared.

"Stay here," he commanded. Not said, not asked, but *commanded*.

My temper flared, flashpan hot. "Like hell I will!" If Beauty had a problem with it, she could come over here and do the job herself. Her concept of safety was absolute crap!

Ken's emotionless face tried to stare me down, but I was too livid for it to have any effect.

"Suit yourself," he said with a barely perceptible shrug. That he made it sound as if he truly didn't give a rat's ass one way or the other only pushed me to boil hotter.

Ken donned a thin pair of gloves before removing several slim black throwing knives from a flush pouch at his belt. They looked sharp and deadly.

He slipped like an eel through water from beneath the table, completely silent. I eased out of my coat, knowing I would make more noise if I kept it on, pulled my can of pepper spray out of my purse, and followed him out. I flinched when something bounced hard against the metal entry door. If the doorman hadn't barred and locked it, we would have been the first thing any intruders saw. Ken didn't twitch or glance back, just continued slithering forward as if nothing else mattered.

The sound of muted gunfire echoed our way, making my gut clench, but it was happening somewhere away from the main dining area. It wouldn't stay that way for long, though. I'd researched Boston PD's response times earlier, and they tended to average over seven minutes. With whoever this was coming in from the alley entrance, and the fact that it was rush hour, there was no telling how soon the incident would be reported or when the police would be able to get here.

Even though the city had ShotSpotter to help send the cops to areas with probable gunfire as quickly as possible, the system also had a terribly high false alert rate. Regardless, the sooner we got away from here, the better.

Ken had stuck to the front side of the bar, bent in a crouch to make sure he wasn't visible to the bartender, then slithered to the opposite side once we neared the back hallway area. I was on my hands and knees, trying hard to keep up and keep my breathing even, cringing every time a gun or other loud sound went off.

Swinging doors on the left led into the kitchen. From the louder noises and echoes, whatever was going on seemed to be happening in that direction. It was either a robbery for the funds from the illegal dealings that went on here, or someone had decided they wanted to take out the competition.

My adrenaline spiked as I hurried to cross the space as well, feeling much too exposed. Then the double doors crashed violently open as a heavily tattooed man stumbled through, blood dripping from his left shoulder. He carried a Desert Eagle in his right hand, as if the deadly weapon weighed nothing. Drug-dilated eyes instantly locked on me. A crooked grin settled on the rough face as he raised the gun.

There was nowhere I could crawl fast enough to avoid him, so I lifted the hand with the pepper spray and squeezed. I doubted it would affect him quickly enough to keep me from getting shot, but I refused to go out without at least trying something.

I'd be joining my hermano sooner than I thought.

Two black flashes crossed in front of me as the spray hit the thug's face dead center. An instant later I realized they were knives. One sank into the tattooed man's wrist, making him release the heavy weapon, a surprised look marring his face along with the orange mist. The other blade bit deep into his inner thigh, jerking him back.

A deafening roar came from behind the bar, and buckshot peppered my would-be assailant's right side and head. The force of the blast shunted the tattooed man violently sideways. A scream tried to claw up my throat as drops of blood sprayed out before me in slow motion, the killer dropping to the ground as if lying down to sleep. Half of his face was gone, exposing bone and muscle tissue—things that were never meant to be looked at.

Something clamped onto my arm, and I almost screamed anyway as it pulled me forward. Ken's cold, disapproving visage came close to mine as he dragged me rapidly through the hall. My ears were still ringing from the compressed sound of the shotgun blast. An acrid smell filled the air, mixing with the heavy metallic tang of blood.

"*That's* why you should have stayed behind."

The unspoken accusation that I was only making his job harder couldn't have been more glaring. It stoked the fire inside me and made me want to lash out and spray him with whatever might be left of the pepper spray, which was better than the mind-numbing horror of what I had just seen, or the knowledge that it could have been *me* lying dead over that pool of gore with a bullet-sized hole through my body.

Rancid laughter, exclamations of disgust, and even bored comments filled the air as the number of spirits near the end of the bar increased exponentially. The creatures gathered like grisly spectators about the fallen man and the hyperventilating, wide-eyed bartender. Thankfully, that meant I could no longer see the details of the ugly tableau on the floor behind me. I had never seen anyone die before, and I'd be thrilled never to see it again. The big band sounds continued whispering from the hidden speakers, but the music now sounded more like a dirge.

Ken led us past the restrooms to a door hiding the stairs to the second floor. We went on through.

The access and walls must be soundproofed, as the moment the opening behind us closed, everything turned quiet. I was surprised when none of the spirits followed along. That suited me fine. One less thing to worry about in the deadly farce this had become.

Without being told, I happily rushed up the steps, despite the ache in my knees from all the crawling. It wouldn't be much longer before the cops arrived and the chaos got worse. There was also a chance that if the gangbangers had brought enough muscle, some might come our way.

There was another door at the top of the stairwell, but this one was locked. I stuffed the pepper spray back into my purse, pulled out my lock pick set, and grabbed the credit card blank I kept there. My hands were too unsteady for finer work at the moment. It took less time to open the door than it had for me to take out the card to use on it.

Ken slipped past me on silent feet to check the new hallway. In comparison, I sounded like a wide-eyed, crazed bull let loose in a china shop.

He must have memorized the layout as I had; once he deemed the coast clear, he turned to the left. A broom closet was our next stop. It seemed the most likely place for keeping the security camera recorders, aside from the main office, which was the room further down the hall.

We'd both guessed right: Several recording machines were hidden on a shelf behind cleaning supplies. They were all clearly labeled. Ken popped out the memory cards for the entryway, the restaurant area, the stairwell, and the second-story hallway, and shut off the one for the big office. Rather than hand me the sticks, he hid them on his own person.

Ken left the closet, working around me and acting as if I weren't there. I fought the sudden urge to trip him.

We moved on to the office.

The door was locked here as well, and was of better quality in both its construction and its lock. For this one, I pulled a tension tool and a Gonzo hook from my set to do single-pin picking. While I rarely needed to use this skill, the fact that my fingers were so nimble and sensitive for pick-pocketing helped me "feel" the tumblers in locks. Being able to open them gave me more options for escape if things went south.

I could take care of a standard lock like this in seconds. My hands were still shaking a little, though, thanks to the unexpected excitement downstairs, so it took me longer than usual. Ken's weighted and impatient gaze didn't help me any. Next time, if there ever was such a thing, he could do it all himself.

Once I bypassed the mechanism, I moved out of his way so he could go in first. It was truly unnerving how silently he could move. I glanced down the hall. There were still no hints of any spirits behind us. But if they had been following us to get to a non-existent party, like they'd told Ryo, why hadn't they come upstairs? Did they know or sense something we didn't? A sliver of dread climbed over my spine.

I turned away and slipped into the office.

Once inside, I stopped for a moment, my eyes growing wide—I'd just stepped into a mafioso's wet dream. The room looked like something plucked straight out of a mafia movie. Dark wood paneling with fancy crown molding on the walls.

Thick windows, draped with dark burgundy drapes pulled back with golden tassels, that peered out onto Congress Street.

A giant boat of a mahogany desk, one solid enough to stop a hail of bullets, sat farthest from the door. It had a green felt and leather desk pad. Even an avocado-hued banker's lamp. Two angled leather chairs faced the desk. The furniture all sat upon a huge Persian rug. A couple of places on it were a lighter color than the others, as if they had been scrubbed hard to remove crime-related stains. A weapons collection filled the rear wall, holding everything from a Tommy gun to a Colt M1911.

In one corner stood a tall, old-fashioned green safe with spoke handles and a dial lock. Its door stood wide open, revealing a couple of sawed-off shotguns, ledgers, and some stacks of cash. Surely psycho-boy hadn't been able to crack it that quickly? But Ken was over by the opposite wall, his fingers gliding over the wood paneling, searching for our way out.

Locking the entry just in case and using my sleeve so as not to leave any prints, I walked over to better inspect the safe. There was no sign of Mystic in there, not behind the bundles of money or the stacks of records. Someone had beaten us to the prize but left all these tempting C-notes untouched? It made no sense!

I pulled my phone and took a picture of the interior in case Beauty wanted to see it, and so I could study it once we were out of here. There was a spot at the bottom of the safe by the shotgun stocks that appeared lighter in the photo. Frowning, I scrunched down for a closer look. Then I realized there was something lying there. Something I recognized—but it couldn't have looked more wrong.

Chapter 25

It was Cyrano. Or who I assumed must be Cyrano. The ferret-like spirit lay curled on his side, his suit ripped to tatters, with bloodless, furrowed wounds all over him. Worse, he wasn't as corporeal as he'd been at Last Stop. He was more transparent than not.

A loud click made me glance over my shoulder. Ken had found and opened the secret door. "Let's go. *Now*."

"Wait!" What was I doing? Our safety was at hand. "Can spirits die?"

The cold "are you stupid" look gave me my answer. "This is someone Beauty knows," I said, my stubborn side rising. "She would want us to help him!" When I still got nothing, I added, "Mira, Ryo would want to, too."

Emotion flared in his eyes at last. "Ryo is a fool!"

Red and blue flashing lights flooded in through the windowpanes, though the sounds of sirens were so muted I had to work to hear them.

"We need to go *now*, woman!"

I didn't move. "Is it safe for me to touch him? Will that hurt him? He needs help! If you don't know what to do, put Ryo back in charge."

That earned me a snarl. But an exasperated Ken was slightly less scary than the cold, soulless one.

"Drape him around your neck or stuff him in your bag or whatever, just make sure your hands remain free. Got it? Now move!"

Not daring to think about it, I reached into the safe and scooped up the ferret and draped him over my neck and shoulders like a stole. My cross-body purse wasn't big enough to hold him. Cyrano weighed next to nothing, and if I hadn't been able to see him, I wouldn't have known he was there at all. I tucked him in between my sweater and long johns, hoping that would help keep him in place. If he fell off, I might never know it.

I was halfway to the open panel when I realized I hadn't snatched any of the cash. ¡Coño!

Ken was almost growling with impatience by the time I got there. Without a word, he twisted away from me and stepped into the tiny passageway, then turned sideways to crab walk along a second opening that led downward, the hidden passage not wide enough to walk normally. I grabbed the leather loop on the inside of the panel door with my sleeve and pulled it shut. Rather than throw us into darkness, a string of small, white fairy lights lit up overhead and followed Ken's path, creating an artificial twilight that was bright enough for us to see by.

It was freezing in there, and I had to work at not letting my teeth chatter. If they started, I'd never be able to get them to stop. A musty smell hung about the place, and years of caked dust filled some of the higher beams. Still, the floor and the super-narrow steps were clean as if someone made sure the passage stayed well-kept. Thankfully, that also meant there weren't any cobwebs or giant wasp nests to worry about. Not that they'd be active in this icy-cold weather, even if there were.

Ken disappeared at a turn some ways away from me, the weird, angled crab walk not seeming to bother him in the least. I found it awkward as hell, and so did my legs. One misstep, and I was sure I'd end up with a broken leg or neck, and Ken would leave me there to rot. How a bunch of bigger men were supposed to do this, I had no idea.

At the turn, there was a tiny landing before the narrow stairs continued on. I switched sides to give my body a break and check that Cyrano was still wound around my neck.

A few steps further, a beam of light lasered from the inner wall to the outer. Slowing, I realized it was a hole, and a recent one at that. Noises filtered through, though I couldn't make anything out of them. Taking a peek, I spied the lounge's kitchen spread out before me—or a nightmarish version of it.

A grease fire burned on the far stove, creating black, heavy smoke. Swaths of flour, as well as vegetables and fruits, were flung everywhere. I saw a pair of prone legs sticking out from under a metal table, and a gangbanger lay bleeding out on an island with pots and pans strewn around him. Men and women in the dark navy uniforms of the Boston PD slowly made their way across, their weapons in a two-handed grip as they searched for more offenders and victims.

Blinking rapidly, I quickened my pace, having seen more than enough.

Ken waited at the second landing until I came near, then followed a metal ladder down. I soon followed.

It was colder there than on the stairs. The iron rod ladder sapped what little warmth I had through my hands. My breath coalesced before me as if my soul were leaving my body. Noisy or not, I should have kept my coat on. Boricuas were not made for the cold!

We went down and down and down. It surprised me each time I didn't leave skin behind on the freezing rungs. I'd tried several times to pull my sweater over my palm and fingers, but it wouldn't stay. The minutes seemed to stretch in the odd twilight, making it feel like we'd been descending forever, trapped in a forgotten, bottomless mineshaft in some twisted fantasy world.

My foot hit the ground unexpectedly, sending a jarring sensation up my leg. As soon as my other foot joined it, I took my numb hands off the ladder and jammed them under my pits, hoping to bring them back to life. I tilted my head to the side and thought I still felt Cyrano on my neck.

"It shouldn't be much farther now."

My breath hitched in my throat in surprise. Gone were the clipped tones and cold indifference, the hint of bottled violence. There were emotions in this one. "Ryo?"

The dim light in this new, broader corridor glinted off his large-lensed glasses, which were back in their usual place. His gray eyes wouldn't meet mine, but they were full of energy rather than empty nothingness. "Yes."

"*Good.*" Though they were inevitably the same person, I much preferred to deal with this persona.

But instead of being happy and wagging his imaginary tail, Ryo sagged almost imperceptibly and turned away. He set off down the partially collapsed service tunnel before I could say anything else.

Surely he hadn't thought Ken and I would become BFFs during our time in danger together. No way was I befriending psycho-boy. Not that Ken would be open to anything of the sort in a million years. He'd probably never heard of the concept. We couldn't even finish a little girl's simple unfinished business, so there was no chance we could ever accomplish a crazy miracle like becoming friends.

After several minutes of walking, the corridor ended at a partially rusted metal door. A small niche beside it held a couple of flashlights and a package of batteries. Ryo took one and tested it, the bright beam making me squint. My hands were still sending pin and needle-filled messages as they came back to life, so I kept them under my armpits.

Despite how the door looked, it made no sound when Ryo pulled the lever to open it. The hinges didn't even creak. Cyrano may have called them wannabes, but they sure took care of what they had. A win for us, though it had done little to help those upstairs when they'd needed it.

We stepped onto a tiled walkway with a railing that sat at the edge of a tracked underground tunnel. An active one—as way down thc path I could see a subway platform full of people waiting for the next train so they could make their way home.

I trudged after a silent Ryo as we headed in that direction.

Chapter 26

We got a few stares from commuters as we moved past them, likely assuming we were lunatics for not having coats, but no one tried to stop us. Our foray through the escape route would have put us beyond the Fort Point Channel, making it unlikely that anyone would be looking on this side of the waterway for people involved in the mess back at the lounge.

A groan slipped past my lips as I realized that we'd need to make our way back to Last Stop while exposed to the elements. Although the weather was warmer than during our last expedition, it was still much too cold out there for this chica. Who knew what it would do to an injured spirit?

I must have made more noise than I thought. Ryo glanced over with a furrowed brow and a questioning expression as we took an escalator from the subway platform areas to the higher levels with the trains, the huge, high-ceilinged station itself, and our way out.

"Sorry, I was thinking about the walk back to LS," I said. "Might they have any shops selling coats here?" My quick phone search hadn't shown any, only eateries or places to get snacks and travel-related items, but I could have missed it. The possibility we'd need replacements had never entered my mind.

He gave a small shrug.

"We could grab a taxi, or call an Uber rather than walk?" I suggested. Both were viable options to keep us out of the weather, as long as they took cash. Traffic on Congress near the lounge was likely moving at a snail's pace, though, thanks to the gang attack, so there was no telling how much time it would take to return over there in a cab.

Ryo's brow furrowed further. "It's less than a block away."

"What is?"

We stepped off the escalator.

"Last Stop," he said. "You can't sense it?"

I grabbed his sleeve and moved us to the side out of the flow of people moving around the station's main concourse. If we kept going, we'd end up outside, and I wasn't stopping to ask questions while exposed to the elements.

"What are you talking about?" The question came out more forcefully than I wanted.

His expression turned sheepish, his gaze skipping away from mine. "The mark—it connects us to Last Stop. So we always know where it is. Did Beauty not tell you?"

I gritted my teeth, trying hard not to take my frustration out on him. "It must have slipped her mind." That cursed gata and her damned lack of information! "So, how exactly do I turn that on, then?"

He blinked at me several times as if confused by the question. *¿En serio?* The process was so easy that he had never thought about how to do it? Could this get any more *annoying*?

"I think about where she is, and I know which way to go."

Yes, yes it could.

I closed my eyes to calm myself and gave it a try. In my mind, I saw/sensed a bit of blue flame not too far in the distance. It was in the opposite direction from the Wise Guys Lounge. Last Stop had indeed moved—assuming this blue flame was it and not some figment of my imagination. That this chica had completely lost her mind wasn't outside the realm of possibility at this point.

When I opened my eyes again, I could still feel the direction the restaurant now occupied. A handy trick. One that I would have appreciated more if the gata had deigned to tell me about it in the first place!

I tried to kick my flaring temper to the back, where it could fester awhile, until I could feed it to the person who truly deserved it. Beauty and I would have *words*. Of that there was no doubt. Yes, it might have been an oversight, but it wasn't like she hadn't played tricks at my expense before. This was just another offense to add to the growing list.

"Thanks for that," I said, my voice sounding mostly normal. "If you have any other tips or info Beauty might have forgotten to tell me, I'd appreciate you letting me know."

He nodded, a tiny frown still in residence between his eyebrows. It had not escaped me that he had yet to look me in the face since I welcomed him back in the tunnel.

We set off toward the exit. It helped a little knowing LS was close. I had no idea how bad Cyrano's condition was, so I didn't suggest we grab something hot to drink as we passed the food court with all its tempting smells. Wallowing in the heated water of Last Stop's onsen sounded way better, anyway.

Outside, the sun had already ducked to hide away past the horizon. That meant the temperature was dropping fast. We headed out from the rounded exit of South Station. It was an impressive sight from the outside, with its three arches and columned higher floors that ended with a large old-fashioned clock tower and its eight-foot marble statue of an eagle preparing for flight.

The moment we stepped outdoors, I could feel icy tendrils trying to dig into me. Gasoline fumes and the echoes of quickening steps as the cold grew worse wove around us as we waited for the light to turn so we could cross the street. I shoved my hands under my armpits again and shut my lips tight. We got a lot more stares there than we had inside, as only true lunatics would come out here unprotected.

The warm orange-colored neon of Last Stop beckoned from the other side of the road.

The second the light turned, I half-sprinted across, exposing one hand to set it along the back of my head to keep Cyrano in place. The restaurant's front door slid open for me, so I didn't have to stop or slow down. By the time I made it into LS's warm, welcoming embrace, my teeth were chattering like mad.

"Welcome back." Beauty greeted us from the counter, her emerald eyes bright, her fluffy, long tail wrapped around her feet. "Have some hot tea. You look as if you could use some."

Warmth was the priority, so I kept my festering displeasure bottled away and hurried to where two tall cups sat steaming. I burned my lips and tongue, but didn't care. The heat pouring from the cup into my hands was glorious. Ryo joined me and claimed his, though nowhere near as desperately as I had.

"I take it there were problems?" Beauty asked a few moments later.

I had started to thaw by then, the hot tea working its magic inside me. But her words were like throwing a gallon of gasoline onto a lit pyre. I turned on her. "*Problems*? Oh, they were more than problems. It was a complete shit-show!"

All my pent-up frustration, fear, and anger exploded from me like an erupting volcano. Mt. Vesuvius had nothing on me.

"Some gangbangers decided it was the perfect time to raid the place after we got there! One of them almost killed me! And for what? *Absolutely nothing!* Mystic wasn't even there!"

It was only then that I remembered what we *had* found. It put my fire out with a torrential rain and draped me in a coat of heavy guilt. "Dios mío, Cyrano!"

Was he still with us? Both my hands flew to the back of my neck. A light tingling greeted my searching fingers—his body was still there.

"Let me do it." Ryo's voice whispered near my ear.

Surprise, gratitude, and a bit of chagrined discomfort flushed through me at the close proximity. I held up my hair to make it easier for him to remove my impromptu spirit-fur stole. As he scooped Cyrano carefully off me, it felt oddly intimate, which was loco.

A kitchen towel floated to the counter, and Ryo gently settled the almost invisible ferret on it.

"What happened?" A white and silver-haired young woman with Beauty's eyes and voice, and wearing a flattering sequined evening gown, stood on the other side of the countertop. Concern marred the gorgeous woman's feline-like features.

Mira, yet *another* "surprise." I fought the urge to roll my eyes. So Beauty had a human form. Something else she had *thoroughly* neglected to mention. But even I knew this wasn't the time to bring it up. "I found him inside the open safe in the mobster's office," I said. "Is he going to be okay?"

The question felt stupid as it left my mouth. Beauty's drawn brows and pursed lips, and the way her green eyes were focused on Cyrano, told me how serious his condition was.

"I don't know." The lack of emotion in her response screamed that he wouldn't be. She nestled the barely corporeal ferret in her arms. "Please excuse me."

Beauty rushed past the kitchen curtains and was gone.

Steam wove gently around me as I basked in the heat of the giant wooden tub, staring with half-unfocused eyes at the detailed image of Mt. Fuji on the wall in the communal bathing area.

Once Beauty left with Cyrano, Ryo had disappeared, without a word or sound, before I'd realized it.

He was avoiding me. I was sure of it. Which made little sense. Just like when he had looked away after I'd voiced my single-syllabic pleasure at the fact that he had returned and replaced Ken. I shook my head. The whole day had been a disaster, so I was probably seeing things that weren't there. This chica was well aware that the world did *not* revolve around her. Ryo was likely only tired from all the chaos at the lounge, and worried about Cyrano.

I leaned back against the side of the onsen and closed my eyes. The scent drifting over from the incense burner was a mix of maple and pine, and possibly lilacs? It was incredibly soothing. Maybe I could sit here and indulge in it for a lifetime or two.

The water moved against me as someone slipped into the water beside me, startling a gasp out of me. I shifted sideways, not knowing who or what to expect, one arm raised across my chest to hide my nakedness. I must have drifted off or zoned out, as I'd never sensed or even heard whoever it was come in. So I twisted now that I had more space to see who had joined me, even as a painful kink flared in my neck. My body flushed from head to toe as I used my free hand to massage my neck.

"It isn't healthy to stay soaking for too long, though I understand the appeal," Beauty said. I tried not to stare, realizing she was still in her human form. Her lush mane of hair had been gathered into a loose braid and piled on top of her head. In this setting, with her vertical pupils, her flawless and almost literally white skin, and the wisps of vapor rising from the water, she looked ethereal and more alien than usual.

"How's Cyrano?" I asked.

"Stable," Beauty said. She half turned on the bench to stare at me with her emerald, inhuman eyes. "If you hadn't brought him back with you, he wouldn't have made it. So thank you for that."

"Sure." Her heartfelt gratitude caused odd flashes of happiness to burst inside me. I guess I had never done much to make anyone grateful—except Jay, but he was my hermano, so he didn't count. "Is he here at Last Stop?"

Beauty looked away. "No. I took him to an adjoining spirit realm, despite his not having evolved there. Since he is not bound to a location, he will recover faster there. Their hospitals are better equipped to help him."

So spirits could be hurt, but also healed? "What did you mean by 'his not having evolved there'?"

She threw me a sideways glance and eased herself a little deeper into the water, pleased. "There are many types of spirit entities. But a fundamental difference among them is where and how they came to be," she said. "I was born here on Earth's primary plane. But others, like Desmond, are creatures that came to life in a different realm altogether."

"Is that where Jay went?" I asked.

"No. It is not." Her green gaze locked with mine. "Human and non-evolved animal souls are something else altogether. The power resides in them to make their way to their next destination on their own." She glided her hand over the water. "But if they don't move on and stay tethered to the physical world, they become ghosts.

"Then it becomes a matter of whether they need help to move on, or they refuse to acknowledge the truth and become stuck." She brought her left hand to float beside the first with the palm facing upward. "For those who need and want help, that's where we come in. We are facilitators to help them let go of earthly concerns and get them to where they need to go." She raised the hand facing up, staring at it.

"If we aren't able to carry out or refuse their request, and they can accept it, they're still able to move on. Otherwise, they enter a limbo dimension until they can." She let her left hand rest on the rim of the tub.

"Those who die and deny the truth, or refuse to ask for help will be stuck in the physical realm and will slowly devolve. They can eventually turn into malignant spirits or even monsters." Her right hand sank. "At that point, there is nothing more we can do for them." She stared at the mural on the wall, though I had a feeling she wasn't seeing it. "However, there are humans who have the power to deal with spirits like those by capturing or destroying them."

This all sounded way too complicated. "But who or what hurt Cyrano? And why?"

"Don't fret about that for now," Beauty said. "I have a feeling the culprit will reveal himself or herself before long."

"Leaving me to stumble over every little thing and keeping me in the dark is *not* going to end well!"

"Would *you* show all your cards to someone you'd just met?" Beauty asked, merriment flashing in her eyes.

She had me there. Not that it made it any easier to swallow. I rose to my feet, not bothering to hide my displeasure or my nakedness. The heat left me a little dizzy after standing up so fast. "If it would keep them from getting killed, I might!"

"Is that so?" she said, sounding amused.

I got out of the onsen and sent her a blazing glare. "Yes!"

Why did she aggravate me so?

Though it didn't have the same effect naked, I stomped away in a huff toward the dressing room. Beauty could stay in there and boil the flesh off her bones for all I cared. I dried off, then slammed the divider to close off the dressing area. I put my sweater and jeans back on, but not the thermal underwear.

Under no circumstances was I going back out into the cold today.

Chapter 27

Using the slippers by the changing area's door, I carried my boots upstairs rather than leave them in the shoe cubbies at the bottom of the stairs.

I didn't want to unnecessarily tempt Bruja Ida into doing something I'd make her heartily regret. In my current mood, it wouldn't take much for me to lose my shit.

As I neared my room, I glanced toward Ryo's. Should I try to talk to him? He was a lot freer with information than Beauty. And there was still his weird response in the tunnels to contend with. If I didn't ask him directly, I was pretty sure he'd never tell me.

That was when I noticed something had changed. The doorframe and plaque for his quarters were different from before. Gone were the tiger and dragon, the yin and yang, the oriental flair. Now it looked more like an Art Nouveau piece of décor, grand and full of eye-catching curves and multicolored wooden hues. Carved roses painted white filled the frames for both the sign and the door as if they were lattices for the roses to grow on. The letters on the sign had transformed into a flowery script spelling the name Mizuki.

Had something happened to Ryo and Ken? The question made me more nervous than it should have, making my mouth go dry. Surely I wasn't getting attached. That would be plain stupid.

"Where is Ryo?" I asked the air.

There was no answer. Which was as it should be. *Dani, get a grip.*

Rather than forget the whole thing and barricade myself in my room, I walked farther down the hall. A quick glance over my shoulder verified that Ida's door was the same as before. The rest of the doors in the corridor were all plain.

I had a sudden urge to rush downstairs and check the kitchen. If there were one place I could find him, it would be there. I'd already turned around toward the stairs before I caught hold of myself. ¡Carajo! What was I doing? What did it matter where he was or where he'd gone? It was none of my business!

'*By the way, Dani, there was something I forgot to mention.*' Beauty's thoughts entered my head, making me jump.

My hand leaped to my chest, where my heart now raced at a thousand miles an hour. ¡Coño! She was going to be the death of me. I held back from mentally throwing every cuss word I knew in multiple languages at her. '*I'm listening.*'

'*We're holding a welcoming party in your honor this evening. I'd been planning to wait until after your first mission was complete, but certain parties took it upon themselves to ensure it would happen tonight.*'

She sounded annoyed. I was plain shocked. After today's mess, some big shindig was the last thing I wanted. '*Can't you postpone it?*' I asked. It was weird having a conversation in my head with no one around. At least before, she had been there physically to look at.

'*I'm afraid not.*'

I wasn't sure I believed her, despite her obvious irritation. '*Was it Desmond?*'

She ignored the question. '*Unfortunately, because of who the guests are and the original location where Hokora-chan awakened into awareness, certain traditions will need to be upheld.*'

This brought up a question that should have occurred to me before. '*So there are other waystations?*' I asked. Even if those with unfinished business were few, only one of these places would not be enough to handle them all, not with billions of people living on the planet.

'A few. But that is not important at the moment. You've got other things to worry about.'

That didn't sound encouraging. '*Like what?*' I asked.

'As a new employee, you'll be required to bow and greet our visitors as they arrive, and then take charge of the small offerings they'll bring to honor Hokora-chan, as well as possible gifts for yourself. A formal banquet will also be held,' she said. '*Though it is being thrown in your honor, you'll still be seated at the end of the table closest to the door rather than at the head. You'll also be expected to don traditional Japanese attire.*'

Typical. Show the newbie their proper place in the hierarchy while using them as an excuse to party. Pierson and others had done similar things back in Miami. '*When you say I'll need to wear traditional Japanese clothes, are you talking about a kimono?*' I asked. '*I've no idea how to wear those properly.*'

'Mizuki will teach you what to do.'

I stared over at what had not all that long ago been Ryo's door. '*She's not new, then?*' I mentally inquired.

'*No,*' Beauty said. '*But do not mention Ryo or Ken to her. She's not aware of their existence.*'

¿Qué? My brain locked up. I felt like that old fable—where domesticated turkeys stare up at the rain with their mouths open, too stupid to know they were drowning themselves.

A picture formed in my head, one grain of sand at a time. Ryo had DID, or dissociative identity disorder—what used to be called a split personality. Ken was his alter. I'd seen the change from one persona to the other with my own eyes. And the two were aware of each other.

Ken had tried to warn me away from Ryo, somehow knowing about me, though we hadn't met. Ryo had punched himself to force Ken to back down from harassing me. All of that made a crazy kind of sense. But now… was Beauty saying he had a third persona? One who didn't have a clue about the other two? What was I supposed to do with that?

I reached out to the nearest wall to hold myself up, my whole body feeling like I was standing at the edge of a deep, dark crevice.

'*How... how many of them are there?*' I didn't want to know; I really didn't. But I couldn't stop myself from asking.

'*Only as many as were needed,*' Beauty said simply. '*They've all worked very hard, and most have been cooperative.*'

'*How. Many. Are. There?*' Couldn't she answer me straight for once? I tried to slow down my breathing before I hyperventilated.

That's when I felt eyes on me. Beauty now sat in her feline form at the top of the stairs, her emerald eyes watching me intently.

'*That is not for me to tell. Nor for you to ask. So don't. Their situation is unique, and they've found a way to make it work. Outside judgements are not required.*' She stared with slitted eyes, as if weighing whether to slap me around or not. '*I'd hate to find out that my trust had been misplaced.*'

Trust? What trust? Way too vague answers. Partnering me with someone who had DID without so much as a warning. The list went on and on. "You are such a liar!"

Her tail tip slapped against the wooden floor, her ears turning away from me. '*I find that baby steps are typically required for newcomers to the supernatural. Your view of the true world is so limited that your minds begin to fray when exposed to things too quickly.*'

Now she was just being condescending. Enough was enough.

The tidal wave of cuss words I'd been holding back spewed out of me like vomit. There was some lively foot stomping and hand waving to go along with them, also two simultaneous middle-finger salutes for good measure.

Beauty only tilted her head during my insulting tirade as if observing a monkey at the zoo throw poo around as she sat safely behind a wall of plexiglass. It only wound me up more.

"Are you done?" she asked out loud a few minutes later. "Though I will say, that's an impressive repertoire, especially for a young lady."

I gave her another set of salutes, too busy trying to catch my breath to speak.

A door opened nearby. It was Ryo's—or rather, Mizuki's. I froze in place.

The door didn't open far. Only enough for a face to peer carefully around it. I saw a flash of coiffured hair and wide but shy, dark gray eyes.

"Mizuki-san, what excellent timing," Beauty said. "Come and meet our newest member."

For half a second, I thought she would disappear, but then the door opened a little more, and Mizuki came out from behind it. She wore a wig of slicked-back black hair gathered into a simple bun, as well as black eyeliner with a lengthy feline flick at the ends to highlight her eyes. Slightly pouted lips covered with pink gloss made the mouth appear more petite and girlish.

The demure stance and simple slate-colored indoor kimono added the finishing touches to the illusion. If not for the distinct dark gray eyes and Beauty having warned me, I would never have guessed this was Ryo.

"*Hajimemashite*," Mizuki said, half-bowing toward the floor. Even her voice was different—soft and feminine. Everything about her screamed "girl." "My name is Mizuki. I am very pleased to meet you."

I finally found my ability to speak again. "Uh, hi. I'm Dani." How could she not know she was in a man's body? That she shared it with Ryo and psycho-boy? How did that work?

"I apologize for the short notice, Mizuki-chan," Beauty said, sauntering toward us with dainty cat steps. "But could I count on you to help Dani dress and show her what she needs to do for her welcoming party? I regret to say you'll only have a couple of hours to get her into shape."

"Of course, Beauty-sama." Her eyes darted a glance at me, and she showered me with a soft smile. "It would be my pleasure."

"Thank you." Beauty then turned in my direction. She spoke directly to my mind rather than out loud. '*Do behave yourself, Daniela. And remember what I said.*'

I threw her a dirty look as she swiped at me with her tail and took her leave of us.

My curiosity was on fire, but there was no reason to let Beauty know that.

"Won't you join me in my humble quarters, Dani-san?" Mizuki tilted her head slightly and swept her hand out in a graceful arc.

"Sure." I was a girly-girl, but in front of Mizuki, I felt like a mud-covered tomboy. Seeing her room only served to make it worse.

Chapter 28

Mizuki's bedroom was a mix of traditional and modern Japanese styles with a heavy emphasis on cuteness overload. The floor was made up of light-colored tatami mats with the edges painted an off-white with pink and red petals. A three-section panel of a flowering plum tree filled one wall, above a slightly raised bed with a matching coverlet.

The long table on another wall held the entire cast of Hello Kitty characters—the white cat wearing a big scarlet bow, the spiky-haired penguin, and even the little twin star kids. A round table sat over a red, fuzzy, heart-shaped carpet. Beautiful flower arrangements in elegant small vases dotted her quarters and had cute touches like ceramic ladybugs or dragonfly caricatures. The gorgeous, lacquered vanity with peach blossoms had playful butterflies clipped at the edges.

But more amazing was the fact that a corner of the room opened onto a wooden porch that faced a flower-filled garden. A giant flowering plum tree, almost identical to the one painted on the three-sectioned wall panel, provided shade and gently scented the air.

There was something spiritually soothing and timeless about the place when taken as a whole.

"Do forgive my humble quarters," Mizuki said softly as I took in the room. "If there's anything you require, please don't hesitate to ask."

"Gracias, but I'm fine."

Mizuki half nodded. "If that is the case, should we get started, Dani-san?"

I gave her a thumbs-up. It was becoming harder and harder to remember that she was but a facet of Ryo's personality. What kind of trauma had he gone through to generate such diverse alters? "Just tell me what I need to do."

"Strip to your underwear, please."

My eyes tried to pop out of my head. I must have looked comical, because Mizuki's hand rose to cover her mouth, and she partially turned away. "Are you shy, Dani-san?"

"Mira, it's not like that. Okay?" I had just never been asked to take off my clothes by a woman who was actually a man, even if she didn't know it.

Mizuki opened one of the closet panels and pulled out a simple folding privacy screen of paper and bamboo. She set it close to a corner, creating a mini dressing room. She made another of those elegant sweeping motions with her hand again, mirth still filling her semi-downcast gaze. "*Dozo.*"

I ventured behind the screen with a repressed sigh and started removing my clothing. As I folded my pants, a business card fell out onto the floor. I stared at it in surprise for a moment before remembering I was the one who had put it there, and why.

I'd forgotten all about it with everything else that happened at the lounge. Picking it up, I gave it a more thorough look than the first time. Aside from realizing that it was 14-point card stock, nothing else revealed itself. If I hadn't seen the creature who delivered it, I would have thought it was some kind of scam or joke. I still didn't have the faintest idea what to make of it. The thought of calling the number just to see who answered was tempting.

"Put this undergarment on, please." Mizuki's arm came from the other side of the screen, holding out a long white robe of some sort.

I tucked the business card inside my bra cup and reached for the strange garment.

"Dani-san, fold in the right side first," she said. "I'll need to adjust how the collar sits once you have it on, so don't worry about lining things up. I'll take care of that and the belt for you."

Hold on, there was a right way and a wrong way to put on a robe? I started paying attention to it. The long undergarment was white, soft, and cool to the touch, making me wonder if it was made of genuine silk—something I could never afford. Not only that, but the fabric was stitched with intricate woven patterns of peonies, rivers, and clouds, all in white as well. And this was an undergarment? I was glad I'd gone with my lace underwear this morning; otherwise, I would have felt like a total *jibaro*.

As instructed, I put it on and folded the right side first, then overlaid the left. The stiff hem made the collar stand up, though the fabric felt luscious against my skin. I came out from behind the screen. "This way?" I asked.

"Yes. Just so." Mizuki circled about me, pulling the fabric here and there until the collar lay a little past the nape of my neck, and the tips at the edges of the robe panels were aligned. Then she wound a sash around my middle, starting from the front and then back again. She tied it once and then tucked the ends into the belt.

She then took my hand and gently guided me over to her dressing table and pulled out a stool for me to sit on. She slipped a pair of tabi socks onto my feet, and after draping a protective towel over the robe, got to work on my face and hair.

By the time she was done, I had feline tails shorter than hers around my eyes with a lovely striation of colors over my eyelids that made my brown peepers pop. She'd also gathered my curls into an updo halfway on my head, then decorated it with soft-colored flowers and lacquered sticks with dangling beads.

Her skills were amazing. The makeup application was flawless, eradicating all signs of the bruises on my neck and making it look as if I weren't wearing any at all. I was good with cosmetics and doing my hair, but she took it to the level of an art form. It made me more curious about who the hell Ryo truly was.

"Now for the final piece." Mizuki gently removed the protective towel and then helped me to my feet. Gorgeous or not, the underrobe impaired my movements.

She opened a different closet panel. Inside was a kimono on a stand that showed the colorful fabric and gorgeous needlework in all its glory. It was so beautiful that all I could do at first was stare.

Deep blue at the top, the color lightened as it fell, as if diluted by rain. Japanese cranes stood amidst flowering reeds at the bottom, while others took flight and rose toward the darkness, their bodies white, with their necks, legs, and the secondary feathers on the wings black. Each crane was crowned with a red patch. Their beaks had been stitched in gold.

"Hokora-chan has wonderful taste, don't you think?" Mizuki asked.

All I could do was nod. Excitement prickled my skin and made my heart race at the chance of getting to wear it. Once Mizuki slipped it on me, she added a wide, green-colored belt she called an *obi*, followed by a braided cord, decorated with a brooch of a cat with bright emerald eyes.

Mizuki led me back toward the mirror again, even as she looked me over, making an adjustment here or there.

"Now we will practice walking, sitting, kneeling, and bowing," Mizuki said.

She made it all seem effortless and graceful, but it was actually quite difficult! I somehow bumbled through it repeatedly until she was satisfied I wouldn't completely embarrass myself in front of others.

Then she changed her outer kimono to a green one that complemented mine and was equally gorgeous in its own right.

Mira, the party hadn't started yet, and I was already exhausted.

"Shall we go, Dani-san?" Mizuki asked.

If I couldn't avoid it, I would *own* it. "Let's do this!"

Mizuki's laugh sounded like bells stirred in a breeze. "Yes. Let's!"

We headed downstairs, my hand plastered against the wall the entire time to steady me while I concentrated on taking one step down at a time.

Soft, festival music welcomed us at the bottom. Two pairs of Japanese sandals waited in the cubbies for us to slip on. As we neared Last Stop's entrance, the hallway bloomed with color from a plethora of lanterns and streamers decorating the walls. The wooden walls themselves had transformed into intricately painted panels of different eras, places, and countries, but always with the same central motifs—an inviting open golden doorway with souls and spirits drawn toward it, like moths to a flame.

Things had changed in the front area as well. The U-shaped counter was now more of a C-shape, creating more room for visitors to come through. The stools were gone, and the bench seat coat rack had stretched to accommodate a lot more than before. Last Stop had outdone herself, and everything around us looked brand new. It was almost as if we were celebrating the opening of a new business rather than welcoming a new employee.

Whatever Last Stop was, I no longer had any doubt that she had complete control over her own environment, not just the objects she housed inside. My pulse sped up a little. It was a sobering and scary thought.

One curious change was the tilting mirror on the column closest to the entry—the one that had shown me Desmond's true form and the invisible mark on my forehead. It had elongated to a full-length mirror a couple of feet wide, framed in a fancy red lacquered frame filled with dragons.

As Mizuki showed me where to stand and the easiest, most elegant manner to open the sliding door, I realized the mirror was angled to give me the best possible view of those about to enter. Almost as if I were to be a greeter with a secondary purpose as a guard. Were they expecting trouble? And if it came, what in the world did they think *I* could do about it?

"Mizuki?" I was still trying to figure out how to phrase the question, but I needn't have bothered.

"When there is a knock, open the door, bow, and glance at the mirror," she said. She stood before the closed door so I could catch her reflection. I held my breath, not sure what it would show me, especially as she was but a facet of Ryo. Her reflection only showed what I could already see, but with hints of several silhouettes standing behind her, the closest looking like Ryo wearing his glasses. Weirdly enough, the shapes varied in height and heft, as if who they were mentally gave them different physical forms.

Were they so indistinct because she wasn't aware of the other alters?

"You will see many strange beings, so try not to react if you can. If you can't, use your sleeve to politely hide the expression from them." Her hand rose as if to touch her hair, and the kimono's long sleeve hid her entire face from view. "If the mirror's surface becomes clouded or shimmers, do not welcome the guest or invite them in. Also, if a guest is accompanied, check each person in their retinue. Call for Beauty-sama or let me know if you spot something untoward, and we'll take it from there."

So someone might crash the party? Big guests, big event—I suppose it would make it a tempting target for unsavory types like me. Did spirits have pickpockets and conmen in their ranks? Would they be looking for souls to steal—for example, Beverly's? Or mine?

Chica, calm your ass down!

It felt weird being on the other side of things—being the one trying to prevent problems rather than the person causing them. And since someone had gone through all the trouble to snatch Mystic before *we* could, there was no telling if they might try something here as well.

"A guest's name and rank will appear at the bottom of the mirror if they are of high rank, so be sure to call them by their title when you welcome them inside," Mizuki said. "Once they enter, I'll care for their hats and coats if needed. Our guests will deposit any gifts on the counter and then follow the lanterns to the banquet hall, where Beauty-sama will be waiting to greet them yet again."

It all sounded simple enough. Still, I felt on edge, my shoulders tight. Nothing in my life had prepared me for dealing with spirits, or other-dimensional beings of any kind.

But I'd be damned if I would show any weakness. And there was a lot I could learn tonight. Information was power. It always had been. There was no reason it wouldn't be the same in this crazy situation, too.

There was a knock at the door, and I almost jumped. *¡Cálmate!* I closed my eyes for a moment, pushing everything away except for the focus on getting the job done. The setting was new, the people strange, and some of the rules made no sense, but I knew how to survive. I would get through this just like I had everything else in my life.

One step at a time.

Chapter 29

I slid the front door open and bowed, glancing at the mirror when I did so. The reflection remained clear, and our guest's name appeared at the bottom of the glass—so she wasn't seen as a threat and was someone of note.

Yet despite the expectation of seeing fantastical beings, I was still caught by surprise. Flowing gossamer robes covered our first guest from head to fin, and she wore a crown of pearls and coral. Her colorful scales matched the pastel blues and pinks of her clothes, and her huge turquoise eyes with large black irises almost seemed to glow. The image of a fish walking upright was ridiculous, but that made her no less beautiful.

I straightened and kept my gaze lowered, much as I had seen Mizuki do, but still saw that what I'd viewed in the mirror was how our guest also presented herself to others. I swept my hand in a clumsy imitation of Mizuki's water-like movements to invite her further in. "Welcome to Last Stop, Princess Pearldrop. My name is Daniela. It is an honor to meet you."

A fan snapped open in the princess's semi-transparent fin and rose to hide her protruding fish-mouth, which had been lightly covered with pink lip gloss. "Oh my, so polite. And look at you! How lovely."

She sounded pleased—assuming that was possible for a fish spirit. My incessant, nibbling apprehension at what the evening might bring eased a notch. The princess had come with a couple of fish ladies in tow, but rather than barging in behind her, they patiently waited their turn to be asked inside and greeted. I slid the door closed behind them to await our next set of guests.

Beauty had mentioned previously how beings with higher powers could travel into our world on their own if they came from another plane, like Desmond. Those who lived here on Earth must have the means to travel far and quickly as well. With the short notice they had been given, they would have had to. Was there a way to tell which dimension/plane of existence they came from? Was Desmond's attitude with regard to elementals the norm or just his own prejudice?

There was a knock at the door. *Dani, stay focused!*

I got back to work.

More often than not, our guests' appearance in the mirror matched what they looked like. Most didn't appear human, though the majority were humanoid. You would think that would cause them to seem less strange than our previous visitors (had that only happened this morning?), but being closer to human made them somehow weirder. Fish people, frog people, bird people, the men and the women, some with beauty so radiant you almost couldn't look at them.

Every one of them, even their escorts, was dressed in such finery that my practiced fingers itched to snatch a bauble or two for my own. The size of some of the pearls and gems, or the shimmer of the amazing fabrics, would surely earn enough money to make Pierson forgive me. But then I realized that while it might do the trick for me, none of it would bring Jay back. And without my hermano at my side, what would be the point?

All these beings were high-ranking in whatever hierarchies supernatural entities lived by, and this was obvious from their titles. I greeted lords, princesses, dukes, queens, emperors, and more. Their finery ran the gamut, from magnificent feathered or jeweled headdresses, to ten-thousand-dollar suits, tuxedos, and gowns from all eras and countries. One veiled woman was draped in all manner of colored algae woven together into an unbelievable masterpiece of a dress.

The mood of the guests was jovial—even Desmond's, when he finally showed up in the queue. Last Stop's mirror verified that he was indeed a prince. He wore a black fur-lined cape that somehow attached at the shoulders of his gold double-breasted suit. The reflected light from the metallic fabric doubled when he removed the cloak. He threw it in Mizuki's general direction, forcing her to scramble to catch it before it hit the floor.

If he hoped to get a rise out of me, he'd have to do better than that. I gave him my brightest, most welcoming smile. "Welcome to Last Stop, Prince Desmond. It is an honor to *officially* meet you."

He flashed me a smug smirk, as if he knew things I didn't, and moved on. He was absolutely going on my shit list.

A thing made of mud and formed into the shape of a hand slithered in behind him. The wrist was tilted back, putting the palm face up in a horizontal position with the fingers half curled. Nestled on it was a golden box tied with a giant black bow. The mirror's reflection was normal, though no name scrolled along the bottom. As Desmond moved forward, he reached behind him to pluck the wrapped gift off the open palm. He walked on, but the creature or whatever it was stayed right by the entry.

I'm not sure what caused me to step back from it. Whether it was a subconscious intuition from the fact that he'd left it there, or the slight tremor that suddenly went through the mud-made object.

It was a good thing I did, though, because a second later it lost cohesion and glooped flat, spreading mud all over the entry area. If I hadn't moved, it would have been all over my kimono as well. Thankfully, Mizuki had been hanging his cape and was away from the door, so she hadn't been near the target zone. She stared at the mess with a horrified expression.

I flashed a look after Desmond, but he was already gone, not having waited to see the results of what I assumed was his little joke. The gold box he'd brought with him wasn't on the counter along with the other gifts. The cabrón was up to something. I just had no idea what.

LS quickly absorbed the mud through the floorboards to clear the entry before our next guest arrived. At least, I hoped it was Hokora's doing, rather than the collapsed thing doing it on its own. Beauty needed a heads-up, so I sent a mental warning in her direction.

'*Thank you, Dani.*' Beauty's response rang inside my head. '*Stay alert. I suspect this isn't all he has planned for the evening.*'

Of that, I had no doubt. Maybe I'd get a chance to spill something all over him during the banquet. The thought perked my spirits right up.

Thankfully, the parade of guests dried up not long after that. All the smiling and bowing had tired me out, and I wanted to be near Desmond so I could monitor him.

"Before we go, please let me check you over, Dani-san," Mizuki said. The small frown that had settled on her brow after she overcame her horror at the mud incident was back in full force now that we were alone.

She looked critically over every inch of me, especially at the places I couldn't see myself. After a few strained minutes, she sighed with relief, bowing her head. "Oh, I am so glad! What a horrible spirit he is. You'd think a prince would know better."

Hell, the cabrón *did* know better. He just didn't care.

"We need to hurry." Mizuki took my hand, and we shuffled off, following the route of the lanterns. Kimonos might be beautiful, but you sure as hell weren't getting anywhere fast while wearing one. Our hair ornaments jangled like bells on a cat.

The party path ended at a set of sliding double doors painted in gold leaf, showing revelers on an open field of blooming sakura trees. We were no longer in an eatery, but were now plopped into the middle of some medieval samurai movie. Loud, upbeat music and voices raised in conversation leaked from inside the room. It relaxed me, for regardless of where these people came from or what they looked like, they seemed to party much the same way as humans.

Mizuki stood beside me, and after she gave a slight nod, the two doors slid open on their own. The wave of sound grew exponentially, then the music and spirits quieted into near silence as all eyes turned in our direction. The room was long, and everyone was seated on cushions with small lacquered tables placed in front of them in dual parallel rows only a few feet apart. Jugs floated through the air, refilling the guests' wide sake cups, as well as whiskey and other beverages.

I had thought Akasha's desire for alcohol odd, but it appeared it might be normal for all types of spirits. It would be useful to note whether they could become drunk or not. As we stepped inside, Mizuki sashayed gracefully to the side, leaving me center stage. Applause began at the far end and rolled toward me in a wave of sound. It was rather flattering and unexpectedly welcoming. Being chosen to work at Last Stop wasn't truly *that* big a deal, was it?

All I could think of doing in response was bow. That excited them even more.

As I straightened, Beauty—in her human form—rose to her feet. She too wore a gorgeous kimono, one in emerald green, with white silver-bordered paw prints filling the bottom hem and rising and growing smaller as they wrapped in a loose spiral over the body. Her hair had been braided and coiled around the back of her head. A pair of jade sticks with silver bells and flowers held it in place. She called out in a loud voice, "Let the feast begin!"

This earned a more raucous round of applause.

Beauty's voice rang inside my mind. '*Come, sit next to me.*'

Only then did I notice the two empty places at the ends of the parallel lines. Mizuki was already heading to the one on the left, so I joined Beauty on the right. If I recalled correctly, seating in Japan was typically in order of rank. That I was at the bottom didn't surprise me, since I was new. What I hadn't expected was that all these others would be higher ranked than Beauty.

I hid a snicker behind my sleeve, realizing this was probably one of the reasons Desmond was such a prick. Despite his position near the top, he had still lost his bid to control LS to someone of a much lower rank. I'm sure it had been a terrible blow to his immensely inflated ego.

The doors opened again, and covered, lacquered boxes and bowls floated inside in two rows and settled on the small table before each visitor. The tops popped off simultaneously, revealing the colorful contents all at once. Mizuki had been with me for several hours, so there was no way Ryo had cooked all this. Since Last Stop was much older than the cook, she must be able to prepare food on her own. But how would it know what tasted good and what didn't?

Considering the zeal with which those near me attacked their meal, I could only assume she knew what she was doing. She hadn't skimped either. The servings were generous yet still managed to look like works of culinary art—flowers made from sliced pieces of fish, vegetables cut into all manner of complementary shapes, and ingredients set side by side in contrasting colors.

What few bites I allowed myself were delicious. But after Desmond's previous stunt and my certainty that he was going to pull something during the party, I was in work mode. And I never ate or drank while on the job if I could help it. Restrooms were dangerous places since most had only one way in or out, and a full stomach could make you sleepy or sloppy.

Last Stop had just served a dessert of different colored balls when I spotted Desmond rising to his feet near the banquet's far end. With that gold suit on, he was hard to miss. My insides clenched.

"What a lovely banquet this has been!" Desmond's voice boomed across the room. The smile that followed almost outshone his outfit. "Humans are creative creatures, if nothing else," he said. Everyone grew quiet. I saw a few troubled glances being exchanged. Had Beauty told others about the mud incident? Or were they aware of what a sore loser he was?

"While we traditionally leave our gifts for the hokora and the new servant at the counter when we enter," he continued, "mine is time sensitive, so I brought it along with me." With a flick of his wrist, the box rose from behind him to hover between the two rows of revelers. The large black bow unwrapped itself, and the lid popped off the container.

Rather than remove its contents for all to see, the box tilted sideways and made its way down the line, first on one side, then the other. Confused whispers rang out as it moved along. By design, Beauty and I were the last ones to see what was inside.

I shouldn't have been surprised, as I had expected this would be his "gift," but it still felt like a punch to the gut all the same. Nestled inside the velvet-lined box, wearing an added small golden collar, was Mystic the unicorn.

Chapter 30

He had cojones; I'd give him that. Pulling this stunt to rub our faces in what he'd done. After letting us get a good look at what was in the container, it floated back in his direction. The top and box reattached themselves before settling to rest between Desmond's tray and that of the person across from him.

Questioning whispers zipped back and forth, no one else having any idea what Mystic was or what it meant. It also brought up the question of how Desmond had even known what we were searching for in the first place. I had a suspicion, but no way to verify it. I slipped a glance in Beauty's direction, but the cat in human form was chatting amicably away with her neighbor as if Desmond's "gift" was some kind of inside joke and of little consequence.

The wattage of Desmond's glittering smile dimmed slightly when he didn't get a rise from those of us belonging to Last Stop. He'd obviously hoped to get under Beauty's skin and have her call him out so he could embarrass her in front of what I'm sure he considered her betters. Even *I* could have told him he'd be wasting his time, and I hadn't known her that long.

"It appears that Beauty is too shy to tell you about the importance of my gift." Desmond shook his head slightly as his voice boomed across the room again. While I would have loved to plunge one of my hair sticks in his eye for stealing Mystic, for hurting Cyrano, and for whatever else he was hoping to get out of this little stunt, Beauty only tilted her face and blinked slowly in his direction as if waiting to see if he'd implicate himself or take things a bit too far.

"This child's toy is the missing piece in their current endeavors," he said. "It will allow the new recruit to have her first success in pacifying the human dead."

A few oohs and ahhs rang out here and there, but from the twitch in his jaw, there were nowhere near as many as he'd hoped for.

A man with a colorful feather headdress, a collar of leaves, and scaly skin spoke up from his seat close to the head of the line. "Prince Desmond, I'm sure the Gatekeeper and those who help her are grateful for your unasked-for assistance," the man said with a slight slur in his speech, "but this is supposed to be a party! I would rather concentrate on making merry than watch you pat yourself on the back."

The roar of approval from those assembled was almost deafening. Supernatural beings truly loved their booze. The floating bottles of alcohol had never stopped filling glasses and cups throughout the banquet.

Desmond's smile turned to ash. I saw his eyes blaze for a moment all the way from my seat at the end. He gave the speaker an acknowledging bob. "As you wish, sir," he said, then sat back down and raised his glass before knocking its contents down his throat all at once.

The man in the headdress laughed with good humor and followed suit.

While I was pleased that we had Mystic and Beverly's unfinished business could now be resolved, it all felt anticlimactic and tasted bitter. It didn't help that we would have retrieved the Beanie Baby on our own if Desmond hadn't interfered and put our lives in danger. The fact that he'd flaunted the prize in front of everyone, like he had done us a great favor, churned acid in my insides.

'Desmond has always struggled with the art of timing.' Beauty's amused words rang softly inside my head. *'I also doubt this is his only trick.'*

Sadly, I agreed with her assessment. I would be keeping my eyes on him.

As soon as dessert was over, the drinking truly began in earnest. I'm no lightweight, but the amount of alcohol being consumed would have been enough to kill a normal person. The dishes and trays were whisked away so the guests could mingle. Some started to dance with drunken energy and overly loud laughter.

I took it upon myself to rescue the golden box with Mystic inside before someone accidentally tripped over it. It was heavier than I had expected. What was it made of? Actual gold? If Desmond had any objections, he didn't voice them. He also didn't seem to pay it any attention. Several male and female spirits of lower rank had gravitated into his orbit, trying to get details about the odd gift. From what little I overheard, he was sharing next to nothing about it. They weren't his target demographic, I guessed.

By the time I returned to our side of the room, Mizuki was surrounded by what looked like a cadre of eager groupies.

"Dance for us, Mizuki-san!" "I've waited ages to see it again." "Please honor us with a performance. Please!"

Ever the demure flower, she still deftly deflected their requests for a minute or two before finally caving in and saying it would be her pleasure. As she rose, she removed a pair of colored hand fans from inside her sleeves.

The groupies moved back, sitting and creating a circle to give her a clear stage. A hush settled over this side of the room as more of the guests joined the growing circle. Anticipation filled the air, and my curiosity grabbed hold.

Mizuki stood poised for a moment once things settled, then snapped both fans open simultaneously. More heads turned in her direction with interest. The sounds of a string instrument, flute, and small drums wove around her as she began a set of beautifully fluid movements that gave life to the paper fans in her hands. She would release and recatch them; join them and separate them. The music, the fans, and Mizuki became one. Though she was fully clothed, with only her hands, face, and the back of her neck exposed, the dance felt intimate and somehow sensual.

I kept having to remind myself that this erotic beauty was actually a man. And as a woman, he had me totally beat. Yet at that moment, it didn't seem all that important, as the dance was a wonder to behold.

Despite Mizuki's magnetic allure, I still maintained a wary eye on Desmond. My sorely lacking knowledge of the prince or what kinds of power he or other spirits held gave too wide a range for my imagination. Putting together any worthwhile theories to anticipate what he might be planning and coming up with ways to counter it was an impossible task.

As Mizuki brought her dance to a close amid approving shouts and applause, I opened the box to double-check the contents. The heavy lid came away easily. Nothing jumped out at me or tried to eat my face. The Beanie Baby sat nestled inside, none the worse for wear as far as I could tell. There was nothing else in there.

Yet my instincts said there had to be more. Something about the whole debacle felt off. Desmond wasn't some noob. He was a prince, so he would know a lot about those in higher positions than him. He'd also previously attended banquets at Last Stop, so he already knew everyone who came would be more interested in eating and boozing it up than anything else. The odds that his grandstanding would bear any kind of favorable fruit were slim. Yet he should have been aware of that.

So why do it? Obfuscation? Like how a stick in the wire mob distracted the mark while the mechanic stole the valuables? But to do what, exactly?

The party was growing rowdier, making it hard to think. I sent a mental message in Beauty's direction. '*I'm going to put Mystic away. Be back in a few.*'

'*Have Hokora show you to a secure room to leave it in just in case,*' Beauty said. '*You've done well tonight. Thank you for your efforts.*'

Was that an actual compliment? She must have been dipping into the Bacardi too much. Even so, it was nice to hear. Pierson only complimented those showing possible skills during training. After that, if you heard anything from him, it was purely faultfinding. Still, it would be best not to let it go to my head.

I quietly made my exit with the golden box in my arms. A definite benefit of being at the bottom was being the one closest to the door. Hokora slid the doors open and then shut them behind me. "Gracias. Beauty mentioned something about a secure room?"

A floorboard lit to guide me in the right direction.

The relative quiet of the hallway was a relief. I lugged the heavy container where the boards led me, taking my time, my attire not the best for carrying hefty things around. A cheerful bark greeted me before I had gone far. "Hey, Loaf," I said. He sniffed all around me without getting too close to the kimono, which was good.

It didn't take long before we reached a set of double sliding doors with glowing symbols etched into the supporting wood. The same glyphs also floated parallel on the doors themselves, like added 3D decorations.

Hokora opened one of the doors, and Loaf dashed inside ahead of me. If he stayed, he could help guard the box until the party was over.

The interior of the room was empty, except for a short table in the back. I set the bulky thing on it. Loaf smelled every inch of the golden container, sneezing several times. He was fascinated by it but not alarmed, as far as I could tell. Hopefully that was a good sign.

Loaf settled in front of the table, his entire concentration centered on Desmond's box. He still didn't seem upset, and no weird alarms had rung in the room, so I assumed everything was okay. Had he sensed Beverly's lingering scent on the unicorn hidden inside? Dog noses were amazing things. If they could find buried bodies under mounds of dirt, picking up a whiff of her would be child's play.

Loaf didn't even twitch when I took my leave, his entire focus centered on the box.

As the secure room's door slid closed behind me, I realized this would be a great opportunity to relieve my bladder. I made my slow way upstairs to my room. After taking way too much time to do my business, I double-checked that all my clothes were lying properly and prepared to go back downstairs.

The door to my room started to open for me, then suddenly stopped. I heard light footsteps in the hallway; at the same time, the subtle and slightly fruity aroma of expensive cigarette smoke tickled my nostrils. Was Ida skulking around?

I eased my door open further as her steps diminished down the stairs. As a giant bigot, I doubted she was interested in hobnobbing with spirits or demons, even if some of them were royalty. It would offend her delicate sensibilities. So what was she up to then?

I crept to the head of the stairwell and peeked. Bruja Ida had stopped beside the cubbies for our shoes, keeping out of view of anyone who might be in the hallway downstairs, and seemed to be waiting. Less than a minute later, her whispering voice and someone else's came floating upstairs, whatever they were saying too far away to overhear. I couldn't see who she was talking to as they kept themselves in the corridor.

Then an arm came into view, holding something small wrapped in paper. Because of the width of the cubbies, the hand extended farther than it might otherwise to keep Ida hidden as she moved to take the item. I caught sight of a golden jacket sleeve.

Heart pounding at the discovery, I watched until the secret exchange was over, then pulled back and quietly sneaked back to my room to stay hidden until Ida returned upstairs. Since I couldn't hear through the door, I waited five minutes, then exited the room normally. The hallway was deserted.

I made my way to the party once more, questions bouncing like ping-pong balls every which way inside my head. My suspicions from before had been confirmed. We had a traitor in our midst.

Chapter 31

The party became something of a blur on my return. Everyone suddenly wanted to have a word with me. It was like my leaving before had been a warning that they might not get another chance if they didn't take advantage of doing it now.

I answered crazy questions such as: Were the rumors that we ate our own young true? Could we really change sex at will? Meanwhile, my brain kept churning away at figuring out answers regarding our traitor problem. Beauty had been clear that Bruja Ida was here for punishment and atonement. Not that anyone in their right mind would use the woman to help with anyone's unfinished business. And I was pretty sure Ida wasn't allowed to leave Last Stop. So how in the world had Desmond and Ida met?

She was more a prisoner than an employee, so I doubted she'd gotten a welcome party like I had. Beauty could answer these questions, but then I would have to tell her why I was asking, and I would lose any leverage I might have gained. This needed to stay quiet.

Desmond and some of the other higher beings would have been made aware of Ida, of course. But options for contacting her, let alone meeting with her, were nonexistent. Unless a third person was involved?

¡Sí! That was it! An intermediary of sorts. But who? Surely not Ryo. I also couldn't see Ken wanting to have anything to do with the bruja. And from what I had read about her, she seemed to be a man-hater on top of a bigot, so she wouldn't have reached out herself. You couldn't get into Last Stop without an invitation if you weren't one of the recently dead—or that's what I assumed, anyway, from what little I'd seen.

But we'd had that meeting with all the nearby spirits who'd helped to locate Mystic! If Desmond had any of them in his pocket, he could have learned some of what he needed from them or sent a message to Ida for more information, or even set a time to have her meet him at Last Stop's door for a conversation. That would have given Desmond plenty of time to work his mental mojo on her—just enough to make her more receptive to whatever he was offering, or at least get him past her hangups long enough to tempt her to his ends.

I almost tripped as a crazy idea slammed into my head. What if that was why he had thrown such a stink that morning? To cover up the fact that he'd been communicating with Ida in case other spirits had seen him hanging around? The guy was hard to miss. His having a meltdown about being snubbed would cover up anything else he'd been up to, *and* make for a more distracting bit of gossip.

Then it hit me—the double furball spirit that had been roaming where it wasn't supposed to! It could have delivered a note to Ida to set up the meet. And if Ida showed any interest in the details of the latest unfinished business, there would have been no reason not to tell her about it. If she had asked Ryo, he wouldn't have found it odd at all.

Hell, if she could rein in her nasty tendencies long enough, as she had seemed to be doing lately, she could have asked Beverly about it directly. That's why she had played nice with me before—to make everyone believe she was making an effort and wanted to help. Hell, for all I knew, she could have been eavesdropping during the meeting.

Since Mizuki was the current dominant personality, and she didn't know about the others, I'd need to wait to ask Ryo about this, circumspectly. I could also look for Beverly in the morning to ask whether she'd been approached by Ida or not.

The alcohol finally stopped flowing, and guests started making preparations to depart. After politely turning down three drunken marriage proposals, two to become a concubine, and an offer of a bag of gems if I let one drink a few ounces of my blood, I was more than ready for them to leave. I kept my itchy fingers to myself despite all the easy prey. Eventually, they would be sober again, and they wouldn't have to be geniuses to figure out who had taken their valuables.

Mizuki and I headed back to the front entrance to bid the guests goodnight and return their coats and other personal items. Beauty stayed in the party room to herd those who didn't get the hint that the festivities were over to come our way.

Desmond was one of the last to leave, and he deigned to give me a broad smile, his golden eyes laughing at me, again as if he knew something I didn't. "Do enjoy the rest of your evening, little pet."

"May you get home safely, sir." *And trip and fall flat on your smug face!*

As our front door slid closed for the final time that night, I sighed with heartfelt relief. This kimono might be beyond gorgeous, but it had grown heavier and heavier as the night rolled on.

"Thank you both for your efforts," Beauty said. She had come into the room after our last guest. "Everyone seemed to enjoy themselves."

I pointed at the stack of gifts on the counter. "What should we do with those?" My curiosity about what supernatural beings considered to be gifts begged to be satisfied.

Beauty shrank, transforming into her usual feline form. "Hokora-chan and I will go through them," she said. "Though most should be fine, occasionally the givers forget what might and might not be appropriate. A few like to play little pranks."

"I bet." Why did I get the feeling some of those jests ended with us humans losing an arm or leg, if not our lives? Last Stop was sorely in need of a new employee handbook or a spirit encyclopedia. "Desmond was in a good mood when he left," I said. "He told me to enjoy the rest of my evening."

"Interesting." Beauty's head tilted slightly, her eyes narrowing. "Mystic is in the secure room, correct? Perhaps it's time you and I gave the unicorn a closer look." She glanced at Mizuki and said, "Feel free to turn in for the night. And thank you again for all your help, and your lovely performance."

She bowed, a tiny smile decorating her lips. "*Hai*, Beauty-sama. I was happy to be of use."

Mizuki headed upstairs, and I followed Beauty. From what I could tell, Mizuki didn't seem bothered by being left out of the loop. It would have driven me bonkers.

Once we made it inside the secure room, we found Loaf on his back on the floor, his tongue lolling, while still watching the golden box.

"He's been staring at the thing since I brought it in here," I said. "Is that normal?"

At the sound of my voice, Loaf flipped over onto his stomach and barked a greeting, but his round eyes never left the container.

"He doesn't appear distressed," Beauty said. "Though his fascination with it seems a bit odd." She half-rolled her eyes. "But, then again, he *is* a canine."

Loaf barked again as if happy that she'd noticed. He looked and acted fine.

"Hokora-chan, would you mind lifting the lid for us?" Beauty asked the room at large.

The top floated off the container and settled on the table. Loaf's attention remained glued to the body of the box.

Beauty made her next request. "Would you lift Mystic?"

Though we waited for several seconds, the Beanie Baby didn't appear.

"How odd." Beauty jumped onto the short table. "Hokora is unable to raise it, despite it being in her domain. Yet the container itself did not give her an issue." Her ears tilted forward, and then she carefully peered over the gift's edge. "I see nothing but the doll inside."

Curiosity humming in my veins, I drifted over to peer in as well. Mystic was there, in the velvet-lined box, wearing the golden collar Desmond had added to it and nothing else, the same as before. "Still, it was pretty heavy when I lifted it."

Beauty walked all the way around the container. Then she extended a claw and tore through the wrapping of the box at each corner. The covering peeled away, revealing not a normal carton, but one made of sheets of thin metal. From the reddish-orange color, it might be copper. With the gold paper exterior and the velvet lining inside, no one would be the wiser. But why make a container out of copper, of all things, in the first place?

"Would you mind reaching inside and removing the doll, Dani?" Beauty asked.

I made a face. She was kidding, right? "Why would I be stupid enough to do that? This thing is likely some kind of trap."

"Copper, among other metals, can be used against the supernatural," Beauty said, swishing her tail. "The current configuration won't allow Hokora-chan to remove the contents, since she is a spirit house. Since I'm what you mortals term a mystical being, there's a chance it could affect me, depending on whether there are engravings on the interior sides. But things that affect us don't typically do anything to humans." She tilted her head to look sideways at me. "If there is a trap, it's not meant for your kind."

The metal thing made sense. Cold iron was used against the Fae in the UK, and the Taino people of Puerto Rico had used gold and copper in rituals. So she could be right. I crossed myself, just in case, my pulse speeding up, and then dipped a couple of fingers past the edge into the box's interior. When they weren't immediately torn off or burned, I put my hand inside and yanked Mystic out of the box, in case moving her was some kind of trigger.

Nothing happened.

Loaf gave a soft whine as I placed Mystic on the short table. His gaze had finally shifted from the container and was now locked onto the Beanie Baby.

"Hokora-chan, are you able to lift the doll now?" Beauty asked.

The unicorn rose into the air and pranced around as if being played with by a child.

"Maybe Desmond wanted to make sure nobody stole it?" Even as I said it, I realized it sounded ridiculous. It had to be something else, but what?

"No one would be so foolish," Beauty said. "Well, *almost* no one." That last part had a splash of glee and secret past deeds plastered all over it.

"Then why do it?" I asked.

"That is the question, isn't it?" Beauty's tail swished faster and faster at the edge of the table.

Should I tell her about what I had seen earlier—the exchange between Desmond and Ida? Or continue to hold it in reserve, to put pressure on the bruja later? "Would Ida…?"

"Would Ida what?" Beauty asked, her ears swiveling in my direction.

"Sorry, just thinking out loud." No. I needed to keep in hand all the advantages I could get. Besides, how much could the bruja possibly do for him?

Beauty leapt off the table. "For now, let's leave them here, where they'll be secure. We can revisit the topic again in the morning."

I was more than happy to shelve the questions for now. It had been a long enough day already.

Chapter 32

One second, I was drifting off the edge into sleep; the next, I was falling out of bed onto the floor for a painfully rude awakening. The lights flickered, then came on. Blinking, trying hard to hold back a moan, my hip loudly complaining at the rough treatment, I tried to get back on my feet.

That was when a keening sound full of pain and torment shrieked through the walls and tried to cleave my head in two. I dropped to my knees. Putting my hands over my ears made no difference—I couldn't shut it out. *¿Qué está pasando?* The screams drilled into my brain from all around, causing a deep ache in my teeth and vibrating in the marrow of my bones.

Fear and panic bubbled from deep inside, making my limbs feel shaky, and my heart hammer began to hammer violently in my chest. The urge to run sang like electricity in my veins. But run to where?

Whatever Desmond's plan had been, I knew this was it. Except I had no idea what 'it' was or what to do about it. The floor and walls trembled around me as if made of rubber; the lights flickered on and off in a mad Morse code dance.

This wasn't just affecting *me*; it was messing with Last Stop as well. My chest squeezed. If the spirit house were destroyed, what would that mean for those of us inside it?

Images of Beverly and Mizuki flashed in my head. Beauty and I might have been expecting something to happen, but those two hadn't. Beverly would be terrified. Then I realized I had no idea where she might be. She was only a child! Dios mío, how would I ever find her?

I crawled on all fours toward my door, not trusting the now undulating floor to let me stay on my feet. The desperate need to get out, to search for Beverly, grew exponentially, but even crawling was proving difficult. Whatever this sound was, it appeared to be affecting Hokora as well. The screeching waxed and waned but was continuous; the pain blared through me, making it hard to put cohesive thoughts together. The urge to flee this place only grew stronger.

I yelped in shock when my door slammed open as if kicked, then Ryo filled the doorway, using the frame as an anchor to keep his feet. His hair was tousled every which way, but he had his glasses on, and the worried expression etched on his face told me it was him, and not one of his alters. He wore a pair of black boxer shorts and a matching t-shirt, as if always ready for anything.

He could have had a tutu on for all I cared. I was just glad to see someone.

Ryo thrust out his hand, and I took it. He pulled me to my feet and helped me stay there. The wailing felt stronger at the doorway. Though I had no idea how, I could almost make out the waves of penetrating screams coming down the hall from the direction of the stairs.

"What do we do?" I asked loudly. To my surprise, Ryo heard me. It added weight to the possibility that the overwhelming sound wasn't sound at all.

"We need to find the source," he said.

"It's got to be Mystic! Desmond did something to the doll before he brought it here last night," I said. "Beauty put it away in a secure room. The one with gold symbols carved into the wood."

Following the weird waves would also get us there if the source was somewhere else. Yet every cell in my body wanted to race the opposite way. "Do you know where Beverly is?"

He pointed toward the stairwell.

Claro. Of course, she was in the same direction as where the screams were coming from. My insides twisted into a painful, gnarled mess.

Ryo clasped my forearm and had me do the same to his. Then he sprang to the other side of the hall and placed his palm flat against the wall, and I copied him on this side. Though the walls were trembling or undulating in waves, we could still use them as a brace to stay on our feet. We started inching toward the stairs.

He kicked in Ida's door on the way, but our backstabber wasn't in there. Surprise, surprise. I cursed at myself for not telling Beauty about seeing her get something from Desmond when I'd had the chance. I had hoped to utilize the knowledge as leverage, but a whole lot of good that would do me if I died.

By the time we made it to the stairwell, I was panting hard. Fighting the urge to run away screaming from where we were going was getting harder and harder to do. And it would only get worse the closer we got to it. Sweat beaded on Ryo's forehead and upper lip, proving he wasn't having an easy time of it either.

'*Beauty?*' I sent the mental message, but all I received in return was a brain full of static. It made taking that initial step down the yawning maw of the stairs all the harder. If our boss had been taken out, what chance did we mere humans have? But if we wanted to find Beverly, if we wanted to escape, there was no choice but to go down.

Almost as if our thoughts were in sync, Ryo nodded at me and moved, our arms still linked in the Roman handshake. This chica would not let a puppy like him show me up, so I took one too. Braced against each other and the walls, we crept on, the way more treacherous than before. A misstep here would send us tumbling with a reward of bruises, cracked bones, or a broken neck waiting at the end.

I had to sit for a minute when we made the landing, my knees trying to lock, and my legs shaky as hell. The wailing continued, pouring into us, through us, feeling almost physical in its invasion and making me want to join in the screaming.

¡Dios, por favor, ayúdanos! If demons, ghosts, and monsters were real, maybe He was too? So I sent out a prayer as frightened tears stung my eyes. We needed all the support we could get.

Ryo let go of my arm as I sat, and he crawled forward, glancing both ways down the hall. As I had suspected all along, the rings of sound came from deeper inside the building rather than from the exit. The decision was a no-brainer. Sensible people would run outside, call for help, and hopefully locate someone else to take care of whatever was going on. Moving in the direction of the bad stuff was not how you stayed alive.

"Dani, get out of here," Ryo said. "We'll come find you once it's over." Through the flickering lights, I could see that his eyes were dilated. The guy was scared shitless, but he was going to go anyway.

"Are you *crazy*?" My throat tried to shut closed, making the question squeak out as a screech. My arm flung out. "You don't know what 'this' is, let alone how to handle it!"

He flinched as if I'd hit him but didn't look away. "I owe them. Hokora and Beauty accepted me, *all* of me. Nobody has ever cared enough to bother." Resolve shone on his face. "I won't abandon them. I will fight."

My jaw dropped. Realization smacked me like a shovel to the face, somehow driving the fear, the incessant wailing, and everything else back for a stretched-out moment. The way he'd sagged and looked away when I'd voiced my satisfaction that Ken was gone when we were escaping the lounge. He'd been upset because I hadn't accepted him—at least not *all* of him. Was that messed up or what?

Or was it?

Ryo had turned to go, shuffling on hands and knees over the undulating floor to follow the wails to their origin. Half-muted barks and whimpers drifted toward us. A reminder that there were still others unaccounted for.

I might not owe Beauty or Last Stop anything, but there was a terrified six-year-old girl trapped somewhere in this horror. I wouldn't be able to live with myself knowing I'd left her here just to save my own skin. Fate had already been a total bitch to her; I refused to add to it.

"W-wait! I'm coming with you." My whole body broke out in a sweat as I said it, but seeing Ryo's surprised glance and the momentary wave of his imaginary puppy tail gave me what I needed to move forward.

The waves of screams continued, growing louder and stronger the farther we went. Time became meaningless. The onslaught grew so bad that my brain half turned off, becoming numb, in a possibly futile attempt to safeguard my sanity. Focusing on a list of the million ways I'd make Desmond and Ida pay for putting me through this hell helped—I would stab them, peel their skins off layer by layer, set them on fire after dousing them in gasoline.

Ryo and I had returned to walking side by side, our arms locked once more. The physical contact brought relief, though I couldn't have entirely said why. Just knowing I wasn't alone was part of it. Misery did so love company.

We spotted Loaf on his side before the familiar set of double sliding doors. Its glowing symbols pulsated in counter rhythm to the waves of psychic sounds emanating from within. The room was supposed to be secure. Why was it not working?

I focused on the dog as Ryo and I tried to move faster. Loaf's form appeared blurry at the edges. Would that be happening to Beverly as well? I sure hoped not. We kneeled beside Loaf at the doors. His margins were fuzzy, and he had a long, jagged gash along one side of his body, but he was conscious. A broken cigarette holder sat beside him, a sign of how and by whom the corgi had been hurt.

There was no blood, but I could see the muscles normally hidden beneath his skin, which was somehow more disturbing than the incessant screaming. He gave a pitiful whine, so I forced my hand forward to pat his head, telling myself repeatedly that whatever was wrong with him was not contagious. Thankfully, he was solid, which was a relief. Even his tongue felt rough as he offered my wrist a lick.

This close to the doors, we could hear something other than all the keening. I couldn't identify it, but if I had to guess, it sounded like violent rolling and things smacking against the walls.

I swallowed hard, knowing what the next step should be, but not wanting to be the one to commit us to it. My voice was shaky as I asked, "What do we do now?"

Ryo had an ear to the nearest sliding door, his face a blank mask. His gray gaze locked with mine. "We go inside."

¡Coño! That's what I was afraid of.

Chapter 33

It sounded so easy—slide the door open, peek in, and step inside. Nothing could have been farther from the truth. Not when every primal, hard-coded survival instinct screamed against it. Whatever was going on in that room ran contrary to the reality of anyone living. But I could feel and see Last Stop suffering from what was happening. If the spirit house collapsed, we were all screwed—the spirits *and* the living housed here.

I grabbed Ryo's arm to lock us together again as he reached forward with a trembling hand to slide the door open. The moment it moved, the wailing turned from a supernatural screeching to a physical and cerebral one. Ryo opened the entrance just enough to yank both of us in and close it behind him.

But it didn't matter; I was too shocked by what was happening. I kept blinking as my brain struggled to process it. Two gargantuan beings were locked in mortal combat, flailing across the floor, the walls, and the ceiling as if gravity meant nothing to them. One had white and silver fur made of smoke, with claws and teeth the size of swords. Its eyes were green, glowing orbs.

The other was… was… a horror from someone's darkest nightmare. Built roughly in the shape of a human, it comprised hundreds of tormented and angry souls. A thousand eyeballs stared out from it in pain, hatred, or madness. Those that formed the fingers had mouths, and they bit and snapped as they grappled and rolled with the other creature, both struggling for dominance.

At the far corner of the room, above the remains of the small table and the golden box, a black plant had taken root, tendrils crawling like a malignant disease to entrench itself in the walls and floor. A blood-red flower with sharp edges sat open like a mouth, bordered by razors, and trumpeting the foul mental and physical screams. Looking at it made my skin crawl with revulsion. Whatever it was, it had never been meant for our world.

Only a few feet from it, Ida lay unmoving, blood trails drying at her nose and ears. Mystic the Beanie Baby sat beside her, a silent witness, the gold collar Desmond had placed on the unicorn now discarded. Rage burned through me at the sight of the traitor. She'd been given a second chance at life, a place and means of possible redemption, and she'd *thrown* them away like garbage. If this stupidity hadn't killed her, I might put an end to the bruja myself. But first, we had to survive this.

I tried to mentally call out to Beauty again. '*Tell us what to do! How can we help? And where is Beverly?*'

Ryo pulled us to the right to avoid being crushed by the flailing combatants.

'*Bring sea salt!*' A roar shook the walls. '*Purify and kill the Death Blossom. It must not be allowed to leave this room!*'

We were forced to dive back toward our previous position. Arms, legs, and mouths clamored for us as the pieces of the creature Beauty was fighting became aware of our existence.

'*Hokora was able to get Beverly out before things got completely out of hand, so the child is no longer in immediate danger.*' Her mental voice rang with strain. '*If you can, drag Ida and Mystic to safety. And I forbid* either *of you to allow yourselves to be killed!*'

The last dragged a rough laugh out of me. Gata mala. As if just ordering it would make it so.

Ryo brought his mouth close to my ear. "There's a bag of sea salt in the pantry." His voice sounded strained, as if having to force the words out one by one. "Bring knives back, too."

My pulse jumped with joy at the thought of getting out of this room. But there was a problem with that. If I left, I wasn't sure I had the fortitude to force myself to come back—just the idea of having to do it left me panting again. I'd only made it this time because there were two of us. "You, you can't trust me with that." I shook my head, the skin over my face tight, letting the deep-seated terror and panic show on my face. "I'll take care of dragging Ida and Mystic out."

Whatever he saw must have sent the right message, because he nodded a moment later. "Here," he said. He pulled out one of those thin black knives he'd used at the lounge and handed it to me. Where he'd been keeping it, I had no idea. "Steel has iron. It will hurt them." He flipped the blade so I could grab it.

It didn't look like much, but I was grateful all the same. The pressure around me eased a microscopic bit. "Gracias." I'd never meant it as profoundly as I did that moment.

Ryo nodded again, then slunk off toward the sliding doors. I turned away, biting my lip, so as not to see him leave, knowing it would chip at what little resolve I still had about me. Keeping one eye on the thrashing combatants and the other on Ida and that hated flower, I crawled forward following the wall.

More than once, I had to scurry onward or jump back to avoid being crushed. More and more of the souls making up the creature noticed me, sending chills and goosebumps creeping all over my body. A few of the faces cried tears, while others assaulted me with expletives, as if their plight were my fault. They would close their eyes, look away, or struggle to submerge into the seething mass of the gigantic body whenever the fight turned any of them in the direction of the Death Blossom.

Whatever the flower truly was, not even the dead wanted to be anywhere near it. Yet here I was, inching ever closer to the thing.

Dani, what the hell are you doing? I didn't have the faintest idea. But this Boricua didn't back down from anybody! I gripped the knife in my hand more tightly, trying to make myself believe it.

I was a foot or so away from Ida when my ears popped and a wave of vertigo hit me with such force I could no longer tell up from down. Nausea swept through me, and I dared not move for fear of impaling or hurting myself. My chest tightened, ice flowing through my veins.

¡Carajo! What was going on now?

It took several moments to work out. The wailing—the incessant, terror-inducing, mind-numbing wailing—had stopped. Except it hadn't. I could still see the supernatural rings of sound coming out of that unnatural flower's mouth. But they shot from it in a direct line, growing wider as they went. Because of the ring of petals around the opening and being this close to it, we were in a dead zone of sorts.

While it was great not to be flooded with constant horror, being in such close proximity to the thing and its inching, greedy roots didn't make me feel all that much better. Sweat-soaked and shaky, I watched one root detach from the wall like a finger and stretch out at a snail's pace to touch Ida's neck. What would happen if it did wasn't worth thinking about. I didn't have to be a psychic to know it would be nothing good. Possibly a fate undeserved by anyone, even this traitorous bruja.

Using Ryo's knife, I stabbed a section still attached to the wall, embedding the blade, not wanting my flesh anywhere near the moving tendril. The reaction was immediate. The end part of the root, past where the blade had impaled it, thrashed violently and turned gray before coming apart and dissipating like bits of ash in the wind. The Death Blossom's giant bloom jerked as if slapped, and the size of the rings of sound went momentarily erratic.

¡Sí! Glorious glee slashed my mouth into a nasty grin. It could be hurt! We might actually be able to rid ourselves of the ugly, unnatural thing. Something that, until that moment, I had deep down believed was impossible. Now we could claim our pound of flesh for what it was putting us through. I couldn't wait.

'Daniela, snap out of it! You need to get them out!'

Beauty's mental shout smacked me out of my foul thoughts. I refused to feel guilty about them—the thing would deserve whatever it got—but I had work to do.

I flipped Ida onto her back—none too gently, I might add—then lay Mystic flat on her stomach, before grabbing the bruja's ankles. Taking several deep breaths to steel myself, I then pulled us into the sea of projected fear and horror. It was like taking multiple sledgehammer blows to my brain.

I screamed—the sound absorbed and played back by the Death Blossom and the hundreds of mouths on the amalgamation, who were still grappling with Beauty's semi-gaseous form. I felt like a puppet with its strings cut. The temporary reprieve and then diving back into the worst of it had backfired hard. Black filled the edges of my vision, hungry to take the rest of it.

'*Move, you useless human!*'

A flash of irritation lit through me, driving the darkness back. Some part of me knew that Beauty was only trying to keep me conscious, but her words rankled all the same. My head felt on fire, my brain boiling in its own juices. The spot on my forehead with Beauty's butterfly mark itched like mad. Something warm dripped onto my lip, and I brushed my hand past it and came away with blood. Argh!

I'd willingly trade a piece of my soul to have a chainsaw to ram into that stupid flower's face! I refused to be killed by this moronic plant.

Desmond would pay, Ida would pay, the evil plant would *absolutely* pay! I stoked my anger to energize me and to push the fear, exhaustion, and everything else as far away as possible. Ida was thin, but she was still a lot of deadweight. If Beauty or that blob she was fighting with came our direction, she would be toast. Hell, I wasn't sure *I'd* be able to move out of the way in time.

A litany of curses flowed out of my mouth as I tried to dredge up the energy to move even a fraction faster. *Mija, you're a Boricua! Let's get this done!*

I'd almost reached the doors with my burdens when the one closest to me slapped open, startling me. For a second, I thought it was Ryo, until I realized the glasses were gone, and the teeth-gritted expression was full of dead, icy fury. Ken must have had to take over to make it all the way back here again. This chica was proud, but I was also a realist: I could have never pulled it off. Whether I liked the guy or not, it was good that psycho boy had been there when Ryo needed him.

Ken had brought with him a bag of sea salt, one with a multitude of handles poking out of the top of it. A small hole on the bottom sprinkled crystals wherever he went.

"Make it hurt, Ken," I told him with frothing eagerness. "Make that evil flower pay!"

Our gazes met, and for once we were in complete agreement. His answering feral grin was mirrored in mine.

The gravel-sized pieces of sea salt brought prickles of tiny pain as I stepped over them, but it also pushed back some of the effects of the psychic-sonic attacks, which felt glorious. Ken had spread a ring of salt around Loaf, and the corgi looked better, now sitting on his belly. He barked a greeting, but when he saw Ida, a low growl thrummed in his throat. Good to know the pooch didn't like the bruja any more than the rest of us did.

Once I had dragged the traitor across the threshold, I dropped her feet and moved to close the sliding door. Rather than shut the room and reduce, if only by a little bit, the pressure from the onslaught, I proved exactly how loca I was by stepping inside before closing it.

My brain blabbered like crazy, every inch of me shocked by my insanity and clamoring for me to change my mind. But a small part of me had to know, had to see, needed to witness whether we were doomed or not, rather than cower in ignorance and darkness.

Ken had already made his way to the corner, pitching handfuls of sea salt at the thing grappling with Beauty. The crystals landed in open mouths and eyes. The entire creature shuddered wherever they hit, and parts and pieces stopped moving. Beauty took full advantage and switched to a better hold on the mass, then flipped and pinned it to the ground. The whole room shook from the force of the movement, almost throwing Ken and me off our feet.

With the two fighters no longer rolling everywhere, I now had an unimpeded view of the Death Blossom. The root tendril I'd stabbed to the wall had stopped growing, but all the other tendrils had kept extending, while giving the knife a wide berth. The opposite side was farther along. Three black leaves had sprouted on a thicker tendril, with a small bud rising between them. If *two* of them started howling, it would puree our brains.

"*Ken!*" I yelled as loudly as I could, hoping he might somehow hear me over the never-ending wailing. I pointed frantically at the rapidly maturing blossom.

He pulled out one of the handles I could still see sticking out of the bag. The long carving knife's blade was covered in salt—he must have gotten the blades wet before sticking them in there. As the fact registered in my mind, Ken threw the knife straight at the bud. It plunged into the growing blossom with a resounding thud.

Anchoring roots for the sprout and those extending past it convulsed like angry waves before turning gray and falling apart. The original bloom spasmed as if in pain.

Ken didn't give it time to recover. He pulled a cleaver out of the sea salt and launched it straight at the flower's sharp-toothed maw. Mesmerized, I watched the blade spin across the intervening space and flawlessly enter the thing's dark cakehole.

A true scream issued from the Death Blossom's mouth as all its tendrils thrashed, tearing the walls and floor it clung to into pieces. I clapped my hands over my ears as its convulsions threw me from my feet.

Then came a ringing silence as the bloom and roots lost all color and then turned to ash before disappearing as if none of it had ever been.

Chapter 34

I sat up shakily on the floor, my teeth, bones, and head still aching from the inhuman death scream. Warm tracks coursed down my face, and I realized I was simultaneously crying and softly laughing with soul-wrenching relief. Except, we weren't done yet, were we? There was still one intruder to go.

But when I dared glance in Beauty and the flesh thing's direction, matters had changed. Beauty had shrunk back into her Maine Coon form and was currently busy licking her paw and then passing it over her tousled fur. More blood began to drip from my nose when I sneezed thanks to the tufts of cat hair floating around in the air, now that she'd reverted to normal from the giant cloud-like form she'd had before.

Beside her sat a plain bundle of long sticks tied together—sticks that were crying and moaning. Tiny-sized people who had been stretched into thin stalks with their weeping faces flattened. I quickly crossed myself and looked away.

Did Desmond do that to them? Had that been his plan for us as well? If I ever laid eyes on the pendejo again…

"That was highly unpleasant," Beauty said. "Are both of you all right?"

Was she kidding? Plenty of lovely nightmares would be coming to visit me for a while, thanks to this mess. But I was alive, and mostly in one piece, so this was a win. "Mira, that depends on your definition." I threw a glance at the bundled spirits. "I'm better than they are, but not by much."

A strangled snort came from Ken's direction, startling me. When I peeked, all I saw was his usual emotionless expression. Was it possible the psycho had a sense of humor under there? That was somehow more alarming than this entire mess.

"Those are human souls, right? What made them this way?" I couldn't help asking, still trying my best not to stare at the bundle directly. Their eyes kept attempting to meet mine, pleading. It was disturbing. "How did they go from that to the giant flesh thing?"

"I'll be more than happy to explain," Beauty said, "but aren't you forgetting something?"

Argh. This wasn't the time to be playing games! I wiped at my nose. "No?"

"Are you sure?"

Then it hit me. "Beverly!"

"Hurry to the front and let her in, won't you?" Beauty said, her half-closed eyes watching me intently. "She's probably terribly upset."

I struggled to my feet, glad the floor was no longer moving, or I'd never have made it.

"We'll clean things here and join you presently."

The double doors slid open for me.

Ida was still passed out where I had left her in the hall, which was good, or I might have been tempted to punch her face in. Leaving Mystic there with her was a bad idea, so I took charge of the Beanie Baby before slowly limping toward the restaurant area. I was beaten and sore, but at least my brain was mine once more, even if it was half-cooked. Loaf hobbled along beside me, obviously feeling better.

Halfway to the front, I swayed on my feet as I realized the gata mala might have played me again. Last Stop was more than capable of opening her own doors, despite the ordeal. I had seen it moments before! Hokora could have let Beverly in. So why? Maybe Beauty only wanted the child to have someone there to alleviate her fears rather than have her walk into an empty room? But Beauty could have also sent me off to avoid having to answer my questions.

Just this once, however, I would give her the benefit of the doubt.

I was gasping for breath by the time we got to the restaurant area. Since I knew I was in better shape than that, it spoke of how much the craziness and being batted around inside and out had taken out of me. I already expected bruises galore, and my thinking was still a bit fuzzy. Hibernating under my covers for a week or two sounded heavenly right then.

I left Mystic on one of the barrel-backed stools at the counter, so it would be out of view in case there was anyone else out there, and then slid the front door open. A blast of cold air blew in, making me shiver. I had forgotten it was winter out there. At least it numbed a few of my aches and pains. "Beverly?"

"*Dani!*"

I scrunched down with a moan, and Beverly ran straight into my arms, but not before I noticed the tear tracks on her face. I hugged her little body and held her tight as the entrance closed on its own behind her. She was warm, her tears were wet. I could feel her tiny heart pounding. Like Jay when he had been here, she felt alive rather than dead. Hokora existed under rules not found in the living world. "Everything is okay now, chiquita."

Loaf gave a bark of agreement and licked her leg. She giggled for a moment, then hiccupped. "I couldn't get back inside!" She hiccupped a second time. "Then, and then the store was all wavy and I could see through it! I was scared."

"A warrior princess like you?" I said. "I don't believe it."

Beverly snuggled against me and giggled again.

"Do you want some hot chocolate? Or some ice cream? It won't be fancy like Ryo's, but I bet between the two of us, we could do a decent enough job. What do you think?"

She pulled back, her brown eyes filled with excitement. "Yes!"

I let her go, the offer of sweets giving her more energy than she could quietly hold.

"Can we have both?" she asked with a sly look.

"I don't see why not." I straightened, my body protesting every inch of the way. "We've been through a lot tonight," I said. "We definitely need all the yumminess we can get."

Her little face glowed at the idea. "Could Loaf have something, too?"

"Claro. He was a super brave boy, so he totally deserves a treat."

The corgi barked, the stub of his tail wagging madly as he seconded the motion. I took Beverly's small hand in mine. As we turned to head down the side passage toward the kitchen, I caught a glimpse of myself in the mirror.

I was a royal mess. My hair looked like something that had fought a tornado and lost. My short, blue satin pajamas sat askew on my body, and drops of blood from my nose stained the fabric. I didn't look as bad as when I had first arrived at Last Stop drenched from top to bottom, but it was close. This time, though, I bet I stank to high heaven.

The butterfly on my forehead that marked me as a Last Stop employee appeared none the worse for wear, though the site still itched like crazy. Rubbing it didn't help one bit. But, hold on, had it gotten *bigger*? As if I needed more complications.

I glanced away and got us moving before Beverly noticed and asked if something was wrong. I blindly finger-combed my hair into some semblance of order and tugged my PJs straight. Beverly was the priority at the moment.

"This place is huge!" La chiquita let go of my hand to run around and check out the vast kitchen when we arrived.

I half-expected Ryo to be here, though Ken was the one currently in charge of their shared body, and he was helping Beauty with the cleanup. The room felt somehow empty without him.

Just as I realized that I didn't know where anything was kept, I got some unexpected help. Two large mugs and a couple of parfait glasses drifted from the other side of the divider curtain and landed on the island facing me.

The espresso machine clicked on, and the dispenser for hot milk was selected. A double set of premium bags of cocoa mix and mini marshmallows settled beside the cups. Strawberries and bananas floated over from the cooler, and a small paring knife came out of a drawer and started slicing them. A soft-serve contraption beeped, drawing my attention to it.

It was like having an invisible assistant. All I had to do was bring the different parts together. I dragged a chair over from the dinette set so Beverly could stand on it and help. A large bone floated in from somewhere, much to Loaf's delight. He happily gnawed on it while Beverly and I created our masterpieces.

When we were done, she and I moved our finished products to the table and dug in. The warm, familiar taste of hot cocoa helped push the evening's nightmare back a bit, which was a welcome relief. Sugar and chocolate always made everything better. It also took the edge off the heavy exhaustion trying to bend me with its weight.

'*You seem more settled*,' Beauty's words rang softly inside my head. '*I'll answer your questions now if you like.*'

I did feel calmer. And there was no telling whether she'd ever make the offer again if I didn't grab it this time around. '*That would be great*,' I thought back.

'*The souls you saw were tied together. They were cut away from wherever they were anchored as lingering spirits in the earthly plane*,' she said. '*Or were forcefully kept from ascending to their next destination the moment their bodies died.*'

None of that sounded good at all. Grabbing ghosts that refused to move on was one thing. But the thought that someone might have killed innocent people just to bind their essence to create the monstrous thing made me shudder to my core. I half turned and crossed myself. Thankfully, Beverly was too engrossed in her treats and teasing Loaf to notice.

'*Desmond is able to do stuff like that?*' I asked, tempted to cross myself again.

Beauty's answer was slow in coming. '*No,*' she eventually said, '*those from the spirit world do not have dominion over human souls. They may hurt them, possibly destroy them, and on rare occasions even eat them, but they cannot* bind *them.*'

I knew I would regret asking this, but I did it anyway. '*Who or what could have done it, then?*'

Beauty hesitated again. '*Humans. Only humans can tether human souls.*'

A chill crept through me, one that had nothing to do with the ice cream I had been eating. People had created that horrible bundle? Rather than help those spirits move on, someone had purposely bound them into a terrifying creature to aid in the destruction of the very place that could have helped them? What would be the point of that?

'*That doesn't make any sense,*' I thought back at her. '*Why would a human want to wreck Last Stop?*'

'*Yes, indeed, why would they?*' Beauty countered.

Ugh, the one time my brain cells are fried, and she wants me to figure things out on my own? ¡Coño! '*I have no clue about all this supernatural shit!*'

'*True,*' Beauty said, '*but you are well acquainted with what drives humans, aren't you?*'

She had me there. I shoved some ice cream and fruit down my gullet and tried to kick-start my mind into figuring out some logical motivations as to why a person would do this. Why bind souls in this way and be complicit in trying to destroy this place? '*Because they either didn't know what the bundle would be used for or didn't understand what Last Stop* actually *is*,' I said. '*With enough money or leverage, you can get most people to do just about anything. Like gathering a bunch of restless spirits and not asking questions.*'

And Desmond seemed the type to use such things to his advantage. Or find desperate individuals, nudge them mentally, then flood them with promises he never meant to keep. Like a person in the bruja's situation. Not that I would let Ida off the hook for it.

Beverly had finished her parfait, and now that the mini marshmallows had melted and the hot chocolate cooled, she was taking her first sip. I picked mine up and took a deep breath to allow the soothing scents of the cocoa to work their magic.

'*How did the souls go from looking like bundled sticks to that giant flesh thing?*' I asked.

'*I can't say for certain*,' Beauty replied, '*though I've a feeling the Death Blossom was somehow involved.*'

I swallowed a mouthful of hot chocolate, trying not to shudder before moving on to my next question. '*What happens to them now?*'

'I'll store them away,' Beauty said. *'Only a trained human can free them. Until we find one willing to work with us, they'll remain bound.'*

This time, the shudder tore through me with full force. That was a horrible fate. Might the mysterious Shaman Corps be able to help with that? But how would we know they weren't the ones helping Desmond in the first place? There were too many unknowns.

'What exactly was that flower anyway?' I asked.

Echoes of its screams rang in my head, making me shiver.

'A scourge. An abomination from the Abyss. Something that should never *have come so close to the living world.'* Though her words were telepathic, I felt furious anger behind them. That alone told me how bad it would have been for that thing to get an unchallenged toehold here. Desmond had taken a major gamble with this. ¡Pendejo!

'What would have happened if we hadn't killed it?' I asked.

Beauty hesitated longer on this one. *'Hokora would have disconnected herself from her anchors and cast herself adrift rather than allow it to escape.'*

That sounded super-duper bad. We would have all been trapped inside it, tumbling between dimensions, slowly turned insane by all the screaming and eventually becoming food for that evil weed.

"That was so good!" Beverly's enthusiastic voice dragged me back from the awful image. She beamed from ear to ear. Loaf was still happily gnawing on his bone.

"I'm glad, chiquita." And I was. It would be a pity to send her on, plagued by the feelings of fear and worry she'd suffered during the night.

"So am I." Beauty strolled in from the other side of the partial curtain. "And Beverly, we have a wonderful surprise for you."

The Beanie Baby floated in behind her. She must have found it on the stool. My still hazy brain had forgotten all about it.

Beverly squealed. "You found her!" The girl flew from her chair to intercept it. "Mystic!"

With a second manic squeal, she hugged the unicorn to her chest.

'*Was that a good idea?*' I mentally asked Beauty. '*Desmond could have added other booby traps.*'

Beauty jumped into Beverly's vacated seat. '*It's clean. The mirror showed no warnings now that we could examine it without the gift box's interference. I also sensed no power coming from it. The collar he placed on the toy was what carried and held the Death Blossom seed in check until Ida removed it.*'

'*She's going to pay for what she did, right?*' Just the thought of her getting away with only a slap on the wrist made my blood combust. The bruja had almost gotten all of us killed.

'*Oh, don't worry,*' Beauty said. '*Our dear Ida will get what's coming to her. Would you like to be present when I question her?*'

'*Claro que sí. I wouldn't miss it for the world.*' Watching the bruja squirm as she was grilled by a "lesser species" would be a treat.

'*Good.*' Beauty gave a low purr. "Beverly, can I count on you to guard Mystic for a while? It's been a very long night and trying night, and everyone should get some rest before we try to deliver her."

Beverly was still hugging the unicorn and had been whispering to her as if catching her up on all the things the Beanie Baby had missed. Her eyes sparkled as she answered Beauty's question. "Yes! I'll protect her. Loaf can provide backup."

Someone had seen too many cop shows. But hearing such a grown-up term spoken from so young a mouth made me smile.

"Thank you, Beverly." Beauty turned her emerald-colored gaze in my direction. "Tend to yourself and grab a few hours of rest. Ida has been safely tucked away where she won't be able to cause any more mischief once she wakes. We'll let her stew in her own juices for a while and come at her fresh first thing."

"I like this plan."

Running short on sleep wasn't something new for me, but I will admit it proved a lot harder to get out of bed that morning, despite the added enticement of questioning Bruja Ida. Having crawled upstairs after leaving the kitchen had almost done me in. Despite the sugar and chocolate, exhaustion had covered me from head to foot, weighing me down. I ached everywhere. Hokora or Ryo had left a tin of Tiger Balm Ultra Strength, which I had gratefully smeared all over after a hot soak in the tub. A couple of Advil hadn't hurt either.

Mira, I was so gone that even the jewelry box with the charm bracelet popping open and closed several times in a row, suddenly and frantically vying for my attention, hadn't bothered me. Whatever it wanted to say, I couldn't have cared less about.

Protein would be the order of the day. Loads of meat for breakfast, then Ida's blood for dessert. But first, I needed to make myself presentable. White linen slacks, flats, a red peplum shirt, and a long gold-plated chain necklace to wrap around the bruja's scrawny neck if necessary. Looking good and self-assured would serve to demoralize her a bit. I had no idea where Beauty had stashed her last night, but I was sure it hadn't been somewhere comfortable.

Everything about my rooms seemed and felt "normal"—for this place, anyway, not that I'd been here long enough yet to get used to all the nuances of the building. My old apartment might not have been much, but I'd known every quirky noise and smell to the point where the rooms almost spoke to me. Living spirit house or not, I figured Last Stop also had telltale signs—though last night's throes had been way more than what you'd expect from a regular structure.

The stairs had railings this morning. After the craziness before, I hoped they would become permanent additions. They would have helped a lot last night. Okay, maybe not. With the Death Blossom's induced terror, I might have grabbed onto one and never let go.

A shiver racked me as I rushed downstairs, memories of the evening's horror trying to force their way in. I had carried my flats with me, and at the bottom of the stairs I slipped them on, trying my best to continue to ignore the unwanted, panic-tinged prodding. Out of nowhere, soft, bubbling, cheerful music trickled all around me. Amazingly, it had more of an impact on pushing back the undesirable recollections than I did. I lightly touched the nearest wall. "Gracias."

The volume rose a notch.

Could buildings be traumatized? Could they feel fear or happiness? Why the hell not! Hokora had done her best to hold together long enough for us to come help. She had gotten Beverly out of the danger zone before losing all control. Last

Stop, according to Beauty, would have thrown herself into the void to keep the Death Blossom from infecting other planes of existence. She would have gone above and beyond.

Was it loco that somehow this reassured me? I'd been drinking too much of the Kool-Aid around here, that's for sure. Grinning to myself, I entered the restaurant area.

The scent of freshly brewed coffee and cooked bacon wafted in the air. The answering growl from my stomach quickened my steps. By the time I grabbed a seat, I was almost drooling. The temptation to go down the hall and head straight into the kitchen was strong, but I curbed the impulse. After the previous night, someone invading his workspace was probably the *last* thing Ryo wanted.

"¡Buenos dias!" I figured I might as well let him know I was here. I thought of adding "Feed me," but I was afraid of sounding too much like Audrey II from Little Shop of Horrors. Talk about meat and blood. Plus, I'd had my fill of deadly plants.

A second or two later, Ryo came through the curtain carrying culinary treasures. "Morning." The dapper dark chef's outfit was back, and so were the large, round glasses. In hindsight, he'd looked damn good in his black boxers and t-shirt, with the added bonus of his tousled hair. His normal clothes hid his well-developed muscles, which was a pity.

I mentally kicked myself back to reality. *Sheesh, chica. What's that about?*

Had that stupid weed given me brain damage? My feelings were all over the place this morning. I needed to get a grip. I required food.

Ryo set a carafe of café con leche and a plateful of thickly cut bacon in front of me. "Your omelet will be out in a moment." His gray gaze didn't meet mine, but the slight awkwardness from after our escape from the lounge was gone.

"Thanks for the Tiger Balm, by the way."

That got him looking in my direction. His imaginary tail was wagging. Ryo's tiny smile came and went, his cheeks coloring a little. "Ken thought it would help."

Now *that* surprised me. Had I somehow managed to score some points with the psycho? Was that a good thing or a bad thing? "Tell him gracias for me, then. It helped a lot."

Ryo's tail wagging revved to a mile a minute. He hurried back into the kitchen.

The moment I was sure he was gone, I dug into the bacon like a ravenous hyena. My eyes almost popped out of my head as I realized it wasn't ordinary bacon, but honeyed bacon. Sweet and savory flavors dueled for supremacy over my taste buds. If there was one plus about being stuck working here, it was *this*. That boy could cook!

I was about halfway through the pile when he returned carrying a platter with a huge ham and cheese omelet, accompanied by a side of blueberries and bananas. I almost squealed like Beverly at the sight. It disappeared almost as fast as the bacon.

Beauty sauntered in as I took my last bite, sure I'd soon explode. That honeyed bacon should be outlawed. But I could feel all the protein and carbs going to work.

"Good morning," Beauty said, then jumped onto the counter. Ryo came through the curtains from the kitchen, wiping his hands.

Emerald eyes studied us. "You're both feeling better, I hope?" Beauty asked.

Ryo slightly inclined his head. I shrugged, which I should have avoided since it sent painful little reminders of the abuse my muscles had taken, then added, "Well enough. I'll be even better once I get a crack at Ida."

Beauty's eyes were half closed, her ears forward and relaxed, her tail wrapping around her feet. "I am rather looking forward to that myself," she said. "Let's go indulge, shall we?"

A feral grin settled on my face. "Let's."

Ryo joined us in the hallway at the kitchen's exit, and then Beauty led the way to a sliding door I didn't recall as having been there before. Inside, the small, wood-floored room was empty. Had the bruja escaped? Before I could ask what was going on, a wall slid open, showing a tiny, closed-in compartment. Ida was nestled within it, sitting on a hard armchair.

Dried blood clung to the bruja's ears and nose. Her gray and black streaked hair was in disarray, her clothes rumpled. Ida's face was a rabid dog's as she spotted us, all snarls and hate, hoping someone would come near enough for her to bite.

The chair floated out of the closet and settled in the middle of the room. Nothing held her to the seat that I could see, but aside from her head being able to turn and glare our way, the rest of her was frozen in place.

"Release me at once!" she demanded, her eyes wide, their color showing hints of green and rolling in their sockets. The bruja was almost frothing at the mouth.

I choked back a laugh. She was an entitled bruja through and through.

"My dear Ida," Beauty said, sitting straight in front of her, "despite your timeout, I can see you've not given your predicament any thought at all."

"I didn't do anything!" Ida screamed, the cords standing out on her neck.

"I don't recall accusing you, but now that you've brought it up…" Beauty's eyes turned to slits, the tip of her tail twitching as if she were about to pounce. "Ida Rolls, you've betrayed and threatened our most sacred trust. First, you leaked the details of a *child's* unfinished business to an outsider."

"I nev—" Ida's mouth clamped shut, and from the shock blaring on her face, she hadn't been the one to do it.

"Second, because of your actions, a being who had helped us was nearly murdered."

Ida rolled her eyes, obviously not caring about that in the least.

"Third, you allowed yourself to be deceived and used by one of the males you so despise, and in doing so, almost destroyed the spirit house, nearly killed everyone currently inside her, and risked releasing a Death Blossom into the physical plane."

Ida's chin jutted out, and she stared down her nose at Beauty with a pleased look on her face.

"I see you don't quite understand everything I've just said," Beauty said, her right ear turning to the side. "Let me explain, shall I? You tried to commit suicide when you followed Desmond's instructions."

Ida's plucked brows drew slightly together.

"Don't you find it odd that, after doing what he requested of you, you have no recollection of anything that occurred afterwards?" Beauty asked her, brimming with innocent curiosity. "Maybe you didn't have time to realize what happened before you were knocked unconscious from standing at ground zero?"

"What are you blabbering about?" Ida asked, her lips free again.

I tackled this one. "Do we really have to spell it out for you? Your buddy set you up. Whatever he promised you, he never intended to pay it. He used his demon powers, messed with your mind to sway you, and made you his bitch. You made yourself an easy mark, and after you did what he wanted, you became a loose end. The cabrón meant for you to die."

Chapter 35

There was something devilishly satisfying in watching my words register in Ida's mind, and her bitter dawning comprehension. Her face drained of color as her eyes moved back and forth, not seeing us but replaying all that had happened in her head, and worst of all, realizing that everything I'd said was true. The player had been played.

Tears gathered at the corner of her eyes for a moment, her face twisting with what I guessed was years of buried pain from her repressed childhood, unearthed once more by the fact that she had been used—again.

"You lie!" Ida's admonition sounded more like a child's desperate plea.

Desmond might not be human, but he was still a prince, and could ooze charm when he felt like it. And some of his opinions closely paralleled hers with regard to status and being better than the rabble. Treating her as an equal and lamenting her plight would have gone a long way toward lowering her defenses enough to allow him to give her a mental push. It was the exact type of tactic Pierson would have used, except he didn't have powers to help seal the deal.

Ida's cheeks turned beet red, and a low growl issued from her throat as she intered her pain once again and put more of the dots together.

"You should thank Daniela for her above-and-beyond efforts to drag you to safety," Beauty added, tilting her head. "If not for her, you wouldn't have survived. The Death Blossom was about to use you as food when Dani intervened, at great personal risk." She blinked slowly, enjoying the moment. "It would have been a long and agonizing demise as it drained everything you had to give. As you became just another source of fear, pain, and despair to add to its repertoire."

That's when the bruja lost it. She gave a guttural scream, too incensed for words. If Beauty hadn't kept her body locked in position on the chair, she would have been thrashing all over the place. Though I knew it wouldn't help, I smiled sweetly at Ida. She screamed even louder, the veins popping out near her forehead as her blood pressure spiked.

The woman hated the fact that someone like me had saved her life; hated it more than the fact that Desmond had messed with her head and tried to get rid of her. Now *that* was truly pathetic. ¡Idiota bruja! Delusions of racial superiority had put such large blinders on her that it was the only thing she could see.

That was also when I realized what had made Ida desperate enough to fall for Desmond's tricks. Dani, the lower life form, had come into the mix. *I* could go outside. *I* was allowed to help with the dead's unfinished business. That a "spic" was offered all the things she had been denied must have felt like the worst insult. Desmond knew her, or at least enough to tell what buttons were best to push. Worse, by using my presence to push her, she had thought she'd finally found an ally, perhaps even made a friend. She had grabbed at the possibility and been burned for it.

I wasn't entirely sure how to feel about that.

We all waited patiently for her tantrum to be over. Beauty groomed herself while I crossed my arms and watched the show. Ryo wore a small, confused frown as he viewed her antics. After the Death Blossom, her frothing shrieks were only a bothersome noise and did little to affect any of us. It was too bad the bruja never got a taste of the nasty horror she'd unleashed.

Ida eventually ran out of steam and just glared at us, her lips curled in disgust. Her voice was rougher than usual when she spoke again. "Enjoying yourselves at my expense, are you?"

Ryo's frown deepened. I grinned. Beauty stopped licking her leg and sat as she had before. "Dear Ida, you're not all *that* entertaining," she said. "We were merely waiting for you to get your frustrations out of your system before resuming our talk." She yawned. "Are you ready now, or do you still need a little more time for your hysterics?"

I might have felt a smidgeon of pity for the bruja at this point. Not that she didn't deserve every last bit of what she got.

Ida's features twisted first one way and then another, her eyes smoldering with flesh-stripping loathing. Then, little by little, she sucked it all in, her expression turning into a chiseled, neutral mask. Her gaze continued to burn. She wasn't fooling anyone, but it would have to do. "Talk away, *cat*."

"That's better." A hint of a purr momentarily trilled in the air. "And do buck up. I doubt you'll be happy about what I'm about to say next."

Ida's eyes widened minutely at that, but she remained silent.

"I've been too lenient with you," Beauty said, "so part of the responsibility for this disaster lies with me. I also gave you too much credit, never having thought you were so desperate that you'd fall for such an obvious trick, even if he used his powers against you to make you more compliant."

Ida's lip curled again and twitched erratically for a few seconds before she got it back under control.

"I won't ask what he offered to tempt you onto this foolish path," Beauty continued. "It would only make you look stupider than you do already." She tsked. "You've foolishly forgotten that I am the *only one* keeping you from your original fate. The indignities you suffer here would feel like paradise in comparison to what awaits you. Not even Desmond can stop your reward for the crimes that you've committed."

Beauty's presence suddenly filled the entire space. She expanded in size, and the chamber followed suit, the floor widening and carrying Ryo and me away from her to give her room. Like I'd seen her do once before, she started looking less and less like a cat and more like a giant-sized lion. She continued to change until her fur became more of a fog, her eyes glowing as they became independent orbs. Her teeth grew to the size of deadly swords.

Despite being on the periphery, the sheer weight of her essence was overwhelming. To be the target of her focus would be terrifying. Ida's head was tilted back, doing her best to get as far away as possible. The prickling in my gut told me this message might not be for the bruja alone. I tried to suppress a shudder.

"The *only* means to ease that eventual reckoning is by serving Hokora and me. And at the moment, I'm finding it very difficult to see why I should bother to put up with you rather than send you on your way. Toys like you are everywhere, and oh so easily replaced." Beauty's monstrous form leaned into Ida's personal space until her teeth were but a mere inch away from the bruja's face. "Is that what you want?"

I wasn't sure Ida was breathing anymore. She shook her head so fast it was almost a blur. If she became any paler, she'd have no color at all.

Beauty shrank back to normal size. "Glad to hear it." She stood on all fours and turned away from Ida, bushy tail raised high. Ryo and I followed her out.

As soon as the door slid closed behind us, I spoke. "You really think that will do it? That she'll mend her ways?" The bruja's type wasn't logical even at the best of times.

"Anything is possible." Her tail swayed from side to side as she led us toward the restaurant area. "Like I said, she is not the only one at fault. And as you so aptly pointed out, Desmond likely used his abilities to sway her into going along with his plans." Her tail and ears drooped. "I've grown complacent, and I apologize for that. I'll be monitoring everything a lot more closely from now on."

I slowed, not liking the sound of that. But to stop something as terrible as a Death Blossom from becoming a problem again, I supposed there was no choice. "What will you do about Desmond?"

A drawn-out sigh filled the hallway. "There's not much that can be done directly, despite Ida still being alive as a witness.

Her hatred of men is well-documented. Desmond would insist he'd merely stretched out a friendly hand and that she was only implicating him as a means to escape her guilt.

"He'd also use the incident as a platform to highlight my incompetence in allowing it to happen in the first place. Sending Ida to her just reward now would also be noted. Any attention we bring to this will only end up being to his benefit, just as he intended." Her tail dragged behind her on the ground.

Ugh! I was so tired of backstabbers getting their way. "He won't give up either. He doesn't seem the type."

Beauty shook her head. "I'm afraid you're right." Then she glanced at us and flashed her canines. "But now that we've stopped the main leak, he'll find it harder to get what he wants. His ability to compel others won't sway Ida anymore after this betrayal. And if I have anything to say about it, he'll also discover what it's like to be prey." Her eyes glittered.

That was definitely something to look forward to.

"Wait for me at the counter, won't you?" Beauty asked. "I want to sift through last night's gifts and see if there is anything useful that you can take with you. Desmond likely has lookouts keeping watch for when Last Stop reconnects to the physical plane and to see when you leave to finish Beverly's request. Hokora moving to a different location before and after you exit will prove helpful."

If Ida had given him information about our final destination, I wasn't positive relocating would make much of a difference.

But there was also no point in making things easy for him. "Agreed."

Ryo and I continued into the restaurant while Beauty took a detour upstairs. The cook had yet to say a word. The slight frown he'd picked up while we'd talked to Ida was still there.

"Is something wrong?" I asked him.

He glanced over at me, his gray eyes clouded. "I don't understand."

I grabbed a stool at the counter and motioned for him to do the same. "Don't understand what?"

He blinked several times as if fishing for the right words. "Why Ida did what she did." His gaze met mine. "Life is good here. We have a purpose. There is redemption."

My naïve little perrito. "Some people can't see how great they have it. Others, even when they do, covet more." Ryo's frown deepened. "Humans are innately selfish," I said. "We're wired that way. For survival. Many fight against it, whilc others wholeheartedly embrace it. And the latter fits our bruja to a T."

His brow didn't clear.

I cracked some mental knuckles. "Ida's also the type who likes to be in control. Almost like she needs it to stay sane. So she resents Beauty for forcing her to stay here, despite the fact that it keeps her from something worse and could help reduce her ultimate punishment. So when the opportunity came, she let herself be swayed into a monumentally stupid plot," I said, drawing figure eights on the counter. "Desmond wouldn't normally have been able to win her compliance, but he used her vulnerabilities against her. She went along so she could feel she was back in charge of her own life again."

Desperation and the need for control were weaknesses my old boss loved to exploit when running a scam. Picking pockets was a lot easier and took less planning, but it never hurt to know how and why things were done. Sadly, despite knowing better, Jay never realized Bobby was using those methods on him, and it had gotten him killed. Some people were too trusting for their own good. Jay's misguided love for Bobby and his desire to help me be free had doomed him. Ryo looked to be the same, though I doubted Ken was. How that was possible—I had no idea.

"Do you feel that way too?" Ryo asked me.

Now, there was a tricky question. "I don't know, to be honest. Full control over my life hasn't been something I've ever truly experienced. I was quite young when Abuela got really sick. We had no other relatives or money, just the little house we lived in." It felt weird talking about this. It surprised me to be doing it at all. "There was this local man everyone knew about. Someone you could go to when you had no other choice. So I went to him, and we made a deal. He would help Abuela and keep me out of the system so we could be together again once she got better. While she was away, I joined the other kids he was helping. We took tests, learned things, ran errands, and did a bunch of other things until he decided the best way for me to pay him back."

Not that it had turned out like I'd hoped in the end. Abuela had died, and the debt had still needed to be paid. Still, I'd been lucky. Small as I had been, I could get into all sorts of places. Listen in on conversations and report what was said. People didn't pay a lot of attention to kids and typically underestimated what they could do. That they discovered I had a talent for pickpocketing also helped a lot in the long run. A way to pay my debt without having to sell my body to do it.

Why in the world was I telling him this?

"Anyway, because of all that, being able to make my own choices and having control over my life weren't something I had a lot of." I swept my hand over the counter where I'd been making the figures eights.

I glanced over at him. "Did you have control over yours?"

His eyes took on a faraway look.

"Do as you're told. Question nothing. Perform beyond your limits. To fail is to die." The phrases slipped from his mouth like chained weights—as if they had been pounded into him and carved onto his flesh.

I repressed a shudder. "I'll take that as a "no" then." Was that why he had DID? How bad had things been to push him to it?

He shrugged. "It's better now."

'Daniela, please refrain from asking him any further questions on that topic.' Beauty's voice poured softly into my

mind. '*As I am sure you've guessed, his existence has not been an easy one. And he is but one of thousands of children swept into illegal programs to create controllable soldiers or assassins. Most never even reach puberty.*'

Her voice grew soft, and it made what she said next all the more horrifying for it. '*They broke him into pieces, but rather than fall apart, those pieces banded together through harmonious internal cooperation to help Ryo survive. A rare feat for those with this affliction to manage without outside help. In the end, integration or continued cooperation will be up to them to decide. Regardless of what they choose, I'm hoping that here, he at least has a chance to live a better life and have more control over it.*'

I had to look aside from his earnest face before I inadvertently gave something away. "I'm glad."

"Thank you for waiting." Beauty sauntered in, tail high, as if she hadn't just delivered me a mental bomb. She jumped on the counter between us, with a small, familiar lacquered case floating behind her. "Most of the gifts were for Hokora or the group—decorations and the like. But a couple of items were meant to be added to a previous gift from years ago." Her eyes glittered as if laughing at an inside joke.

I tried not to react as I realized she had probably told others that the crazy bracelet had taken an interest in me. But why go to the trouble to do that? "I thought you said I couldn't use it?"

The box settled before her. The bothersome lid popped open on its own yet again, as if eager to get on with things. Aside from the charms I'd noted on it before, it now also held a silvery snowflake. Had Akasha given a gift as well? Despite not being invited to the banquet?

"Things have changed," Beauty said with a purr. "The requirements are no longer an issue." She blinked slowly. "Put it on. If it still wants and accepts you, I will explain further."

I sat back and threw her a look. Mira, that did not sound exactly kosher. This thing had been "stalking" me since the first time I'd seen it. The cursed thing had even planted itself in my bathroom, trying to tempt me to put it on. And what did Beauty mean when she said the requirements were no longer an issue?

But if it would help… I held my breath as I took the bracelet out of the case and slipped it on. It tingled for a moment on my skin, then it felt like it wasn't there. Despite all the charms, there was no weight to it at all, and it made no sound. It would be easy to forget that I was wearing it.

"Excellent." Beauty tapped the lid of the lacquer box closed. "Artifacts can be a bit choosy at times, but it seems its interest in you was genuine." She gave a soft purr. "Most of the trinkets attached imbue passive protection for different things—mental attacks, evil spirits, curses, that sort of thing. But a few of them will need to be activated in order for them to work. The bracelet itself will show you which might be helpful in various situations. It's my understanding that the charm suggested will glow."

¿Qué? It could do that? Maybe it wasn't such a good idea to have the thing after all. While I considered removing it, the chain shrank to fit against my skin, and the clasp disappeared as the bracelet made itself a connected whole.

"How do I take it off?" Dread filled me to the brim, sure I already knew the answer, but I had to ask.

"You don't," Beauty said. "And no one else will be able to either, unless you're dead." She looked smug again.

¡Qué mierda! Why did I keep falling for her tricks? I kept my expression purposely neutral. No point in giving her the satisfaction of seeing me upset. ¡Gata mala!

Beverly walked in from the right hallway, Mystic nestled in her arms. Loaf trotted along, bringing up the rear. I would have to save some choice words to serve Beauty later in private.

The chiquita bit her lip when she stopped before us. "It's time?" she asked.

"Yes." Beauty jumped to the floor. "We do appreciate your patience, little one. Ryo and Dani will go deliver Mystic for you now. Linda's currently at home, so we'd best get on with it."

How did she know that? Did Beauty use the local spirits for keeping tabs on others as well as for information? Like Desmond did?

Beverly nodded, looking somber, and held out the unicorn like an offering. I stood, then kneeled before her to take it. "Anything you'd like us to tell Linda for you?" I asked.

Her little brow furrowed as she thought about it. Then her brown eyes glimmered. "Just that I'm sorry, and that she was the bestest friend ever."

I gave her arm a gentle squeeze. "I'm sure that'll make her very happy."

Beverly jumped forward and wrapped her arms around my neck, hiding her face in my shoulder. "Thank you."

Then she let go and ran off. Loaf let out an excited bark before giving chase.

I straightened, my eyes itching, and wondered if she'd be gone before we made it back. It would be for the best if she were. Watching Jay leave me behind had been hard enough. Getting attached only brought heartache.

Chapter 36

Gearing up to brave the frozen wasteland outside didn't take long. I'm not exaggerating, okay? To me, that much white and cold was unnatural.

Luckily, it was another cloudless day without wind, so I could manage. Ryo had brought out a bag with a flap to keep Mystic dry and hidden. Last Stop opened its doors a block or two away from Linda Fletcher's house, which was on the same street as Beverly's. Driveways and sidewalks had been shoveled, and rock salt was seeded everywhere, so my footing was steady, which was a relief.

Since we were in the suburbs rather than the city, it was a lot quieter. A streak of crimson caught my attention and turned out to be a red cardinal flying from one tree to another.

Nothing else was moving about. After the number of spirits that had followed us the day before, I was surprised not to see any today. Were they steering away because of what had happened the evening before?

Beverly had said that Last Stop's façade had shimmered in and out, and that had scared her plenty. Perhaps it had done that to them as well. It was also likely that Akasha's predilection for wanting people to dance for her discouraged minor spirits from rolling around anywhere near her turf.

It was either one of those, or they knew something we didn't. My gut kept insisting Desmond wasn't finished. I wanted desperately to be wrong. From the slight tension I could sense coming from Ryo, I had a feeling his instincts were also full of misgivings.

Would Desmond make a move before or after we completed Beverly's unfinished business? I doubted he would gain anything from making us fail at this point, but I didn't know enough about demonic psychology to have a clue.

A murder of crows flew by overhead. I hadn't thought to look under Last Stop's awning to see if the pair I'd glimpsed before were still there—maybe they'd joined with some friends. My abuela would have called seeing them a bad omen. Hopefully, it meant nothing at all.

We walked on to the Fletchers' porch without incident and rang the bell. Ryo turned his back on me as we waited, keeping his eye on the street and nearby yards for unexpected surprises. I took a deep breath to steady my jittery nerves.

The front door opened, answered by a portly woman wearing jeans and a space-themed t-shirt with a wolf on it. "Hey there. May I help you?"

Dios mío, how was she not freezing? My body temp fell ten degrees just seeing her with nothing else on in this weather. I'd have put on a coat before answering the door! "Hi! My name is Maria Gomez. I work at Linda's school. Can we come in for a minute?"

She stared at me, then Ryo, a crease forming on her forehead. "Well, her parents aren't home right now. Could you come back later? I'm just the babysitter."

"Honestly, how do you *do* it?" I asked, ignoring her suggestion while making my eyes widen a little.

"Do what?"

I gave a shudder. "Survive in this cold!" I waved my arm around. "In this warmth-stealing weather. I only moved here recently, and nobody warned me how glacial it would be. Winter wonderlands might be nice to look at on TV, but being out in it? Not so much."

The woman laughed. "You get used to it." She grinned. "We don't even call this cold. Thirty is balmy."

I didn't need to fake my horrified expression. She must be part Inuit.

The babysitter chuckled again and waved us in. "I can make some hot tea or coffee if you want it. Help you thaw out a little."

"No, that's okay," I said. "This shouldn't take long." Once I got back to Last Stop, I'd be having a gallon-sized cup. Maybe take a bath in it. I lowered my voice a little. "You know about Beverly Price?"

The woman's expression drooped. "I couldn't believe it! That girl was so full of energy and was as cheerful as could be," she said. "I've babysat for the Prices as well."

The woman glanced back over her shoulder as if to check that no one was around. "That's where the Fletchers are—checking up on them. Linda wanted to go, but they said no. She's pretty upset about it."

"I understand where they are coming from, though. For Linda to see Beverly's devastated parents wouldn't have made grieving easier for her. Though I still think they should have let her attend the funeral for the burial part, so she could say goodbye. But what can you do?" She shrugged, her mouth twisting.

I nodded. "Well, I was the one tasked with clearing out Beverly's personal items."

The woman flinched. So far, so good.

"Among them was a Beanie Baby that Beverly's parents insisted didn't belong to her. But they were pretty sure it was Linda's."

The babysitter's eyes grew wider and wider as I spoke. "OMG! It's a unicorn, right?" I nodded again. "Do you have it with you? Linda has been frantic to find the thing. She's been super upset about it. With her gran gone and now her best friend…" She grimaced, but her eyes shone with hope.

I held up the bag.

"Thank you, Lord!" She turned around. "Linda, come quick! They found Mystic!"

A somber little face peeked out from the nearby family room. The young girl studied the three of us for a moment before stepping out. With twin braids, her dark hair, and closed expression, she reminded me of a young Wednesday Addams. The poor thing had had too much reality dumped on her too quickly.

I knew the feeling.

I scrunched down and signaled for her to come closer. "You might not believe it, but Beverly left a message for you. Do you want to hear it?" I opened the bag and removed Mystic so Linda could see it.

Her little gasp echoed around us at the sight of it. The babysitter stepped out of the foyer to give Linda some room.

I held the Beanie Baby out with both hands, much like Beverly had done not too long before. Tears welled in the girl's eyes, then fell unimpeded. Step by hesitant step, she came closer, as if imagining this to be a cruel trick, some grown-up scheme to try to placate her.

Linda took a last step and gingerly reached for the Beanie Baby. The moment she touched it, all her doubts disappeared. "*Mystic!*"

She hugged the unicorn to her chest, also much like Beverly had done.

I straightened and put my hand gently on the girl's head.

"Beverly said she was sorry she grabbed it without permission and didn't get it back to you," I told her. "And she wanted you to know that you were the *bestest* friend she's ever had."

Linda's little face bunched up, but miraculously, there were no more tears. "She's with Gran now. I hope she becomes her best friend, too, and keeps Gran from being lonely."

"You know, Mystic could do the same for you," I said, my heart squeezing inside my chest. "She can remind you of both of them and all the fun you had together. I think it would make them both very happy, don't you?"

Linda bobbed her head, then walked away with Mystic cradled in her arms, not as somber as before.

Though Linda had held back her tears, the babysitter couldn't. "That's so sweet!" she blubbered, pulling a wad of tissues from the pocket of her jeans. At least she was prepared.

"Thanks so much for letting us talk to her," I said, meaning it. "We really appreciate it."

"No, thank *you*!" She noisily blew her nose. "I truly believe you've helped her a lot today. That was very kind."

"That's nice of you to say. But we couldn't have done it without you. So thanks for that." I smiled, an honest-to-goodness real one, for once. "We should be going now." Ryo had already opened the door behind me.

For once, I didn't mind the cold—my insides were nice and toasty. My first unfinished business mission was over. And it left a different, more profound feeling of satisfaction than all the other jobs I'd done before. I could get used to that.

As we stepped off the Fletchers' porch, though, it also felt a little anticlimactic.

Not that it stayed that way for long.

Chapter 37

Once we made it to the street and about halfway down the block, my left wrist, where Beauty's charm bracelet sat against my skin, grew hot. ¡Coño! I'd jinxed myself. Something was up. "Ryo!"

"Over there." His gaze cut to a large oak in a nearby yard. The air near it shimmered like a curtain for a moment before Desmond stepped out, seemingly from nowhere. I spotted the double furball who had threatened me inside Last Stop and who had turned out to be doing Desmond's bidding, rolling for all it was worth in the opposite direction.

The *chota*. He had been lying in wait to narc us out to the demon prince the moment we left Linda's. If I ever got my hands on it, it would pay for being a shitty little snitch!

Unlike at the party last night, Desmond's three-piece suit was now a muted brownish-gray. Kind of like the half-melted slush I'd seen on the busier streets in town. His human guise smiled in our direction. "Beauty's two little human helpers! What a coincidence running into you here."

As if. I wasn't sure why he bothered with the shallow subterfuge. Neither of us was going to buy what he was selling. Though the BS could be for someone else's benefit. Just because I couldn't see them didn't mean they weren't there.

"I doubt that very much," I said. "So let's get this over with, shall we? What do you want?" Turning our backs on him or ignoring him would be monumentally stupid, but I didn't have to like the necessary interaction.

"Such hostility," he answered with a tsk. "Do try to remember who you're talking to. You may be under Beauty's purview, but it won't stop you from getting hurt if you blatantly offend your betters."

Pressure built inside my head, whispering that I was in the wrong. I should drop to my knees and beg for his apology. But I found it easy to backhand the suggestion into oblivion. Beauty's claim that the bracelet imbued the wearer with several passive protections seemed legit. It pissed me off that he was trying to mentally sway me again, though. *¡Pendejo!*

I held back the urge to give him the finger. He would have to try harder to push this Boricua around.

I threw a glance in Ryo's direction to see if he was affected, but like before, he seemed to be holding his own. "Sorry, it's hard to show respect to someone who's tried to twist our will and kill us."

The demon prince had the gall to raise a splayed hand to his chest and look shocked. "Are you accusing me of something?" He took several slow steps toward us.

We had no choice but to stand our ground or step out into the street. No one was around, but cars could drive by at any moment, so the second choice was out. "I'm just stating facts," I said. "And you still haven't answered my question. What do you want?"

'*Beauty! Can you hear me?*' I asked mentally. I heard nothing back.

"Stalling for time, are we? How quaint," Desmond said. "And I see you've garnered a protection or two. Not that they will do you any good in the end."

Mira, what was up with this guy? Sheesh! "What. Do. You. Want?"

Ryo smoothly half-stepped in front of me when Desmond got close, every muscle taut. It was awfully sweet of him. Somehow, I doubted it would stop the demon for more than a moment if he attacked us—though I would be more than happy to be proved wrong.

A grin tugged at the side of Desmond's mouth as if Ryo's repositioning amused him. "I want the two of you to work for me," he said. "I can be quite generous when I choose to be."

"Like when you left Ida to become plant food after she did as you asked?" How stupid did he think we were?

"Come now." Desmond's eyes shone. "I was doing the world a favor. It doesn't have to be that way for you," he said.

Protected or not, it didn't stop him from pushing his will on me again, trying to entice me to see him in a favorable light. Did he have to force Ida's cooperation along as well? Or did she fall for his bullshit without prompting? Not that it mattered.

"And if we say no?"

"It would be in your best interest not to consider that answer." His golden eyes turned cold. "Things could get messy if you do."

Like I was going to let this cabrón push me around. He kept forgetting I was a Boricua, and a stubborn one at that. A glance from Ryo told me he was all in. I guess I might be joining Jay sooner than I thought. "N. O. No."

My wrist burned, not that I needed the bracelet to tell me to move when Desmond reached out to grab me. I threw myself to the right while Ryo went to the left, even as he threw a couple of those thin knives of his into Desmond's side, eliciting a faint hiss.

The demon took umbrage at that and swept out his hand, nails extending to sharp points. Though he wasn't near Ryo, I saw an afterimage of the sweep extend straight toward him. Ryo leaped higher than I would have thought possible and to the right to avoid it as he sent more blades flying in Desmond's direction.

But Desmond was ready for them this time, and he brushed them aside as if they were nothing. We were so screwed.

I scrambled to take cover behind a tree, racking my brains about what I could do rather than cower, waiting for my turn to die. ¡Mierda! Last Stop had internet and cell reception. Did that mean Beauty had a phone? Might she be in my contacts?

Before I could pull the phone out, my wrist warmed again. The snowflake charm on my bracelet was glowing. Too desperate to freak out about it, I yanked off my glove and squeezed the ornament for all I was worth. A woozy sensation whooshed momentarily through me as if something had been sucked out. Hoping I wasn't wrong about who had given this to me, I called out, "Akasha! I found someone to dance for you!"

The effect was immediate. The temperature dropped fifteen degrees in seconds, turning my breath almost solid as my lungs tried to shrivel inside me. Snow and wind blew around us in a sudden storm, then parts of it drew together, coalescing into Akasha's angular, icy blue-skinned form.

"Girl of fire." I couldn't help but shiver as she smiled at me with her jagged, icicle-like teeth. "I have come."

Struggling to put my glove back on, I tried to ignore the fact that I couldn't feel my fingers anymore. "Thank you for that."

Ryo flew backward and rolled several times on the snow-covered ground before springing once more to his feet, his coat and pants torn in several places. Knives flew from him faster than I could count, then he dived sideways away from us, having spotted us and trying to buy us more time to come up with a plan.

Akasha watched them go at each other with interest. Ryo fought with everything he had, keeping his distance from the prince, but aside from a tear or two on the demon's suit, he wasn't getting anywhere. Desmond appeared to play at it, as if Ryo were but a momentary amusement.

"What kind of dance is this?" Akasha asked.

"A bad one," I said. "Desmond means to brainwash or end us to get back at Beauty. But if he does, Ryo won't be able to make his special drinks for you anymore." I was reaching, not having the faintest idea whether this would prove to be an impetus for her, but I knew of nothing else she cared about.

"No more gingerbread martinis?" The angles of her icy face grew sharper and more pronounced.

"Not if Desmond kills him, no." I took a deep breath. "Will you help us?"

I swear the temperature dropped another ten degrees, the surrounding storm expanding and growing more intense. Akasha stepped away from the tree and glided in Desmond's direction. He noticed her immediately and looked her up and down with contempt, while still easily defending himself from Ryo's continued attacks.

"You'd best run along, elemental," Desmond said to her. "This does not concern you."

"This is my domain, not yours, little princeling." She gave him a jagged smile and performed a perfect pirouette. "And I want you to dance for me."

"As if I'd ever stoop so low." He stared down his nose at her. "Begone before I lose my patience and destroy you."

Ryo crouched and started making his way toward me, using whatever cover he could find, while Desmond had his attention focused on Akasha. Blood trickled from several places on his person, leaving bright red dots on the fresh snow. The elemental spirit giggled with amusement. "Now I want you to dance for me more and more!"

Desmond raised his foot and stomped the ground. I gave a startled yelp as the terrain shook beneath me, almost throwing me off my feet. The few parked cars in the area rocked on the street as if pushed, setting off at least one car alarm. This insanity was getting out of control! These two could destroy the entire neighborhood if they went at it!

What had I done?

"We should go." Ryo's warm breath tickled my ear, and I nearly yelped again, not having noticed that he'd reached me. The wind and snow were picking up, rattling the trees and cutting visibility. Icy fingers crawled inside every nook and cranny, but my insides had already turned to ice for other reasons.

Akasha's excited giggles echoed in the air, completely unaffected by Desmond's blow to the ground, despite it having left a slight crater behind.

I grabbed his arm. "We *can't!* We have to stop this. People could die!" Our mutated milk run was now turning into a possible death spree. Instead of completing someone's unfinished business so they could move on, I would be responsible for sending a few more of the living to an early grave. Including Beverly's friend, Linda.

The demon prince sent two of the odd sweeping blows in Akasha's direction, but she avoided them with ease. The unlucky lawn gnome tucked on the edge of the nearest porch wasn't as fortunate, slashed into pieces and flung all over the lawn.

Ryo frowned, blinking rapidly, his glasses still miraculously sitting on his face, despite his having been thrown about at least once. "I don't have the power to stop them. Ken can't help." Puppy dog eyes stared at me in entreaty. "Tell me what to do."

He was the one with experience and knowledge about all this craziness. I threw my hands in the air. "*How the hell should I know?*"

Yelling at him wouldn't get me anywhere, but *come on!*

I thought I heard a car engine and the sound of a door, but it was hard to hear clearly over all the screaming wind and sounds of battle. Adding innocent bystanders to the mix was so not what we needed right now!

My wrist grew warm again. The crystal cube charm was glowing. I hesitated, as following its prompt the last time was how we'd gotten into this current mess. I might inadvertently make matters worse. I didn't exactly know how it might do that, but it could!

But I really didn't have any other options.

I took off my glove again, found the ornament, said a quick prayer, and squeezed.

Chapter 38

Mira, I don't know what I was expecting, but what we got wasn't it. The moment I put pressure on the charm, a semi-invisible box grew and grew and grew from it until it had all of us inside it with room to spare. The woozy feeling returned, worse than before, forcing me to lean on the tree trunk to keep my feet. Neither of the supernatural combatants seemed to notice the field, or if they did, they didn't care that it was there.

The storm was trapped inside the cube, and it raged even harder. The giant box rattled and shook as the attacks within increased in intensity and blowback. It had gone up just in time, but why had it put Ryo and me inside it?

From the strength of the blows Akasha and Desmond were now trading with each other, the neighboring trees and homes should have been blown to pieces, sending deadly shrapnel everywhere. But that wasn't the case. The tree I was hiding behind felt different than before, less substantial, and it was unaffected by the storm or the fighting—as if everything inside were now slightly out of phase with the physical plane and could no longer be directly affected.

Might this be the parallel dimension Beauty had spoken of, where most of the spirits here spent their time? Whatever the truth was, the effect was keeping the area within it safe and also preventing the combatants' powers from leaking out. But how long the encasing field would hold, I had no idea.

Glancing past the tree, I saw that Akasha and Desmond were going at it with no signs of stopping anytime soon. Pleased, bell-like laughter echoed through the storm.

Glad somebody's enjoying all this. I sure wasn't.

"Ryo, does Desmond have any weaknesses that you know of?" I asked. He had hunkered down beside me, using the tree for what little protection it might provide, while still keeping an eye on the fight. "Can any of your weapons harm him at all?"

He slipped me a glance, then returned to watching the combatants. "Yes. But getting close enough to slip a blow past his defenses was proving difficult. His reaction times are too fast."

Ryo removed one of his flat-black blades and handed it over. "If he comes for you, wait until he's close and use it. He won't be expecting you to have it."

I palmed the knife and hid it in my sleeve. The cold metal almost burned my skin like a brand as it drew heat from me as it warmed.

Ryo then removed his glasses and tucked them away. His features smoothed into a mask and his eyes became bereft of emotion as Ken took over. He reached over to the back of his neck inside his coat and unsheathed a black metal sword that seemed to expand as he drew it out. It looked sharp and deadly. "We might have just been given an opportunity," Ken said. A fierce hunger flashed in his eyes. "*If* you dare to take it."

I glanced past the tree again, squinting to make out details past the swirling storm. Akasha and Desmond were now facing each other, their hands locked as they both pushed at one another, engaged in a battle of wills and strength.

Desmond's human guise had dropped, and his moving flesh, tall spiral horns, and weird flaming crown were now visible. Fighting the elemental appeared to require all of his focused attention, despite his boasting earlier. The mad, unnatural storm raged close around them. Akasha's mirth rang louder than before. They both looked as if they could keep this up forever.

My insides knotted and cramped as I realized what Ken meant—psycho-boy wanted us to go out there and attack

Desmond while he and Akasha remained locked with one another. But I wasn't a combatant. He was the one with fighting skills. Exposing myself to be pummeled by Desmond was *not* how I would survive this. But letting Ken go at it alone also meant a reduced chance of him—and Ryo—coming out of this alive. And if they were killed, we would be no closer to getting rid of the demon prince.

Gritting my teeth, knowing I was being the biggest idiota in the world, I gave a nod. "What do you want me to do?"

An eager, savage grin split his face. I held my breath, knowing I was not going to like his answer.

"Follow the sidewalk and get behind him, then run in and slash his flesh if you can," Ken said. "I'll do the same from the opposite side."

Desmond's true form didn't have eyes. "Won't he sense us coming?"

Ken's savage grin grew wider. "As long as she's holding onto him, it won't make much difference if he does or not. Now go!"

He dove into the storm on the left. I started toward the right but found my way impeded. The snow from the raging storm had piled fast and now reached almost to my knees, forcing me to struggle for every step. I would never make it over there in time, plus there was no telling how long Akasha and Desmond would remain at an impasse.

Swallowing hard, numb to my core, I cut a diagonal path toward the demon instead.

The closer I got, the colder the storm became. I could feel my lungs slowly freezing from the inside. I clumsily pulled Ryo's borrowed scarf out of my coat pocket and shoved it against my face and into my hood. At least the effort of pushing forward helped my blood keep flowing. But how much longer that would work was anyone's guess.

Despite his wearing black, I couldn't spot Ken anywhere. For all I knew, he was burrowing beneath the snow to get closer to Desmond. I'd about reached the demon's side when I felt his mind lash out, trying to pierce through into mine.

"Banish the elemental this instant!" The accompanying mental suggestion to see things his way came razor-sharp and barbed.

I dropped to one knee, but not from the attempted mind manipulation. His efforts bounced easily away without effect. No, the reason I almost hugged the ground was due to another swoosh of wooziness as the bracelet on my wrist grew warm, but in a different way from before. I staggered upright and gave the pendejo a pair of single-finger salutes to make my feelings on his attempted manipulation clear. I followed that up by stabbing him in the leg with Ryo's dagger.

That was when Ken's black blade shot out from beneath the snow on his other side and straight into Desmond's side.

A howl of pain and rage blew outward from every pore of the demon's undulating skin. A swath of fire flared out of his fiery crown. I'd never been so happy to be short, as the thing radiated outward horizontally and singed the top of my hood, throwing it partially back. Keeping her hands locked with Desmond's, Akasha still somehow managed to duck enough not to take a direct hit, even as the storm made a wall to intercept it.

Then Ken rose from the piled snow, drove the blade deeper into Desmond's side, and pushed it downward.

Greenish ichor flowed from the widening cut and began to bubble like acid when it hit the air, instantly boiling away the snow it fell on. Ken was forced to let go of his blade as the ichor burned through it, dissolving it. The stench of rotting eggs suffused the air, making me gag.

Desmond swung his arms, taking advantage of Akasha's momentary imbalance to drag her off her feet with pure force. I couldn't jump out of the way in time; her body plowed into me like an avalanche and sent me flying.

I hit the cube's field, which fortunately had some give. It felt more like hitting a hard mattress than a solid wall. Then gravity asserted itself and I fell face-first into the snow. Hitting a real wall with the force at which I'd been flung would have split my head open and busted my spine. As it was, I ached all over and barely clung to consciousness, the yawning darkness terribly tempting.

The wind shrieked as if offended, and Akasha sounded much the same. Crawling on top of the snow, I saw that she'd somehow hooked her foot claws in Desmond's suit at the armpit to stop him from spinning her around anymore. She was now using her other foot to kick at one of his horns, his hands still locked with hers.

Of Ken, there was no sign. He was either hiding in the snow again or had been flung clear across the other side of the cube.

There had to be a way to get Desmond to leave before he got one or more of us killed! He'd been hurt—I could still see his bubbling blood. Surely he wanted out by now! So why wouldn't the pendejo leave?

'*Dani, drop the field.*'

'*Beauty?*' A flood of relief washed over me at hearing her voice. '*How do I do that?*'

Before she could answer, the bracelet warmed, drawing my attention. The cube was lit again. *¡Qué idiota!* I smacked myself on the forehead, suddenly feeling incredibly stupid. I should have thought of that! After a bit of fumbling, I was able to remove my glove and squeeze the charm.

The moment the field dropped, my ears popped again.

"ENOUGH!" Desmond's flesh expanded, tearing his suit apart and losing his humanoid shape. He heaved Akasha away from him with his bulk, his hands and arms shrinking into the main body as the air behind him shimmered like a curtain. Before the elemental could regain her footing and launch herself at him, he rolled back into the opening he'd made and closed it behind him.

Released from its cage, the storm stretched out and began dissipating almost immediately.

"Gracias a Dios." I let myself fall back into the snow, suddenly worn out and exhausted. '*How did you know we needed help? I couldn't reach you before.*'

'*Our messenger crows told me,*' Beauty said. '*They were keeping an eye on you. Once I was able to physically touch the field, I was able to contact you because of your link to it.*'

I forced myself to sit up, groaning all the way. I spotted her in her human form by the tree I had hidden behind, wearing a white coat. '*Are Ken and Ryo alright?*'

'*They're over there.*' She pointed somewhere behind me.

I slowly turned around. Akasha was twirling and skipping in our direction. Ryo limped gingerly behind her, his glasses back in place. Somehow, we'd all survived.

"He didn't even say goodbye," Akasha informed me, a huff of frozen air forming before her. "And after all the fun we'd been having." Her ice-blue eyes flashed. "Will the fire girl dance with me now?"

Was she never going to let that go? "No can do. Sorry." She drooped in disappointment like a rag doll.

"But some drinks might be doable," I added.

She perked back up. "Yes! Libations!" She made a pirouette. "*Now.*"

I closed my eyes for a moment to reach out and sense Last Stop's location as Ryo had taught me. I found the blue flame in my mind almost immediately. "It's that way." I pointed down the street.

"Do make yourself at home," Beauty added. "We won't be far behind you."

Akasha clacked her teeth together as if biting off a chunk of air and took off, her feet gliding over the snow as if it were ice, while she tittered with anticipation.

Once Ryo joined us, Beauty reached down and helped me to my feet so we could make our slow, meandering way back.

Chapter 39

With Last Stop's welcoming frontage in sight, I found the energy to quicken my steps by a fraction or two. I didn't even mind the creepy statue with its big belly and knowing smile staring at me. Soon, we'd be safe again, surrounded by heat, and hopefully spirited away from this deadly frozen wonderland.

The cuddled crows in their nest cawed a greeting as we stepped within the awning's protected area. Beauty slid open the door and stepped inside, a wave of warmth flooding us with welcome.

I was about to enter when I felt a tug on my sleeve.

Surprised, I turned around to look at Ryo. "What's wrong?"

His grey eyes wouldn't meet mine. "I noticed something during the fight." His voice was barely above a whisper. "Your mark. It's changed."

Dread poked a finger at me. I swallowed hard. "Changed? Changed how?"

His gaze rose to my forehead, then he glanced away. "It's grown bigger, and it's a lot more than an outline now. I thought you'd like to know."

The finger of dread turned into a fist. "Yeah, well, it doesn't matter. I'm sure it's fine." Or so I hoped. Summoning elementals, creating giant force cubes, and fighting against a demon prince were more than I could stomach already—I didn't need more to worry about. I turned back around and rushed indoors, not wanting to hear anymore.

Dani's yellow! Running from the poor perrito with her tail between her legs.

¡Callate! I wasn't running away, I just needed to thaw out. This chica had had more than enough cold for a lifetime.

It was a relief to step inside, to push away, if only for a moment, everything we'd gone through. But though the embrace of warmth in the entry area was as comforting as always, it couldn't thaw the ice shard now embedded in my gut.

A trill of music whispered through the air as Hokora greeted us back. That was new.

The weirdness never stops around here.

I stubbornly refused to look in the special mirror on the nearby column. It wasn't the time.

I shook off my winter armor slowly and hung it up, the forgotten aches and pains making themselves felt at full blast now that we were somewhere safe. Beauty had already shed her gear and returned to her feline form before jumping to her usual perch on the counter. Ryo had removed his at top speed and disappeared in the direction of the kitchen, shoulders hunched.

There was no sign of the elemental. "Where's Akasha?"

"Hokora has tucked her away elsewhere and is satisfying her thirst as we speak." Beauty's emerald eyes half closed. "Though you wouldn't dance for her, she mentioned she would still be more than happy to be called on again. She appears to have thoroughly enjoyed herself."

I resisted the urge to roll my eyes. "Good for her."

Beauty blinked slowly, and I had a strong feeling she was laughing—at me—again. Gata mala.

I shook out my hair now that it was free. The hood of my coat was toast. That pendejo almost killed us. "Will Desmond die from the damage Ken did to him?"

Say yes, please say yes.

"It's doubtful; demons are a hardy breed. But at least it will remove him from the board for a while," she said.

"His wounds will doubtless be remarked upon," Beauty added, "but he'll likely concoct a believable story that places him as coming out on top. And he's bound to try his luck again sooner or later." She extended her claws as if envisioning what she would do to him when she saw him again. The tip of her tail jiggled in anticipation.

I would totally pay to see that.

Still, a chill crawled over me. Dishing out payback was the kind of maneuver Pierson, my old boss, typically lived for. And he never minded doing so to an extreme, as I was only too aware. It was the reason Jay was dead. I would be too, if he ever got hold of me.

I didn't think Beauty would act the same, but it wasn't like I knew her or had the faintest idea of how monster cats behaved. Suddenly, I felt weighed down, the emotional and physical punches of the last few days all piling together and catching up with me.

"Are we done here?" I asked. "I just want to go to my room and crash." Bone-tired didn't begin to cover it.

Before Beauty could answer, Beverly and Loaf ran in from the hallway with Ryo not far behind. She stared at us with big eyes, biting her lower lip.

"Beverly?" A bolt of adrenaline shot through me. I was shocked to see her—I'd been sure she would have moved on the moment Mystic was back in Linda's arms.

"Did you meet her?" the young girl asked, her expression tense. "Was she mad?"

I gingerly kneeled before her and took her small hands into my own. Though I wasn't sure why, seeing her suddenly made all we'd gone through seem… not so bad.

"I did. And she wasn't angry at all. She's even hoping you'll keep her grandmother company and become *her* best friend too, so she won't be lonely."

A surprised smile lit Beverly's young face. "I can do that! I'll look for her. I promise!" She wrapped her arms around my neck and gave me a hug. A rare and different kind of warmth flowed through me. I was forced to blink back tears.

Beverly then let go and ran over to Ryo, signaling for him to kneel as well. He appeared dazed by the request, but did as she asked. When she hugged him, his face convulsed through several permutations, as if not having the faintest idea what she was doing or what it meant. I could see his imaginary tail wagging, however, as he tentatively hugged her back.

Loaf barked and ran circles around the three of us, happy as could be.

Beauty leaped down from the counter and sat with her tail curved about her paws when Beverly finally let Ryo go. The young girl shyly approached her. "Can I hug you, too?" Beverly asked, her hands bunching the skirt of her dress.

Beauty's ears flicked first one way and then the other. "I suppose. But please do mind the fur."

Beverly gave a strangled squeal before she ever so gently wrapped her arms around the cat. Beauty pointedly looked away as if distancing herself from the show of affection. A grin grew on my face at the sight.

Beverly let go of Beauty and then stared at the room. "Thank you, too, Hokora!" Several floor, wall, and ceiling slats flashed in bright colors, making her giggle.

Unlike when Jay had gone, Beverly stayed solid and didn't seem in a rush to leave. Was her unfinished business not over?

"Come on, everyone. We have a last stop to make." Beauty stood on all fours and, with her tail held high, led us off down the hallway on the right.

Beverly placed her tiny hand in mine as we started forward. Loaf trotted along on her other side. Ryo silently brought up the rear.

I was desperate to know what we were doing and where we were going, but I was too afraid of the answer to ask.

We hadn't been walking long when the corridor intersected with another—one I could have sworn hadn't been there before. It was twice as wide as the hall we were in, and rather than being made of wood, it was composed of polished stone. Stone I recognized from the night Jay had left me. Except back then, it had blocked the normal wooden hallway and stopped me from following after him. This time, I was being allowed to see beyond the curtain.

The large three-by-three blocks were the same as the wall I'd seen before, made of obsidian or black tourmaline, and were polished to the point that they acted like mirrors. Lit fire sconces made the reflections shimmer and waver. The scent of aromatic oils tickled our noses. Trapezoid-shaped doorways lined both sides, offset from each other. Only light-sucking darkness lay beyond the openings.

Unlike the rest of Last Stop, there was an odd feeling of antiquity running through the place. The unseen weight of millennia was piled all around it.

I crossed myself as every hair on my body stood up on its own.

The stone bar over the trapezoid doorway in the middle started to glow, thrumming with power. There was so much of it, it made my teeth ache. The darkness inside it lightened, becoming a glittering curtain, but we could still see nothing of what lay beyond.

Beverly stared at the opening as if she could. A big smile crowded her face. She took a tentative step and then another, her body slowly becoming more and more insubstantial before she ran full tilt for the doorway, laughing with joy-filled glee. She never once glanced back, as if all that had gone before no longer mattered. She was barely visible as she went through the arch, and we could still see nothing of what lay beyond.

My insides twisted left and right, the moment full of déjà vu and bittersweet. Whatever waited for her there, I hoped it would make her happy and keep her safe. Maybe she'd meet Jay and tell him I was okay.

Instead of disappearing and returning to a dormant state, the ancient portal stayed active. Was there someone else needing to go through that I didn't know about?

Beauty glanced at Loaf. "You helped defend Hokora from Desmond's machinations. Was that not enough?"

My eyes widened. The corgi had unfinished business, too?

Loaf sat on his haunches and looked at her, his tongue lolling out the side of his mouth.

"Stubborn canine." Beauty shook her head. "Do as you wish then."

The glowing stone over the doorway turned back to normal, and the glittering curtain disappeared, leaving behind only yawning darkness.

"Do these activate on their own like that a lot?" I asked in a whisper. It was the kind of place you instinctively knew that raising your voice could have unwanted consequences. It was way more intimidating than the pink-colored Gesù Catholic Church in Miami, where Abuela used to go.

"Hokora controls them," Beauty said. "She can open them when someone needs to leave, and she can sense when someone is on the other end needing to come through. Frequency depends on need. Some of the portals are only one-way, like the one Beverly used. A few have arranged times for traffic." She tilted her head to stare at me and my reflection on the floor simultaneously.

I couldn't tell if she was quietly hinting that what we were seeing was purely for our benefit or that the ground and walls could do the same as the mirror at the restaurant's main entry, and she had seen things in them I wasn't ready to discuss.

"This corridor is typically sealed, so anyone traveling through has no access to the rest of the place," Beauty continued. "Hokora creates whatever hallways she needs to show them out if they're looking to enter the spirit dimension adjacent to the physical world. Rarely would she deign to open a way into our section from here. So, for the most part, we are unaware of those coming or going."

I turned to my left, something catching my attention from the corner of my eye. The stone over one of the other doorways had lit up. Yet the ends of the corridor of doors remained open—the *opposite* of what Beauty had just told us would happen. I threw a quick glance in her direction, but she appeared unconcerned. What was she up to now? I got my answer a few moments later, when a small, furred creature wearing a hospital-like gown hobbled out—one I recognized.

"Cyrano? What are you doing here?" Beauty asked, her ears slightly flattened. "The healer clearly stated you were not to get out of bed. That staying in the spirit world would help you heal faster."

He hopped in our direction, wielding a pair of crutches like a pro. "Too much pampering is not good for my image, see.

And while that joint might be nice to visit every once in a while, it's not home."

The ferret was in a lot better shape than when we had last seen him. Cyrano had cojones, if nothing else. He had tried to keep Desmond from taking Mystic despite not being as powerful as the demon prince. It was lucky that Desmond had left him in the safe, leaving him barely alive to taunt us rather than destroying him outright.

"And thank you, miss," Cyrano said as he tilted an imaginary fedora in my direction. "I hear you're the one who kept me out of the pearly gates."

Would an animal spirit like him have gone to Heaven if he had died, or was he saying that as a figure of speech? I might be able to read micro-expressions on people, but with furred spirits, I was out of my league. "It was a group effort."

He tipped his nonexistent hat at Ryo and Beauty. Loaf was busy sniffing Cyrano's crutches and feet. "If any of you ever need me, give me a ring, and I'll be there. I pay my debts, see."

He wouldn't have been hurt if not for us, but if he wished to owe us a debt, who was I to stop him? Desmond was still out there, and we also had the nasty shaman who had gathered and bound all those helpless souls to contend with, to say nothing of whoever had left me the Shaman Corps business card. Everyone had an angle.

My gaze drifted toward Ryo, who was watching Loaf trying to nibble on Cyrano's left crutch, while the ferret attempted to unobtrusively push the dog away with his foot. His face shone with the fascination and delight of a kid getting an unexpected present at Christmas.

Okay, maybe not *everybody* had an angle.

Still, being that innocent was almost a crime in itself. Ryo was fairly begging to be taken advantage of. Not that Ken was likely to let anyone get away with it. I blinked twice as I realized I might not allow it either. Huh.

Getting attached is dangerous, chica. Had I learned nothing from how Bobby had used Jay's infatuation with him to destroy us?

Growing soft was for suckers. This Boricua wasn't falling into *that* trap.

What I needed was options. It might be time to call the number on the mysterious business card. Maybe hearing from someone not tied to this place would give me some badly needed clarity.

I turned away from the antics and spotted Beauty eyeing me with her inscrutable emerald-green eyes. '*Leaving so soon?*' she asked in my head.

¡Coño! For someone who couldn't read minds, she sure seemed to be good at it. '*I'm dead tired. Figured I'd take a nap. And to be honest, I've had more than my fill of supernatural stuff for one day,*' I said. '*Plus, if she sees me, Akasha might demand that I dance for her.*'

'*We couldn't have that, could we?*' Beauty said.

The gata mala was laughing at me. I was sure of it.

Beauty tilted her head, watching me sideways. '*Running away won't get you very far, Daniela,*' she said. '*Especially if it's from yourself.*'

Chapter 40

My brows drew together as I walked on past her. Running away from myself? What the heck was she talking about? Daniela Maria Martinez Colón didn't run from anyone or anything! Not unless my life was on the line and there wasn't a way to win. That was what surviving meant. And a poor job I had been doing of that lately, taking all these crazy risks.

So what was Beauty going on about?

I stomped upstairs, my mood growing darker by the second. She always seemed so sure about everything. Why did I keep letting her get under my skin? I had finished the mission. The nightmare milk run was over, and we'd won. Beverly had moved on to a "better place." Then Beauty throws this running-away bullshit in my face? Ay, bendito, what more did she *want* from me? Heat flushed through me from head to toe.

And why was I getting so mad about it?

My room door opened for me and then closed silently behind me. In a fit of pique, I turned around, yanked it back open, and then slammed it shut. The loud sound was strangely satisfying, even if it did make me seem like a five-year-old throwing a tantrum. Hokora had done nothing to me, but I was taking it out on her, anyway.

I tromped into the bathroom, seriously thinking about slamming that door, too, and screaming at the ceiling for a while for good measure. Maybe I'd finally work up the gumption to call the Shaman Corps number and find out what that was about.

But three steps in, I came to a total stop. Something weird caught my attention in the mirror.

As if I were a puppet manipulated by strings, my body turned of its own accord.

Movement. What had poked at me to look was movement. Movement *in my reflection.* After finding out I had been marked, I had only been able to see the proof in the mirror downstairs. But that wasn't the case any longer.

I could clearly see the supernatural mark sitting in the middle of my forehead. And as Ryo had mentioned, it was no longer an outline anymore. The image had changed, grown larger and more detailed. And it had *color.* It resembled a peacock butterfly, with its blood-red wings and its four white, multicolored circles on the upper and lower wings. Except here, they looked more like open eyes, the irises a deep blue.

I was *changing*. But changing into what? And why?

Jay, hermano, I appreciate you wanting me to live after your plans went sideways, but I don't think this was what you had in mind. Right?

As I stared wide-eyed at the thing on my forehead, bile burning at the back of my throat, the eyes on its wings blinked. I twisted away with a chill, no longer wishing to look at it.

Mira, this wasn't what I wanted for me, either, not at all. But what the hell could this chica do about it? Deep down, I was sure that whatever was happening, it was already too late for me.

But no way was I going to just wimp out and take it. Someone was going to pay!

The End

Thank you for reading **Last Stop—The Dead's Unfinished Business—Book 1**! If you have a minute, I would love it if you left a review. Just a sentence or two will do!

You'll be helping other readers find stories to love!

If you want to find out more about Ryo and his mysterious past, join my newsletter and receive **Death Stop—The Dead's Unfinished Business prequel novelette** as a gift. A newsletter members exclusive!

Glossary

Ay, bendito—in Puerto Rico, depending on context, it can mean 'Oh my God' or 'Lord have mercy' as in surprise/shock or 'you poor thing' or similar when employed as a lament. Also, 'Aw, come on' or 'For Pete's sake', etc.

Ay, Dios mío—Spanish for 'Oh my God.'

Bakeneko—from Japanese folklore. A monster or ghost cat.

Boricua—a term used by Puerto Ricans when referring to themselves. A native of Puerto Rico or of Puerto Rican descent. It comes from the island's original Taino name of Borinquen.

Bruja—witch.

Cabrón—Spanish for 'bastard.'

Cabeza—Spanish for 'head.'

Café con leche—'coffee with milk,' a popular beverage in Puerto Rico.

Callate—Spanish for 'shut up.'

Cálmate—Spanish for 'calm down.'

Carajo—A more vulgar expletive in Spanish for 'damn' or equivalent.

Chica—Spanish for 'girl.' Also used as an informal form of address.

Chota—'snitch' in Spanish.

Chiquita—Spanish for 'little girl.'

Claro—Spanish for 'of course.'

Claro que sí—Spanish phrase for 'absolutely' or 'definitely.' Adds more emphasis than just saying 'claro.'

Comprende—'understand' in Spanish.

Coño—mild Spanish curse word meaning damn.

Dios, por favor, ayúdanos—'God, please, help us' in Spanish.

Dios mío—'My God' in Spanish.

Dios protéjame—'God protect me' in Spanish.

Dissociative Identity Disorder—DID is a mental health condition characterized by the presence of two or more distinct personality states, each with its own unique characteristics and behaviors.

Dozo—Japanese for 'please' or 'after you.'

El tonto—Spanish for 'the fool.'

El Coco—'The Boogeyman' in Spanish.

¿En serio?—Spanish for 'Really?' or 'Seriously?'

Embuste—literally translated to 'lie' but also used in Spanish to express surprise. Equivalent to English's 'no way' expression.

Estas loca—'You're crazy' in Spanish (feminine)

Fagin—an older pickpocket who is a mentor or boss of a wire mob.

Gata—Spanish for female 'cat'.

Gata mala—Spanish for 'bad girl cat.'

Gorda—feminine Spanish for 'fat.'

Gracias a Dios—'thank goodness' or 'thanks to God' in Spanish

Hermano—Spanish for 'brother' or 'compatriot.'

Hola—'Hello' in Spanish.

Hajimemashite—a formal Japanese greeting used during first-time introductions.

Hokora—a Japanese 'spirit house' or small Shinto shrine. They house minor spirits and also bring protection to travelers.

Jibaro—traditional, self-sufficient farmers of Puerto Rico.

Lambón—toady or bootlicker in Puerto Rican.

Llorona—Spanish for 'weeping woman' or 'crybaby'. It is also the name of a folktale about a weeping ghost.

Loco/Loca—Spanish for 'crazy' for male and female.

Madre de Dios—Spanish for 'Mother of God.'

Malo/Mala—Spanish for 'bad' for male and female.

Mentiroso/Mentirosa—'Liar' in Spanish.

Mi—Spanish for 'my.'

Mierda—'shit/crap' in Spanish.

Mira—Spanish for 'look.' Also used as an exclamation to bring attention to something.

Mi corazón—Spanish for 'my heart.'

Mi hermano—Spanish for 'my brother.'

Muchacho—'guy' or 'young guy' in Spanish.

Muñeca—Spanish for 'doll.'

Niño—Spanish for 'boy child.'

Niña—Spanish for 'girl.'

Niños—Spanish plural for children that can include both boys and girls.

No hablo Ingles—Spanish for 'I don't speak English.'

No me gusta—Spanish for 'I don't like it.'

Nueva—Spanish for 'new' in the singular/plural feminine.

Pendeja—Spanish insult meaning 'stupid' or 'asshole' in the singular feminine.

Pendejo—Vulgar Spanish insult for a 'stupid' or 'asshole' person in singular male.

Pendejo Cabrón—Compounded vulgar insult meaning 'effing asshole' or 'effing bastard.'

Pequeña niña—'A small girl' in Spanish.

¡Pero no me gusta el frio!—'But I don't like the cold!' in Spanish.

Perrito—Spanish for 'puppy.'

¿Por qué?—'Why?' in Spanish.

Princesa—Spanish for 'princess.'

Problemas—Spanish for 'problems.'

Puto/Puta—Spanish for 'whore.'

¿Qué?—Spanish for 'What?,' as in the surprised exclamation.

Qué chulo—Spanish for 'How cool!'

¿Qué está pasando?—Spanish for 'What is happening?'

¡Qué extraño!—Spanish for 'How strange!'

Qué mono—'How cute' in Spanish.

Qué pena—'What a shame' or 'too bad' in Spanish.

¡Qué precioso!—'How sweet/nice/precious' in Spanish.

¡Qué rico!—'How good/delicious' in Spanish.

Sí—Spanish for 'yes.'

Spic/Spick—a derogatory term used for Spanish-speaking people.

Stick—pickpocket term for a stall—the wire mob member who distracts the mark.

Tonto—Spanish for silly, foolish, or stupid, and can be used as an endearment or for teasing as well as an insult.

Wire mob—a group of pickpockets.

Working single o—a pickpocket good enough to do the work without the need for a shadow

or stall.

Also by Gloria Oliver

Daiyu Wu Mysteries (Historical Cozy Mysteries)

Black Jade—Book 1

Jacques—A Prequel Short

The JOY of Murder—Book 2

Romeo's Revenge—Novelette

Music of Death Blues—Book 3

The Prince and Dai—A Prequel Short

The Discoveries of Julia Xero (Urban Fantasy Thrillers)

The Secret Humankind—Book 1

Pay It Forward—A Prequel Short

The Secret Aftermath—Book 2

Kara—A Prequel Novelette

The Secret Countdown—Book 3

Penny—A Prequel Short

Young Adult Fantasy (Standalone Novels)

In the Service of Samurai

Cross-eyed Dragon Troubles

Willing Sacrifice

Fantasy (Standalone Novels)

Vassal of El

The Price of Mercy

Inner Demons

Jewel of the Gods

Science Fiction (Standalone Novels)

Alien Redemption

Horror/Alternate History (Standalone Novelette)

Charity and Sacrifice

Happy Reading!

About the Author

Gloria Oliver lives in Texas with her family and her masters (three cats and two dogs). She is the author of several novels in the genres of fantasy, YA fantasy, science fiction, urban fantasy thrillers, and historical mysteries. Many of her speculative fiction short stories can be found in a handful of anthologies. She is a proud member of Broad Universe, though she has yet to work her way into the top list of Cat Slaves R Us.

When not busy working on novels, she enjoys reading, as well as watching movies, Korean dramas, and Japanese Anime. She also loves to play PC games. To find out more, please visit www.gloriaoliver.com

Gloria Oliver
Unveiling the Fantastic

www.ingramcontent.com/pod-product-compliance
Lightning Source LLC
LaVergne TN
LVHW030907080826
845145LV00010B/2800

9781957230276